Fleur McDonald has lived and worked on farms for much of her life. After growing up in the small town of Orroroo in South Australia, she went jillarooing, eventually co-owning an 8000-acre property in regional Western Australia.

Fleur likes to write about strong women overcoming adversity, drawing inspiration from her own experiences in rural Australia. She has two children and an energetic kelpie.

Website: www.fleurmcdonald.com
Facebook: FleurMcDonaldAuthor
Instagram: fleurmcdonald
TikTok: Fleur McDonald (Author)

OTHER BOOKS

Red Dust
Blue Skies
Purple Roads
Silver Clouds
Crimson Dawn
Emerald Springs
Indigo Storm
Sapphire Falls
The Missing Pieces of Us
Suddenly One Summer
Where the River Runs
Starting From Now
The Shearer's Wife
Deception Creek
Broad River Station
Voices in the Dark
Out in Nowhere

DETECTIVE DAVE BURROWS SERIES

Fool's Gold
Without a Doubt
Red Dirt Country
Something to Hide
Rising Dust
Into the Night
Shock Waves

FLEUR McDONALD

OUT IN NOWHERE

ALLEN&UNWIN
SYDNEY • MELBOURNE • AUCKLAND • LONDON

First published in 2024

Allen & Unwin
Cammeraygal Country
83 Alexander Street
Crows Nest NSW 2065
Australia
Phone: (61 2) 8425 0100
Email: info@allenandunwin.com
Web: www.allenandunwin.com

Allen & Unwin acknowledges the Traditional Owners of the Country on which we live and work. We pay our respects to all Aboriginal and Torres Strait Islander Elders, past and present.

A catalogue record for this book is available from the National Library of Australia

ISBN 978 1 76147 010 3

Set in 12.4/18.2 pt Sabon LT Pro by Bookhouse, Sydney
Printed and bound in Australia by the Opus Group

10 9 8 7 6 5 4 3 2 1

The paper in this book is FSC® certified. FSC® promotes environmentally responsible, socially beneficial and economically viable management of the world's forests.

To every single person from Allen & Unwin
with whom I've worked over the past fifteen years,
I am incredibly grateful.

And to my True North.

AUTHOR'S NOTE

Detective Dave Burrows appeared in my first novel, *Red Dust*. Since then Dave has appeared as a secondary character in sixteen contemporary novels, including *Out in Nowhere*, and seven novels set in the early 2000s in which he stars in the lead role. These novels are *Fool's Gold*, *Without a Doubt*, *Red Dirt Country*, *Something to Hide*, *Rising Dust*, *Into the Night* and *Shock Waves*.

In these earlier novels, Dave is at the beginning of his career. His first marriage to Melinda has ended due to issues balancing their careers and family life. No spoilers here because if you've read my contemporary rural novels you'll know that Dave is currently very happily married to his second wife, Kim.

I had no idea Dave was going to become such a much-loved character and it's reader enthusiasm that keeps me writing about him. Dave is one of my favourite characters and I hope he will become one of yours, too.

PROLOGUE

'Stop it. Don't do that!'

The man stirred as a panicked voice filtered into his dreams. He was glad of the intrusion. His dreams were never nice. Usually, they were something about droughts and stock dying of starvation, their carcasses spread over the orange earth, little black spots, flies, buzzing hungrily over the rotting flesh.

'No!'

He frowned. That woman sounded as if she meant what she was saying. Was it to him? What did he have to stop?

Something was sticking into his back. Not just sticking, jabbing at him. His whole body felt as if it was weighed down with iron. He tried to wiggle out of the way, but as soon as he shifted, spikes dug into him once more. What the hell was that? Branches, maybe? Was he lying under a bush? How had he got there?

Opening his eyes, the world spun and spun until his stomach felt queasy and he thought he might throw up.

'Don't do that!'

The woman's voice again. A fury and terror.

'I'm going to report you. Fuck off and leave me alone.'

Geez, just stop, be quiet, he thought. *My head hurts enough without your bitching.*

'What's the matter, sweetie? Why are you acting like that? Can't you see I want you?'

In among the nausea and dizziness, the man frowned. The male voice was familiar.

There was the sound of a hand slapping skin and the rumble tumble of two bodies rolling together, then a squeal.

'Stop it, please!'

She was begging this time.

Unease flickered. Was that woman okay? He should help! That's what good men did. Help when ladies needed it.

'Hey,' he tried to call out.

The words died before they even left his mouth. Vomit rose in his throat and he rolled quickly, turning his head to let the vile liquid onto the ground. Instead, it pulsated onto his chin and down his chest.

The heaving stopped and he lay there, exhausted, the world still spinning, albeit more slowly than before.

He could hear sobbing now.

'Don't, just don't!'

Another yelp. This time male.

'What'd you do that for? Bitch!'

The man frowned and tried to push himself up. He really did know that voice. Who was it? What was going on?

'You all right?' he called, weakly, so faintly his words would have been drowned out by the passing traffic.

Okay, he was near a road. Now he just had to work out where and how he'd got here.

He remembered music. And beer. And then . . . rum, maybe? Shots. Oh yeah, he remembered the shots. Tequila. Salt. Lemon. Not in that order.

Running now, footsteps and fast breathing. Whimpering.

He struggled to sit up then pushed some branches out of his face and away from his body. That's right! It had been his mate's twenty-first. He was the youngest of their group. Twenty-one and there'd been . . . strippers?

'Bitch! Come here, you little tart!' Whose was that voice? He knew it for sure. Who . . .

Heavy, clumsy steps. Chasing. Heavy breathing. A girl whimpering as she ran; it sounded like she was running in circles around where he was half sitting, half lying.

'Don't!' The woman's voice was loud and high. 'Don't come near me, you fucker!'

'Come 'ere.'

Was that a stumble and then a fall?

'Do you need help?' he called out. Except the words ran into each other, and even he couldn't understand them.

Silence. Not even footfalls now. Only cars. The ever-constant hum of cars.

A high-pitched yelp. The woman.

Brakes screaming through the night and a sickening thud.

He finally got himself upright and staggered out into the open. A grassed, wooded area, like a park with scrub, opened onto a highway. The space was only lit by a few streetlights lining the footpath.

Cars stopped, lined up behind one another. Blinkers flashed; spotlights on. There was a bundle lying on the ground in shadows on the road.

'Oh my god, oh my god, I couldn't stop, I couldn't stop!' This voice was fearful. A man, standing zombie-like, staring at whatever was on the ground.

Someone came running from the car line-up. 'Call triple zero! I'm a doctor!'

Then another person came running, and another, and another.

Too many people surrounded the front of the car to see no matter how much he squinted.

A heavy hand landed on his shoulder, and he blurrily turned.

'Mate, what are you doing here? How'd you even get here?'

'Maaaaate,' he replied, swaying slightly. How to answer the question? 'Too much piss! Time for more.' Narrowing his eyes, he tried to bring his friend into focus. 'What're you doooin' 'ere?'

'Looking for you! You deserted us at the party. Come on, let's go.'

'What's goin' on over there?' His speech was slurred. He didn't even really care, being seen like this. Perhaps he was still too drunk to give a toss. That was it, he guessed.

'Whatever's happening has nothing to do with us,' the man answered comfortingly. 'Come on, let's get you back to the dorms. I reckon a sleep is what you need.'

There were red flashing lights on the road now, and an ambulance had pulled up, sirens wailing. What was on the ground?

And where was that woman? Her voice echoed through his brain. What he thought was a smile was really a grimace, and it slipped quickly away to a frown.

'What'd you do there?'

His finger didn't line up as he pointed, then touched his friend's cheek. Fingers came away red and bloody.

'Must've caught myself on a branch. Like you have. Here.' A finger jabbed at his own face. 'Don't worry about it. Come on, mate, it's time to go home.'

'There was a woman,' he mumbled, his eyes heavy now. 'Needed help.'

'In your dreams I reckon, fella. Let's go.'

A strong arm around his shoulders, guiding him away from the road and towards the college.

That's where he was! At the back of the college. In the bush near the sheds. Because that main road ran to the back of the campus.

'She needed . . .'

'She needed nothing.' His mate's voice hardened. 'Nothing at all.'

CHAPTER 1

The toddler banged her hands down on the highchair. Peanut butter was spread over her cheeks, hands and every surface in sight, while her face was alight with laughter.

'Ruby! What in the world are you doing?' Hallie Donaldson, wipes in hand, came rushing across the office to where her daughter was strapped into her highchair in front of a computer screen.

'Mumma!' Ruby said, grinning at Hallie. Her smile fell away when she saw the wipes in her mother's hand and her arm flew across her face. 'No!'

'Oh, yes. You need a big clean-up, Ruby-girl,' Hallie said, gently taking hold of her daughter's arm and making one quick swipe across her face. 'Have you been watching Daddy on the screen?' she asked, with a quick glance across to the footage from the water-monitoring cameras that showed a coloured image of a trough and tank. The lower half of a windmill could be seen in the background, although the base of it was obscured by red dirt and bushes. A white piece of rag attached to the ladder flapped gently in the breeze. Alex had tied it there to give them an idea of which way the wind was blowing when they checked the screen from inside the office.

'Dadda!' Ruby pushed her mum's hands away quickly as a man's face appeared on screen.

Hallie turned. Her handsome husband, with his wide smile, two days' worth of stubble over his jaw, and red dirt and sweat leached into the felt of his hat.

'Dadda!' Ruby banged her spoon on the tray.

Taking the utensil from her hand, Hallie sighed at the noise. 'Ruby-rubes, a bit of quietness wouldn't go astray.'

'Dadda!'

'Yep, that is your dad.' This time, instead of being annoyed, Hallie pulled the office chair next to Ruby and sank into it. She pushed her hair back from her eyes and looked up at the air conditioner to make sure it was still on. The room felt unusually hot for mid-morning. The blue ribbon attached to the vent streamed into the room, signalling the air conditioner was working.

Hallie frowned and wiped her forehead. She got up and dragged the stool over and climbed up, holding her hand in front of the stream of air. Cool enough.

Must be her. Probably a hangover from last night's lack of sleep. Ruby had woken up six times and Alex hadn't heard her once. Every time she'd slipped out of bed to soothe the cries of their toddler, her husband had given a deep and long snort that any boar would have been proud of and rolled over.

How did men sleep through a baby crying? she wondered. This was quite normal, according to her friends in the city. Jasmine's husband never moved from when he went to sleep until the next morning, waking fresh and bright, wondering why Jasmine was bleary-eyed and exhausted when she'd been up to their two-month-old six times.

Skye's partner, Craig, was another. He tended to be a bit more restless at night, apparently, but he still didn't wake. Skye had been so annoyed one night, she'd brought their bub into the bed with them and when Craig had woken with the alarm at 6.30 a.m. and rolled over to kiss her good morning, he'd got such a fright to come face to face with a screwed-up little boy's nose rather than Skye. She'd told their group later, as they'd sipped lattes in the park and rocked prams back and forth with their feet—while Hallie had watched on in envy over the Zoom call—that Craig had been totally bewildered. He'd not heard a thing.

Alex worked hard and often it was so, so searingly hot in the Flinders Ranges that Hallie could understand why he would feel drained every night. She certainly didn't begrudge him his sleep. However, it would be nice if he woke up one morning and told her he'd heard Ruby crying in the night. Or even better, mutter at 11.24 p.m. that he'd get up to her this time. Then again at 2.56 a.m. Maybe even at 5.23 a.m., too. After all, he was usually up by 5.30 a.m.

Huffing another sigh, Hallie went to the window to draw the curtain and try to keep the worst of the heat out. *Still,*

I might be too late, she mused. Gathered under the hot tin verandah roof were the tiniest of black flies and any other insect looking for shelter away from the forty-plus-degree heat, a sure sign it was already 'bloody hot', as her father-in-law would say. '*It's bloody hot, Ruby*,' Rod would tell his granddaughter unnecessarily when he sat at the kitchen table for his morning smoko. As if the heat were a surprise, after living out in nowhere for all his nearly seventy years. '*Hmm, bloody hot*,' Alex would agree before Hallie had a chance to have input. She was always at the stove waiting for the massive kettle to boil so she could pour the steaming water into their teacups, little beads of sweat on her forehead. It wasn't just outside that was always 'bloody hot'.

No matter how many times Hallie sprayed the verandah or had the bug zappers out, there would be another wave of insects ready to invade her home whenever she opened the door. Still, she was happier to have the insects inside than the dogs, which usually smelled because they'd either rolled in something dead or gone for a swim in a creek with rancid water. The smell that clung to their long, shaggy, black and white coats never seemed to bother Alex; he happily let them sit under the table or alongside him in the lounge room, his hand straying down to pat their silky ears. Not that there was any carpet for the smell to seep into. Lino or plain cement floors kept the house much cooler, Nicole, her mother-in-law, had told her. '*And the dust is hard to get out of the carpet pile*.'

Unfamiliar with dogs, let alone their smell, Hallie wanted to kick them out. If she was honest, though, perhaps she was a bit jealous of the way that Alex gave his attention to those dogs and not always her. Farmers did that, her friend Maggie, from the neighbouring station, told her.

Dropping a kiss on Ruby's head, Hallie checked the screen to see what Alex had been doing since he arrived at Red Dirt Bore.

'Seriously,' Hallie muttered, 'Red Dirt Bore. That could be any bore on this place! There's red dirt and dust as far as I can see in every direction!'

'Mumma?' Ruby spoke around the spoon she was forcing into her mouth now.

'Yes, darling?' Hallie answered in that tone all mothers have they haven't really heard what their child said, but knew an answer was required.

Alex had disappeared from the screen, presumably unpacking all the equipment he needed to make sure the windmill was pumping properly. The bullbar of the ute was just visible in the picture and every type of bird had flown in to perch on the trough or the tank's edge. Those birds were savvy, knowing the appearance of a human usually meant water. Alex would undo the bung and all the dirty liquid would run out onto the ground, a river of life-giving water, an opportunity for baths and squawking. Lots of squawking.

With the water spreading out like a small flood, the birds would flock in, ignoring the person who was close by, scrubbing at walls of the cement trough and getting rid of all the algae. Their happy, loud cries alerted their mates, and finally, after they all arrived, and following a few little tiffs to work out the pecking order and who was able to be in what spot, there would be a blissful silence, broken only by contented, muted bird song as they warbled softly from the back of their throats and preened themselves in the cool water.

'He'll be back soon,' Hallie murmured to Ruby as she read her notes in the diary.

Anthea Crawford has been changing the way Australia looks at fashion since 1976. She mouthed the words, practising her introduction to the next episode of her podcast. Hallie hoped that Alex would keep popping up in front of the screen, just the way the galah had been lately, and entertain Ruby from a distance, so she could run through the information that Jenna had forwarded to her.

'Mumma!' Ruby was determined to get her mother's attention.

'What, Ruby?' Hallie turned to her daughter, with a frown. 'I've got to do some work.'

A very quiet noise behind Hallie made her turn around just as Ruby started to giggle and point at the screen. Expecting to see Alex, Hallie grinned as she checked what Ruby was pointing to. Their resident troublemaker was staring through the screen.

'Birdie!'

A wild, mischievous, pink and grey galah leaned over the top of the camera, so they had a close-up of its beak and one shiny, dark brown eye as it pecked at the glinting lens of the camera. Suddenly the bird's claws came over the top, trying to find a grip. It slipped, regrouped and tried again.

Ruby let out another giggle as the bird disappeared.

The screen now showed only blue sky, troughs and a tank. Ruby made three very hard taps on the highchair's tray with her spoon. 'Gone!'

'Yep, it's gone. Don't worry, it'll be back, if the last few weeks are anything to go by,' Hallie said. She reached for her diary and pen, and flipped through the pages. The words *Anthea Crawford* made the bubble of excitement that had been sitting in her stomach for two weeks bounce. The well-known designer had finally agreed to be interviewed for the podcast that Hallie had started six years ago.

She had taken *The Threads Code* from having two or three listeners, which she was sure had been her mum and aunty and some other family friend, to over one hundred thousand subscribers. It blew her mind every time she looked at her diary and saw which amazing Australian fashion guru she was going to interview next.

Even living out here, seven hours from Adelaide and two hours from the closest town, with cattle, sheep and kangaroos, along with the odd camel, for neighbours, her podcast had thrived. Thank goodness she'd made the choice to keep Jenna on in the office in Adelaide. Having her PA and best friend there meant she could meet personally with the sponsors and link Hallie into a Zoom meeting if needed. They'd had to work hard to get Anthea on board. Brand protection was important to the designer and, wow, how loudly Hallie had shrieked two weeks ago when Anthea's own PA had emailed her with a time and date. Did that suit Hallie?

Wouldn't have mattered if it hadn't, Hallie moved heaven and earth to make sure those times didn't change. Including extracting a promise from Alex that he would take Ruby for a drive so Hallie had peace and quiet, and could be focused during the interview.

Ruby's wicked giggle broke into her thoughts. 'Dadda!' her daughter said again as her annoyed thumping became happy thumping.

Learning to tell the difference was Hallie's new skill, just as telling when Ruby's cry was only half-hearted or if there was truly something amiss, although she wondered of what use that skill would ever be outside of keeping Ruby happy.

Hallie gave her diary and the hard copy of that precious email one last read through and went to sit alongside her daughter while they waited for Alex to show his red, sweaty face on the screen again.

CHAPTER 2

''Nake!' Ruby had looked away from the screen, towards the office desk.

'Hmm?' Hallie answered distractedly. She'd started to make some notes on a pad on her knee as she sat alongside Ruby, working out how the interview with Anthea would go.

''Nake!'

This time Ruby whispered and that made Hallie aware there was a problem.

'What? Snake?' She shot up out of her seat, looking around wildly as ice dripped through her stomach. Hallie felt violently ill as sweat broke out on her forehead. She needed to get Ruby out of the office! Still, she was in the highchair, so she'd probably be right. Unless it curled itself around the legs and climbed upwards.

'Where? Where is it?'

'Dere!' A chubby finger pointed towards the wall.

Standing like a statue, Hallie followed her daughter's finger. The space between the floor and wall was empty. Maybe Ruby had made a mistake? Maybe she'd just seen a leaf or something blow in the air conditioner breeze.

Not moving her head, only her eyes, she swept over the area that Ruby was pointing to. There wasn't a snake.

She closed her eyes. Snakes were supposed to be soundless. Noiseless. Hallie knew that wasn't the case. They always made some type of disturbance, and it was that sound which alerted everyone to their presence. Different types of noise depending on what the bloody things were sliding over. In the grass it was a sort of rustling sound. On the lino or cement, it was swishing. There was never anything silent about a snake, you just had to know what to listen for.

Hallie began to relax. 'Are you sure? I can't see anything.'

Ruby had lost interest and was looking back at the naughty galah, who once again was giving the viewers a close-up of the inside of its beak as it chewed the camera.

'Where did you see it, Ruby-girl?' Hallie, still nervous, turned slowly again without moving her feet, trying to see into every crevice and underneath and between the pieces of furniture that lined the wall. Being still was essential when dealing with snakes.

Not a thing, not the tip of a tail, not the flick of a tongue. Nothing.

The tension left her shoulders as Ruby laughed and pointed at the galah once more.

''Illy birdie,' she said, looking at Hallie for approval.

'That is a very silly galah, you're right.' Gingerly, Hallie took a step towards the desk and bent to peer underneath. Maybe she should get the shovel just in case. But what if there *was* a snake and it escaped into another part of the house while she was gone?

She could ring Rod and Nicole.

Hallie imagined her mother-in-law's thin lips pursing in disapproval.

'*Hallie*,' she'd say, '*you need to understand that this is now your life. The men are out in the paddocks and often hours away. You have to be able to deal with whatever comes up. That means snakes, floods, dust storms and anything else this land throws at you. Could be as minor as a mouse or grasshopper plague. We get everything out here in the middle of nowhere and if you can't deal with everything, you won't survive.*'

Annoyance flickered through Hallie's stomach. Her two closest neighbours and most frequent visitors were her in-laws, and she was torn as to whether she liked them much at all. Either of them.

She tried not think about that bloody piece of paper Rod had put in front of her, only days before she and Alex were married.

'*I know you won't mind, love*,' Rod had said with a lopsided smile that was a carbon copy of the way Alex did. He handed her a pen, indicating she sign at the bottom of the page.

'*Mind what?*'

'Oh, it's just what all we station owners do out here. Nothing out of the ordinary.'

Hallie had smiled back, glad they were including her—she was convinced her in-laws-to-be had questioned their son's choice of bride. Especially when she'd turned up for her first visit in white linen David Lawrence pants and top with a bright green belt around her waist. Hallie hadn't realised the red and purple dirt would seep into everything she owned even if she only stepped from the ute into the homestead. Nicole had been kind and offered to wash her filthy, red-covered clothes before she left Tirranah Station for Adelaide. There was dust even in the water out here. Her clothes had come out from the machine a light blood colour.

'I'm glad to be involved with whatever all you station owners do,' she said, taking the pen, wanting to fit in. Hallie had sat down, ready to read the document before she put her signature to it.

'Now, there's no need to talk to Alex about this,' Rod had said just as heat flooded her cheeks. What the hell?

The top line of the agreement read: *Binding Financial Agreement between Rod and Nicole Donaldson, Donaldson Grazing Pty Ltd, and Hallie Jemima Foster.*

''Nake. Mumma,' Ruby said, breaking across her anger.

This time, Hallie turned fast enough and saw the tail end of a brown snake disappearing under the bookcase. Involuntarily, she screamed and leaped onto the chair. Ruby screwed up her face and started to cry.

Alex had been insistent that they teach Ruby as soon as she was able to understand that snakes were 'very bitey' and 'very dangerous', and this wasn't the first time she'd pointed one out. Hallie should have believed her the first time and not dropped her guard.

'Shit! Bloody hell!' Hallie wanted to jump onto the desk and wait until the snake had slithered away, but that would only cause problems down the track, not knowing where it was in the house. No, she'd have to get rid of it.

Again!

'I'm going to murder Alex when he gets home,' she muttered above Ruby's banging. 'Ruby, darling, stop it. I have to think.'

''Nake, 'nake, 'nake!' Ruby yelled at the top of her voice. 'Bitey!'

Hallie had lost sight of it now and terror swamped her body. Was it behind her? Had it slithered out when she wasn't looking and was now under the table? What happened if it wrapped itself around the highchair legs and started to climb towards Ruby? That was possible; Alex had showed her photos of huge, thick snakes winding their way slowly around the top wire of a fence, metres from the ground. She'd never understood how they got there in the first place.

Alex had told her never to take her eyes off a snake and now she couldn't see the damn thing!

Her hands shook wildly as she searched for something to strike it with.

Hallie heard her husband's calm voice. '*All you have to do is break its back.*'

That's all well and good for you, she retorted silently, almost hysterical with panic.

'*You break its back and it can't go anywhere. Then you can get a shovel and finish it off.*'

If only Alex was here to do it for her.

'You are in so much trouble,' she muttered, hoping her husband could hear all the way out there at Red Dirt Bore.

'Mummmmaaaa!'

Another flick of the tail and the snake moved along under the bookshelf. Only half its body appeared in the open. Then the snake froze, its head lifted in the air, watching. Waiting. Assessing the danger. Tongue flicking in and out, in and out.

Apparently, it wasn't happy, because as quick as Hallie could blink, its supple, agile body turned back on itself and disappeared.

'Where the fuck is it?' she screamed, even though she knew.

'Mummmmaaaa!' Ruby had started to sob, red-cheeked, with real tears running down her face. Using the spoon, she banged on the highchair table time and time again.

Wanting to put her hands over her ears, Hallie tried to calm herself. She was the only adult within a thirty-kilometre radius. If she called Rod, it'd take him half an hour to get here, and the snake would have disappeared and none of them would feel safe until it was found and dealt with.

'Where is it? Where is it?' she begged the bookshelf, pleading for it to throw up its unwanted occupant. Her eyes fell on the gun cabinet.

Of course! Why hadn't she thought of that before? The .410 would be in there. Another of the first things Alex had showed her when she'd moved in was how to load and fire the snake gun.

Hallie could do it. And she absolutely would. This would prove to Nicole she could cope.

Alex had told her, '*You'll be right*,' after she'd managed to annihilate the thick rope he'd put out for her to practise shooting at.

'Ruby,' she told the toddler, 'Ruby-girl, you have to be quiet so Mummy can think. Okay?' She turned to face her daughter for only seconds as she dropped a kiss on her head and whispered, 'Quietly does it. Quietly does it.' Hallie didn't feel quiet or calm but she tried to act like she was for her daughter's sake.

Ruby was clever and refused to be tricked by her mother, continuing her onslaught of screaming and yelling.

Why hadn't she taken up Alex's offer of bringing her a long piece of wire from the shed to keep in the house? Wire acted as a whip and had the strength to break a snake's back. She could have kept a piece in every room without upsetting the decor too much. Instead, now she'd have to run to the bedroom and get the gun cabinet keys and hurry back again. Not ideal.

A glance at the computer screen, a snatch of Alex's tanned forearm wielding a trough broom and waves of water, told her he was still cleaning out the trough, oblivious to the chaos inside his house.

'You are going to hear about this later,' she told him as he looked up at the camera, knowing that Ruby would be watching. He gave her a thumbs up and a smile. Hallie wanted to snarl.

Edging towards the door, she kept talking to Ruby, her eyes on the bookshelf. 'Okay. Okay, here's what I'm going to do. I'm going to get the keys and then I'll be straight back. You must watch that snake, okay, Ruby? Don't take your eyes off it. Watch the snake!' She talked through her action plan more for herself than Ruby.

Perhaps she should take her daughter with her, but common sense told her that Ruby was probably safer staying there. The highchair was just that, high, and if she took her out, she'd have a toddler on the loose on the ground while she was about to try to shoot a snake.

Shaking her head at the horror of the choices, she ran out the door, slamming it shut behind her. After dragging the hallway mat to cover the gap between the floor and the door, Hallie raced to Alex's bedside table. She tried to pull the drawer open but her hands were shaking so badly she couldn't hold the little teardrop-shaped knob. With a scream of frustration Hallie dropped her hands, taking two deep breaths just as Ruby yelled, 'Bitey!' from the office.

Shit, the bloody thing was obviously on the move. This time, Hallie tried to close her mind down and concentrate on the task.

Keys. She found them in a box under Alex's jocks.

Hallie couldn't allow herself to think, she must only act, so she turned and ran out into the hallway, back to the office door. Now what? The snake could be right behind it.

Another deep breath.

Slowly she turned the handle and pushed the door open a crack, peering in.

'Mumma?'

'I'm coming, darling. Can you tell me where the snake is?'

'Dere.'

Hallie couldn't see it from her position, so she shoved the door enough to get her head into the room and look around.

'Are you okay, Ruby-girl?'

''Nake,' Ruby said quietly. Her sobbing had stopped as if she knew her mum couldn't handle anything more right at this moment.

The snake was lying without moving against the skirting board where the floor met the wall. Its body was as thick as Hallie's forearm and it was longer than she was tall—a metre and a half, if not longer. It would take only a drop of venom to kill Ruby and Hallie, yet if they were to get bitten, they would have a whole lot more unloaded into their bodies; the Royal Flying Doctor Service would have no chance of getting here before they died. The scales glistened, reflecting the light from the ceiling. With horror, Hallie realised the snake wasn't just a brown, it was a king brown. Somehow even deadlier than 'just' a brown.

Right now, deadly just meant deadly to Hallie. While Alex continued to clean that bloody trough.

This was up to her.

She held a finger to her lips. 'Shh, Ruby-girl,' she whispered.

With her back to the wall and her eyes never leaving the snake, Hallie slid into the room towards the gun cabinet. She'd never been more grateful that the cabinet was on the opposite wall—hopefully the snake wouldn't feel her movement.

Key in the lock. Gun withdrawn. Ammo . . . Where? Which one?

Panic flared through Hallie's stomach as she looked helplessly at the different boxes. Which bullets did she need?

A shuffling noise alerted her that king brown was sliding again. Her head whipped around and she watched as the snake moved away from the wall towards Ruby's highchair. Bile rose in her throat.

'Think, for god's sake, *think*.'

Fumbling with the first packet, she realised the bullets were too small. The next ones were too thick.

'Mumma.' Ruby suddenly banged her hands on the highchair and kicked her feet against the legs.

Once again, the serpent glided to a halt, forked tongue cautiously poking in and out, feeling the air.

Hallie grabbed the last packet and opened it, almost groaning with relief as she recognised the thin shotgun shells. Inserting one in the barrel as Alex had taught her, she raised it to her shoulder, lining up the snake.

The king brown turned its head and its dead, black eyes stared into hers.

Hallie didn't even hesitate. She pulled the trigger.

As the bullet hit, blood sprayed from its body. The mangled snake continued to writhe and twist in one spot.

Hallie reloaded and took aim again, firing off another round. This time its body split in two. Each part moved as if possessed. The head and part of its body jolted in short, sharp movements towards Ruby, and the other end went backwards, towards the wall.

Ruby screamed and clamped her hands over her ears, sobbing loudly, kicking her legs out and squirming, trying to get away from the noise echoing around her head.

Hallie knew how she felt. Her ears were ringing and her shoulder was stinging from the slight kickback from the release of the bullets. She dropped the gun and ran towards her daughter, her brain knowing the snake was dead and the movement afterwards was entirely normal, yet her body couldn't catch up. Her maternal instinct told her she had to get to Ruby as fast as she could.

Yanking the little girl out of the highchair, she climbed onto the desk and watched as the snake continued to slither and slide and spread blood across the floor.

'Ugh,' Hallie groaned, realising she was crying. Her chest heaved as the adrenalin left her and she held her little girl tightly to her, rocking back and forth.

Once in her mother's arms, Ruby started to calm, and Hallie hung on for dear life, taking as much comfort from her daughter as Ruby was from her.

Minutes passed, maybe longer. Hallie didn't know. It took king brown's body to stop moving before they both became calm enough to speak.

'Mumma?' The little girl's voice was quiet. 'Okay, Mumma? My ears sore.'

Another few moments passed before Hallie could answer.

'Mumma?' The little girl touched her mother's face.

Gulping air, she put her hand over her eyes and leaned her head onto Ruby's. 'Yes, darling?'

'Dadda dere.' She pointed at the computer and they watched as Alex leaned down from the ladder to wave to them then continued up and out of sight towards the top of the windmill.

CHAPTER 3

'Um, hello. My name is Constable Mia Worth.'

'Good morning, Constable Mia Worth,' the children from Barker Primary School chorused.

Mia tried to smile through the butterflies flapping in her stomach. Kids were the hardest of audiences. Unforgiving and merciless. If she didn't catch their attention in the first three seconds of her talk, then she'd have to speak over fidgeting, whispered conversations and kids calling out interruptions. The impact she was hoping to make wouldn't be there.

Trouble was, she didn't know much about kids and she wasn't really even sure how old these Year Fives were. Maybe she should have asked the teacher before she started. Her partner, Detective Dave Burrows, usually attended the career days for the kids in high school but he'd insisted she do this talk to the primary-school kids. Looking at the wriggling, squirming, talking bundles of energy, Mia was fairly sure she understood why now.

Maybe she should have brought some props other than her taser gun. Not that it was a prop, more a necessity on her work-issued belt.

Linking her fingers through the loops of her police pants, she found the handcuffs on her belt and touched them for comfort.

'Can we try on your handcuffs?' a boy yelled. His friends giggled while casting wide-eyed glances at each other.

Mia swallowed and removed her hands, grasping them firmly behind her back for two seconds, before deciding she needed to adjust her hat. In doing so, she locked eyes with a little girl at the back of the room who was staring at her like she was a goddess. That was pretty good for her share price.

Smiling at the girl, Mia gave a little wave and the girl dropped her gaze to the floor. But not before Mia caught a large grin on her face.

Damn, she wished she knew how old these kids were. Eight? Nine? Perhaps as old as ten or eleven. Okay, who did she know that was eight or nine? Or ten.

For once, Mia's brain went blank, other than to register that she didn't recognise one face in this classroom. Not surprising, though. Since she'd been in Barker, the whole twelve months, the only kids she'd had anything to do with were the Stapleton twins and they'd been four last year and a handful and a half when she and Dave had been investigating an elder abuse case in their family.

Miss Travenski held up her hand. 'No calling out, thank you, Michael. You need to put your hand up and wait until you're asked to speak. And the rest of the class, please be quiet and respectful towards our guest.' The teacher was standing at the back of the classroom and had obviously realised Mia needed help.

Mia waited until the teacher nodded at her before speaking again. She summoned a smile.

'I'm a police officer here in Barker and I work with Detective Dave Burrows.'

'He's a good bloke,' another boy said, repeating what he'd obviously heard his parents say.

'James,' Miss Travenski warned. 'The same goes for you. No talking without your hand up.'

'Yeah, a real good bloke,' a girl said this time.

Miss Travenski sighed and motioned for Mia to continue.

One girl decided she'd had enough of Mia's stuttered start. 'What's a police officer do?'

'Well,' Mia said, 'I check that people are driving at the correct speed—'

'You pulled my dad up the other day,' another child said. 'He was angry with you.'

Heat flooded through her cheeks. She'd known the conversation today would be difficult, but not this hard. Damn Dave!

'Did I? Well, he must have been going over the speed limit. See, it's very important that you drive at the speed limit. If you don't, there's a higher chance of an accident.' Mia knew she was babbling and using words that probably weren't suitable for the Year Five kids, but if she kept talking, they might stop. 'And accidents aren't very nice to attend. I've been to quite a few now, and sometimes people get hurt in them.'

'My dad's a good driver.'

'My mum is a better driver than yours.'

'Enough!' Miss Travenski called, clapping her hands together.

'It doesn't matter how good a driver you are'—Mia raised her voice—'the fact is that if you speed, then you're putting not only your own life but also that of others at risk. People could die. That's a very irresponsible attitude to have.'

Mia saw Miss Travenski stiffen when she mentioned dying, but she couldn't stop. Not when the room was finally quiet.

'Often, when people ask me if they should become a police officer, I ask them two things. Firstly, are you prepared to kill someone?'

There were gasps across the room. Shocked faces and wide eyes told Mia she'd definitely overstepped the mark.

'Officer Worth, I wonder . . .' The teacher stood and looked around, but three boys shot their hands up in the air.

'Do you get to kill bad people?'

'Is that why you carry a gun?'

'Have you ever killed anyone?'

Mia shook her head. 'Hold on, I'll answer your questions in a minute. The second thing I ask them is if they're prepared not to go home after a shift.'

'Why wouldn't you go home?' a girl wondered. 'Don't you need to have some dinner and go to bed?'

'You're an idiot, Susan,' Michael told her. 'They *die* when they're out working. A baddie can kill them. Sometimes they get hit by a car. I saw that on TV once.' The boy got to his feet and within seconds had put his shoulder to the floor and executed a perfect roll, pretending he'd rolled from the bonnet of a car.

'Well, thank you, Officer Worth,' Miss Travenski interrupted, moving towards the front of the classroom.

'Can I ask a question?' It was the girl Mia had smiled at earlier. A small girl with bright red hair and vivid blue eyes. She was sitting cross-legged on the carpet and started to bounce on her bum. 'Please, Miss Travenski, I've got a question.'

Mia realised the teacher was looking at her warily. The previous statements were true, even if they were too confronting for primary-school kids. To become an officer, you had to be prepared to change. The police see a different side of life that the public doesn't, and it's a life that a recruit may not be prepared for. You might be put in a situation where you must protect or defend yourself. In the academy, one of the lecturers had said to the cadets: *'Are you willing to shoot someone?'*

Her words had given Mia pause, but not as much as the ones that had followed.

'Are you prepared not to come home from your shift? Are you prepared to die? See, when people join the army, they expect at some stage of their career they will see

active combat. That is not something our police cadets give enough thought to. Consider whether you are prepared to not come home from your shift. Because that's how policing is these days.'

Biting the inside of her lip, Mia gave a tiny nod, acknowledging the teacher's warning glance. 'What's your question?' she asked the girl gently.

'What made you want to be a police officer?'

Mia linked and unlinked her fingers again. Why indeed? 'Well, um, what's your name?' she stalled.

'Skye. I'm Skye Maddison.'

'Well, Skye, being a police officer is a whole lot of fun, but it can be a bit dangerous.'

'Is that why you have a gun on your belt?' James asked.

Deciding to ignore him, Mia kept her eyes on Skye. 'Because we chase, ah, baddies.' She grabbed a word already used. 'We have to be prepared. But as to why I chose this as my job? Well, every day is different. One moment I might be patrolling the highway for speeding cars and the next I might be here at the school, giving a talk, like I am today. Sometimes I get to go and visit other towns and talk to other police officers.'

Miss Travenski's body relaxed slightly as Mia talked, and she realised she was on the right path.

'And with every day being a bit different, the other big reason I wanted to work with the police is that I get to travel a lot. If I didn't want to stay here in Barker, then I could ask for a transfer to another town or even another state. I asked to move to Broad River for a while, because my nana was there, then I was assigned to help Detective Burrows here in Barker. So you see I can ask for a transfer to anywhere in South Australia, really.' She cocked her head to the side. 'I could move interstate, but I'd have to get clearance and do some more training.'

Skye was staring, transfixed. Mia felt the weight of expectation in her bright eyes. Maybe she wanted to join the force and what Mia said today might sway her for or against.

Taking a breath, she tried to remember the day she had decided she was going to apply to the academy.

'Let me tell you a story,' Mia said as she moved from the edge of the teacher's desk to the floor. 'Here, let's sit in a circle.' She made a circle with her finger and sat down as all the children shuffled around. Her cuffs were sticking into her side, so she adjusted them, just as a little hand reached out to touch the badge on the arm of her shirt.

Mia caught the look from another girl, who seemed fascinated with her uniform.

'Why do you have to wear all of that stuff?' the girl asked.

'This is so I have tools to help me when I'm chasing the baddies,' Mia said. 'I'll tell you about all these things in a sec, if you like.' Mia realised she should use the same sort of words the kids were using because that's what they'd understand. 'What's your name?'

'Chloe.'

Mia smiled. 'Hello, Chloe.'

'What's the story?' one of the noisier boys asked. He was leaning back, arms crossed, assessing her—one of the cool kids for sure. Someone Mia would have avoided when she was in Year Five.

'I wasn't very old when I had to move from Barker to Adelaide.'

'Did you live here when you were a kid?' someone asked.

'Yeah, I did. With Nana and Mum—' Mia opened her mouth to continue with her story, but another kid got in before she could say anything.

'Where was your dad?'

'He, uh . . .' Mia's mouth twisted as she caught the teacher's eye. Nana had always told her to tell the truth, which sometimes seemed to get her into a whole lot of trouble, like before. And because people didn't like it when the truth called out their bad behaviour. Inwardly she sighed. 'Well, my dad died when I was just a baby, so I don't remember him at all. But as I was saying—'

'Why did he die?'

'Did someone shoot him?'

Mia's mouth went dry. A few moments passed before she answered. 'He hadn't been very well for a while.'

That was a sort of truth. Enough to get the kids off her back. The fact that her father had a severe mental illness was too hard to explain, especially when Mia herself had only found out a year or so ago and the story of his life was still raw.

'Back to why I wanted to be a police officer. Like I said, I was still young when I moved from Barker to Adelaide, and it's a big move for a young kid. I was a bit older than you guys, but not a whole lot. And the city is a lot different from Barker, too. Who's been to Adelaide?'

All the kids' hands shot up.

'I went to the zoo once,' a boy who hadn't spoken before said.

'Well, then you know there are lots of people and cars. Buses and noise. Trams! On this particular day, I got lost. I thought I knew the way home from the park, but I didn't. All the corners and streets looked the same. Not every kid had a mobile phone back then, so I couldn't call my grandmother, then I remembered from when I was at school in Barker, a teacher told my class that if things weren't going right, we should never be frightened to approach a police officer.'

Now the classroom was silent. Every single face was turned to her, listening. Even the most fidgety child was still.

Mia leaned forward with a smile. 'I wasn't frightened to ask a police officer in a uniform for help because all the ones I'd known were nice and kind to us kids. I'm not sure how I did it, but I found a police station and went inside, and the lady behind the counter took one look at me, got me an ice cream and a drink, then organised for a couple of officers to drive me home. Because you see, I knew my address, so I could tell the police, but I didn't know where the street was.' Mia paused and looked at every single child in the circle. 'I wanted to be like those officers. Helping kids who needed help. Being kind to families. Those two constables who took me home, they were awesome.' She gave the kids a large smile. 'They turned the siren on so I could hear it, even though they weren't supposed to. They showed me the switch inside the car that made the lights work, and let me flick it. I thought I was the coolest kid ever!'

The Year Five class laughed, enthralled with her tale.

'The experience they gave me as they drove me home made me want to do what they were doing.' She paused and grinned. 'I hope that what I say to you might make you want to become a police officer, too.'

Mia leaned back, pleased with herself. Although she really wished she could take back the first few sentences of the day, perhaps her story had made up for them. How could she convey, though, the relief she'd felt when Nana had opened the door? Mia had watched the tension in her grandmother's face ease.

How, too, could she explain the diary entry she'd found after her grandmother had died?

Thanks didn't seem to be enough for the lovely young police officers who brought Mia home today. I mean, how do you explain to people who know this place like the back of their hand that even to an old duck like me, let alone a young girl, the streets all look the same? The houses all look the same. That the city streets don't have the personality that the country town ones do and it is very easy to get lost.

In the country, our deep thanks would come from being practical. Dropping excess eggs around or a bale of straw if it was needed to mulch a veggie garden. Here in the city it's harder to know what to do. Maybe I'll cook cakes and biscuits and deliver them weekly? My veggie garden will provide produce but not soon enough for a thanks.

I guess that's it. Cakes and biscuits. And the occasional jar of strawberry jam.

'Do you have any questions?' Mia asked.

'Is there much money? 'Cause I want a two-storey house, and Mum tells me I have to pay for it myself!'

Mia smiled. 'By the time you guys get to being a police officer, I hope the pay is more than it is now. Any other questions?'

'What's on your belt?'

Mia ran through all the pieces of equipment that were around her waist. She'd taken the service revolver off and locked it in the gun safe back at the station, but she still had her taser.

'Cor, can I have a look at that?' one boy asked, pointing to it.

'Nope, sorry. It's not allowed to come out of the holster unless I need to use it.'

'Does every copper get to have one?' another boy asked. He rolled 'copper' around as if it were a naughty word and he loved saying it.

'Yes, every *police officer* does. And we all get one of these.' She touched the hat she was wearing. Distraction, distraction! 'Does anyone want to try it on?'

'I do!' Skye and Chloe spoke at the same time.

Mia smiled and took it off her head, placing it first on Skye's then on Chloe's as everyone stood and moved away from the circle.

'I think you two will make the most amazing police officers in time to come,' she said. Then she leaned forward and whispered to the two girls, 'Would you like to come for a ride in the police car later on?'

CHAPTER 4

'This "problem",' Hallie recited, practising her words to tell Alex when he came home, 'has to stop. I can't live in a house where snakes come and go as they please. This is the second time it's happened! And the one that's dead in the office is massive! We could all die.'

She could imagine Alex now, laidback, languishing in a chair with the dogs at his side. He would pour her a brandy to calm her nerves and ignore the fact that her hands were still shaking. He certainly wouldn't be able to feel the nausea in her stomach, though her pale face might give him a clue.

Last time Hallie had yelled at him, Alex had looked across to where the body of another snake had lain in about one hundred pieces. Blood was smeared across the kitchen floor, the shovel still where Hallie had dropped it after massacring the creature.

'Seems you dealt with it as you deal with all problems,' he'd said mildly. *'Very well.'*

Hallie had wanted to smack him. How dare he bring her out here to this godforsaken joint, in the middle of nowhere with no one to talk to except flies and snakes and a two-and-a-half-year-old toddler. How dare he bring her to a house that seemed to have a draught blowing from one end to the other, where dust entered from minute cracks she hadn't yet found and the walls creaked and moved as much as the tin roof did.

Her mother-in-law had smiled happily when they'd first walked through the house together. *'This house has a personality, Hallie,'* she'd said, almost in a reverent tone. *'It speaks to you, with every creak and groan. I loved it when I lived here.'*

'Stuff the personality,' Hallie had said to Alex after the first snake. *'There must be air vents or holes or something to let a snake that size in. And the dust, let's not forget the dust.'*

'Not a chance, sweetness,' he'd said, taking her hand in his.

Hallie had realised within the first two months of dating Alex that he only called her 'sweetness' when he was calming her down. Distracting her. Now, five years into being married to him, she was aware of his tactics and called him on them.

'I know what you're doing! Don't "sweetness" me, Alex, you're only distracting me,' she would say when he called her that tonight. *'I might be a city slicker, but I know that*

it's not normal to have a snake in a well-built house, even out here in the bush. There must be holes somewhere. I can't put Ruby on the ground, and I'm too scared to even walk without shoes! What if it had a friend?'

Alex would smile in the unflappable way of all good country blokes. '*If he had a mate, I reckon you got it a few weeks back. Wear your shoes in the house if it makes you more comfortable.*'

Ruby hadn't been on the ground since that first one and there was no way that was going to change now. The poor child was sick of going from the cot to the pram to the highchair. Even after Hallie had killed the snake today, Ruby had asked to be put down in her funny, little toddler way.

'Down. Down, down!'

Hallie couldn't put her daughter on the ground.

She glanced at her sturdy boots, which she'd washed to make sure she didn't track dirt inside. Why had she bothered? Because when the lazy easterly from the desert blew under the door, the kitchen filled with dirt that crunched underfoot.

The door into the office was tightly shut with a rolled-up towel placed at the gap with the floor even if, as percentages would have it, there probably wasn't another king brown anywhere near the office. But that wasn't a risk Hallie was prepared to take. Images of the serpent curling its thick body around her daughter as it struck her face, once, twice and a third time, made Hallie shudder and want to throw up.

'I'm sorry, Ruby-girl, that's a no-can-do.'

'Dadda!' Ruby called, wriggling in her arms and pointing at the office door. 'Dadda!'

'I know you want to see Dad.' Hallie fought to hold the little girl upright as she threw herself backwards and screamed. 'But I can't let you down, Ruby-girl.'

'Dadda!'

Hallie felt like growling, '*Yep, he's all yours when he gets back tonight, Ruby. You can have him.*' Instead, she said everything in a singsong voice that would hopefully calm Ruby down. 'You can tell him how much you'd like to crawl around on the ground like a child without a house that has resident creepy-crawlies.'

Unlikely, but she could always hope.

It was time for a distraction. 'I know.' Hallie made a face as if she'd had the best idea in the world and opened her mouth like the clown in sideshow alley games. Then she put her head into Ruby's chest and shook it, trying to make her laugh.

The reward came when Ruby stopping fighting her and let out a surprised giggle.

'Let's go outside and put the sprinkler on. Let's get you all cooled down because, Miss Ruby-girl, you're looking mighty hot to me!' She put on a very bad American accent.

Hallie spun around and half walked, half ran to the outside door then stopped, taking a breath before she yanked open the door.

Loud buzzing rose around her and she felt the flies hit her face as they swarmed, parting ways so she could get through. For a moment, Hallie felt like having a temper tantrum just as Ruby'd had. Never once, while she carefully planned her life, attended the Australian Academy of Fashion and fought her parents, who insisted she study marketing or 'something that will set you up for life, Hallie!', did she think she would end up killing snakes and swiping flies that were bombarding her head, while the sun slowly cooked her.

Funnily enough, Hallie didn't want to cry. A few years ago, she may have, but not now. Living out in nowhere had hardened her, just as the sun had hardened her skin. She shrugged at things that, before she moved out in nowhere, she hadn't known of. Certainly the journalism degree she'd managed to study while she also studied a fashion designer postgraduate certificate was strangely not useful when it came to battling against mice plagues and feeding shearers or bore runners or fencing contractors. Or marrying her wonderful, gorgeous, annoying husband.

Ruby reached out just like Hallie, except she was trying to catch the flies with wild swipes of her hand. She giggled when they hit the windows with a light popping noise, all the while buzzing angrily as they were dislodged from the coolest place they could find.

Hallie closed her eyes, hoisted Ruby a little higher on her hip and ducked her head before heading towards the edge of the verandah. She didn't even stop to peer over the edge in case there was another snake sunning itself against the hot cement wall. Instead, pretending her age wasn't twenty-eight but five, she leaped onto the lawn.

They landed heavily, stunning Ruby into silence momentarily, then she put her head back and laughed.

'Me fyy!'

'Fly? I don't think so!' Assessing the lawned area, Hallie turned on the tap and waited for the fffft, fffft, fffft of the reticulation sprinklers.

''Arter!' Ruby struggled to be let down again. Hallie set her on the ground and she crab-ran along the lawn to sit under the closest sprinkler, her face awash with pleasure.

'How about we sit under the tree?' Hallie said, pointing to the bench. She gasped as the cold water touched her boiling hot bare legs. Bliss! 'Away from the sun. Come on, you don't want to get burned.'

Toddling over, Ruby gave Hallie a toothy smile, just as a round of barking started from the team of mustering dogs Alex hadn't taken with him. Which was unusual, because he always took at least one, if not two.

Hallie glanced at the gate that cordoned off the house yard from the wide-open paddock and saw a plume of dust with a white speck at its base.

'Well, you're only about half an hour too late,' she said to herself.

Ruby clapped her hands and squealed as the water hit her body with a thwack. Hallie, knowing her husband was nearly home, relaxed and closed her eyes, grateful for the cold arc showering her. The sun, fierce and unrelenting, dried her thin t-shirt in a matter of seconds and she was left wanting—wanting more cool water, a husband that was around, or at least close by, more often than Alex was, and a house without snakes.

When Hallie opened her eyes, she saw a white Toyota LandCruiser identical to Alex's, covered in the same red dust and aerials. The red toolbox on the tray was the same, as was the bar spotlight.

'*This baby*,' Alex had told her, patting the spotlight as he walked around to the driver's side door, '*is a 24-inch, 130-watt insurance policy against kangaroos, cattle that turn up in the middle of the road and the occasional camel.*'

Hallie had been incredulous to hear camels were part of the bush out here. How naive she'd been.

However, this Toyota wasn't Alex's.

And, thankfully, it wasn't Rod's. If it had been, Hallie might get a talking to about having the sprinklers on during the day.

'*No point in watering while the sun's up, Hallie*,' he'd say. '*I'm sure you've heard of evaporation. Just a waste of precious resources.*'

The number plate made Hallie realise her visitor was their neighbour, Danny Betts. That and his big grin through the insect-splattered windscreen. His hand was up in a pointer finger wave.

She instinctively looked to the passenger's seat in the hope that Maggie was with him. Some friends were just what she needed right now. Her heart sank a little further at the emptiness.

Danny parked and ambled over to the fence, adjusting his hat before leaning on the white-painted post underneath the pepper tree. 'G'day there, Hallie. And you, too, Miss Ruby. Looks like you've got this hot weather sorted.'

'Hi, Danny,' Hallie said, not moving from the seat. 'Is it always so hot?' Then she waved her hand in a *don't worry about it* gesture. 'Don't reply to that. I already know the answer.' Closing her mouth quickly, she bit down on the words, *Please, there's a massacred snake in my office, can you get rid of it for me?* Alex wasn't one for involving the neighbours when it wasn't needed.

Ruby came up, now, sucking her thumb, and climbed into Hallie's lap. 'Sweep, Mumma.'

Smoothing her daughter's wet hair back, Hallie kissed her hot forehead and, as the water sprayed over them again, thought maybe they could both go to sleep out here in the shade, with the sprinklers going.

'Alex around?' Danny asked, looking towards the workshop and then the car shed.

'He's gone out on a bore run, should be back any time. Actually, I thought you were him.' Hallie didn't ask if her husband knew Danny was coming. That might seem rude. Everyone in the bush was welcome at any kitchen table, at any time. Nicole had made that clear when she had arrived unexpectedly one morning about a month after Ruby had been born. Hallie hadn't managed to do the dishes, or sweep the kitchen, because she'd still been in bed. Recovering from a sleepless night.

'*That's no excuse, Hallie,*' Nicole had said firmly. '*People in the bush arrive unannounced and unexpectedly. You don't want to be thought of as a slovenly housekeeper and wife, do you? And make sure you have something in the freezer you can just pull out for smokos when people arrive. Banana cake freezes well. Get yourself out of bed, shower and clean the kitchen. I'll watch Ruby for a while.'*

It was about then that Hallie would gladly have murdered her mother-in-law—not for the first time. But what was the point in reminding her it might be weeks before someone called in? Nicole would just say it was better to be prepared than not. '*Imagine what the neighbours would say if they arrived to see this mess in your kitchen, and there was nothing to eat.*'

'*I'd hope they might understand that I have a new baby and offer to help,*' Hallie had snapped.

Her words had been water off a duck's back. '*That's not how we do things out here.*' Nicole's back had straightened and a look of irritation had settled on her face.

Danny glanced at his watch. 'I was supposed to meet him here about half an hour ago but I was running late in leaving home. Bloody dingo killed the chooks last night and I needed to clean out the pen. Didn't want Maggie to have to.'

'That wouldn't have been a nice job in this heat.' Hallie stroked Ruby's hair and wondered where the pram was. If Ruby would sleep in that, then Hallie wouldn't have to keep watch over the cot in her bedroom; she could wheel Ruby everywhere she had to go.

'Doesn't take long for the blowies to find the carcasses.' Danny glanced at his watch again and then at the house.

'There's a snake in the office,' Hallie blurted out. Danny would think her rude if she didn't invite him inside soon. 'That's why we're out here.'

'You've had your dramas this morning, too, then,' he said. 'Where's your shovel? I'll get it.'

'I got it.' A hysterical giggle erupted from her at the same time tears sprang to her eyes. 'I shot it. With the .410.'

Raising his eyebrows, Danny said, 'You shot it? Good job! Any holes in the wall after that effort?' He gave a soft chuckle, his fingers rolling the leaf in his hand back and forth.

'No, I didn't make a hole in the bloody wall,' Hallie snapped, trying to get up with Ruby heavy in her arms. 'The only hole in the wall is where these bastards get in. Do you have any idea what it's like living with snakes in the house?' Red fury seeped out of her now as she stomped towards the house. 'Why the hell should I have to do that?'

The creak of the gate indicated Danny was following her.

Shit, shit, shit! Hallie thought. *Now he'll tell Alex I've been completely emotional and unreasonable.*

'The hormones were running wild today, Alex old lad,' Danny would say.

Except Danny wouldn't because he was kind and thoughtful. Those words would be from Rod.

All she wanted to do was curl up in a ball or sink down at the kitchen table and cry. With a large glass of wine. A bottle even. Hallie wished Maggie had been with Danny.

'Snakes shouldn't be in the house, Hallie,' Danny said quietly. 'I'll get rid of it for you. Is there a shovel around?'

'Around the back, next to the laundry door.' Hallie cast a long glance at the kitchen floor before she set foot over the threshold, realising she sounded terribly ungrateful. 'Sorry. Thank you. Would you like a cup of tea?'

'No bother,' Danny said with a nod and a look at the sleeping Ruby. 'That'd be nice.'

He disappeared around the edge of the verandah and, moments later, Hallie heard the back door slam shut. His familiarity with the house had unnerved her at first. Danny seemed to know more about her home than she ever would; he and Alex had spent loads of time together as kids, then as teenagers at boarding school, and then again at ag college. They were blood brothers, Alex had told her when he'd introduced them.

Hallie placed Ruby in the pram, which she'd found in the walk-in pantry, and lit the gas stove.

From the office, a scraping sound echoed through the rambling homestead and then the back door slammed again. Hallie imagined the snake, still wriggling as Danny tried to scoop it up, then it falling off, the actions being repeated until finally, it was still.

Some moments later, Danny appeared at the kitchen door and let himself in. 'All fixed. Did Alex tell you what time he'd be home?'

Hallie shook her head, getting the cups out of the cupboard. Something moved next to the bench and she screamed, jumping backwards.

Danny darted forward as Ruby started to cry at the noise, her hands clamping over her ears.

'It's okay, it's okay.' Hallie raced to the pram and snatched her daughter out, spinning around at the same time to see what Danny had killed.

He stood there, grinning, a long, wet piece of bark dangling from his fingers. 'Don't reckon this will hurt you. Musta hooked a ride when you came in.'

Hallie couldn't say a word. She patted Ruby's back in a slow, calming manner and wished someone was doing the same for her.

CHAPTER 5

'Are you sure that Alex said one o'clock?' Hallie asked as she laid out tomatoes, lettuce, white bread and cold lamb. For what seemed like the hundredth time, she glanced at the clock, which was now reading nearly 3 p.m. 'It's so unlike Alex to be late for anything. What did he need to talk to you about?'

Her heart had finally settled and Danny had kindly rocked Ruby back to sleep before depositing her in the pram and pushing her under the air-conditioner vent. The little girl's cheeks were still tinged with heat, despite the cool air blowing on her.

Danny took the knife Hallie offered and buttered a piece of bread. 'Not sure what he wanted, just asked me to come over because he had something he needed to talk to me about.'

As he finished speaking, the dogs set off another round of barking. Hallie glanced at Ruby, hoping she wouldn't wake.

'Finally! There he is,' Hallie said. 'Must've got held up somewhere.'

The gate creaked and then Hallie heard footsteps on the verandah. She flicked the kettle on, then went to the fridge to get out the jug of cordial. Alex was the only adult male she knew who still loved green cordial with ice. And just like when he'd been a kid, it made his tongue green and he loved poking it out at Ruby and listening to her giggle.

A loud knock and the buzzing sound from the flies disturbed from their cool place reached Hallie's ears. Confused, she turned to look at the door, expecting to see Alex but also knowing he wouldn't have knocked.

The door swung open and, not waiting for Hallie's invitation to enter, Rod walked in.

'Bloody hot out there,' he said by way of greeting. 'G'day, Danny, Hallie.' He looked from one to the other and across to the sleeping Ruby. Pulling out a chair, Rod sank into it, wiping his forehead. 'There's another six days of this bloody heat forecast before it drops back into the late thirties. I always used to say that I didn't think there was much difference between forty degrees and about forty-five, but I'm not so sure now. Cup of tea on the go there, Hallie? Thanks, love. Nothing like a cup of tea to quench the thirst.'

'Hello, Rod. Do come on in.' Sarcasm laced her words. Clenching her teeth but making her mouth smile, Hallie rounded back to the cupboard and pulled out another cup.

'How are things at your place, Danny?' Rod asked. The scraping sound told Hallie he'd grabbed the salt and pepper shakers and was turning them in his hands. She couldn't clench her jaw any tighter so, instead, she mashed her lips together and breathed in heavily through her nose. Not that her father-in-law was a bad person. Rod was quite nice mostly, until he got heavy-handed with what he thought his rights inside her house were. His assumption that he could walk into where she lived and treat her like a . . . well, housewife, annoyed her.

Annoyed was too nice a word.

It pissed her off. She was not just a wife or mother, Hallie wanted to shout so often. *Ever heard of Anthea Crawford? No? Well, google her. And while you're at it, google me and then you might realise who your son has married, not the other way around.* Her in-laws would have no idea how many people listened to her podcast nor that she coordinated her trips to Adelaide and Sydney around invitations to fashion-house launches. Hallie was a big deal in the industry.

'You're looking well, Rod,' Danny said with a grin.

'Gotta look after yourself when you've got to drive a ten-inch nail,' Rod joked.

Hallie wanted to throw up at the thought of her father-in-law's penis and sex life. Seriously, this man lived back in the seventies and eighties. Someone needed to tell him how inappropriate his comments were. That no one spoke like that anymore.

'Anyhow, you know what it's like this time of the year. Not much we can do 'cause of the heat. Check the waters, make sure there are no problems and that's about all.

Is there anything I can do to give you a hand, Hallie?' Danny was sounding uncertain.

'Ah, if you—'

'Mmm, mmm. And how're your parents?' Rod interrupted. 'I haven't heard too much of them recently.' The shakers th-thunked again against the wooden tabletop.

'They've been holidaying up at the Whitsundays. Due home tomorrow. How's everything with you and Mrs Donaldson?' He caught Hallie's eye. 'What did you need me to do?'

'Nothing. I'm fine.' Hallie put the cup of tea down in front of Rod and forced a smile. There was no point in trying to show up her father-in-law's manners, he wouldn't even notice. 'Did you need some lunch, Rod? We were going to wait until Alex got back from the bore run, but he's taking his sweet time, so we've started.'

'Too late for lunch, love. By my watch it's afternoon smoko. Anyhow, Nic fed me a while back. All those cakes and sponges she puts out. No wonder I'm the size I am.' He patted his stomach. 'And she wins all those cooking competitions at the ag shows. Not a single person could fault that woman's scones, ay, Danny?'

Hallie tried not to take his comments as a personal insult. The first batch of scones she'd baked were legendary in Tirranah now. Rod and Nicole joked they could have used them to measure the depth of the house well they'd been so heavy. 'Or chucked 'em at the dogs when they were in the wrong place in the sheep yards,' Rod had joked.

'Mrs Donaldson fed us boys pretty well when we were growing up. Maggie really appreciated the pavlova she brought over on New Year's Eve,' Danny said.

'How is Maggie?' Hallie asked, with a glance at the sleeping Ruby.

'No kids on the go yet?' Rod again interjected. 'I heard she was going back to work at the council office. Mate, you'll have to be careful. She should be at home with you, having kids. These modern women . . .' His voice trailed off and he shook his head as if he was incredibly disappointed with the female of the species.

Danny cleared his throat and glanced at Hallie, who gave a one-shoulder shrug, despite the tension in her body. She heard Rod's opinion on what women should and shouldn't do every time he dropped by. One day he'd even interrupted her recording a podcast with Alex Perry, fashion designer to the stars!

For the interview, Hallie had tried to buy an Alex Perry jacket, even though she knew they were worth thousands of dollars. Alex had frowned at the price, then smiled. '*I reckon you'd look gorgeous in that*,' he'd said, when she'd showed him the photo.

And, oh, how she'd wanted that single-breasted silk jacket that would have been at home in the boardroom or on the red carpet of the Brownlow Medal. Blue was her colour, too, but . . . Well, she couldn't really justify it, even with Alex's thoughts.

Instead, she'd settled for one she found online in a second-hand designer store.

Rod hadn't cared about the interview and had barely glanced at the jacket she wore as he'd stuck his head into the office and asked, '*Any chance of a cuppa, love?*' As if he didn't know how to boil the kettle himself. Or care about anything so frivolous as a fashion podcast. Which he didn't. In fact, Hallie doubted Rod even knew she had one, or what a podcast was. If it wasn't on ABC Radio, it wasn't worth knowing about.

She'd waved him out of the office, but Rod had kept returning. Finally, she'd had to ask Alex Perry if they could reschedule because something had 'come up'. Rod had been lucky she hadn't filled his tea with arsenic, and Alex had had some smoothing over to do that night.

'Maggie doesn't have to answer to me, Rod,' Danny said, leaning back in his chair. 'She's my wife, not my slave. If she wants to work in the council office during the week and come home on weekends, that's her choice and I fully support her. I don't hold her hostage out here. And really, what the hell is there for her to do so far from anywhere? She likes her work there.'

Rod had put down the salt and pepper shakers now and was turning the cup instead. Th-thunk. Th-thunk.

'Ah, well, don't say I didn't tell you, Daniel. It's not right when married women are living in town by themselves. Gives the wrong impression, you know.'

The use of Danny's full name got Hallie's attention. She smirked and looked over at Danny, raising her eyebrows. *You're in trouble now.*

'All good, Rod,' Danny answered mildly, half closing his eye in a wink to Hallie. 'I'll let Maggie know you were concerned for her.'

Rod took a sip of his tea, oblivious to Danny's sarcasm, and smacked his lips together. 'Boiled with little sticks, this cuppa's that hot,' he said. 'Now, where is that son of mine?'

'I'd like to know that, too,' Hallie said, her eyes straying to the clock again. 'Oh, I'll check the cameras in the office to see if his ute has gone from the bore.'

Danny stood. 'I can do that for you, Hallie.'

'No, no. Thanks. It's okay.' She smiled, grateful Danny hadn't mentioned what had happened earlier and appreciative he had also realised she would be nervous to go back into the office.

'I don't know why Alex thought it was a good idea to install those cameras. It's nice to be able to check the waters without leaving the house, but there's nothing more fertile on a station than a manager's footsteps.' Rod's judgemental tone followed her hesitant steps down the passageway as she checked for anything that moved.

'You know, Danny, I've been out to check tanks, turkey nests, dams, whatever the watering point, and found there's a wire snapped because a camel has walked through, or I mighta got to shoot a dingo, 'cause I was in the right place at the right time.'

'Mmm,' Danny answered.

'Yeah, you can know there's water in the tank, but what about all the other things you might get to fix by driving out there? I'm not sure this mod-con stuff is the right direction. Makes young fellas lazy, if you ask me.'

Danny murmured some kind of response, which Hallie imagined was appeasing yet let Rod know that a forward trajectory was inevitable.

She stood in the doorway of the office now, her hands on the door frame, leaning in a little to peer to the left, behind the door, and then to the right. She listened. Hard.

Only the hum of the computer. Her heart had picked up its pace now, yet she wouldn't let Rod know she didn't want to walk into that office. If anything, she should be shouting that she'd managed to act just like a farmer's wife. Like Nicole would have, because she, Hallie, had killed a snake. Shot it, even!

But no, she'd slide inside the office, holding her breath, checking every place on the floor where she put her feet. And check the cameras.

The computer's screen was black, so she wiggled the mouse to wake it up and clicked through to where the images were split into six different scenes: Rising Water Bore—no guessing how that one got its name; Sandy Bore—again, it wouldn't take Einstein to work that out . . .

From the kitchen there was a scraping sound as one of her visitors pushed their chair from the table.

'Oh.' Hallie closed her eyes and breathed deeply, opening them as Rod barged into the office, Danny close behind him.

'Come on, let's have a look and see what's going on.'

Hallie stood stock still, not moving. She hadn't had time to check the darkened corners and see if they were clear. 'Um . . .' Finally, she glanced down and saw a red stain moving across the floor. Only it wasn't moving, it just looked like it was. 'Ah . . .'

'Out of the way there, Hallie.' Rod peered at the screen, his finger tracing across each image. 'Red Dirt Bore. Isn't that where you said he was headed?'

Hallie didn't answer. Instead, she cleared her throat and shuffled a few steps out of Rod's way, trying not to move too quickly.

'Hallie?' Rod sounded exasperated.

'What?' Her voice was high and strained.

'Was it Red Dirt Bore that Alex was going to?'

'Ah, yeah.' She glanced back at the screen, then at the floor. 'Red Dirt Bore. But look.' With shaking hands, Hallie pointed to the screen that so often had a galah peering at them through the camera. Instead of seeing its beak, the bird was perched on the edge of the trough, flapping its wings. That's how the motion camera must have been flicked into life because there was nothing else moving in the picture.

The trough was full and the tank was nearly overflowing. All but one of the birds from earlier in the day had disappeared to the shade of the tree branches, and the bullbar of Alex's ute was still in the corner of the frame.

At the bottom of the windmill, way in the distance, lay what looked to be a leg and boot.

CHAPTER 6

'Oi,' Dave said as his wife walked past and batted his feet playfully. He wiggled them at Kim and she shook her head in the affectionate but still exasperated way she had perfected over the ten years they had been together.

'Get those legs off your desk. If Joan sees that, she'll have a fit!'

'Yeah, she's already cleaned your office today,' Mia called from further inside the police station. 'Leave any marks and she'll be chasing you with a duster.'

Detective Dave Burrows looked from one woman to the other as Mia stuck her head through the doorway and winked, then disappeared again.

'Or she might make you sweep the floor.' Kim threw Dave a glance that said she wouldn't mind it if he did a few little things at home. 'In fact, if you're keen . . .'

'Henpecked,' he sighed. 'I'm being henpecked. Has Joan gone home? I'm sure she'll rescue me.'

'Ha! Unlikely! She'd be in agreement with us!' Mia shouted from the back office.

'Not sure you need rescuing,' Kim replied. 'And, yeah, she left as I was arriving. It's her grandson's birthday, so she couldn't stay to celebrate with us.' Reaching into the basket, she handed Dave an envelope. 'This came for you today.'

Dave pressed his lips together as he glanced at the letter. The now-familiar writing looped across the front: *Detective Dave Burrows, C/- Barker Post Office*. This was the second invitation he'd received in the last six months. The first had been an engagement party invite.

'It's here.' Stating the obvious, but the words slipped out before Dave could stop them. 'Thanks.' He took the letter and looked at it for a long moment. Opening it in front of Kim might cause her a whole lot of hurt.

Kim was studiously unpacking the picnic she'd brought, giving him the time and space to do with that invitation just as he wished.

'I gave Joan a card with a gift voucher for little Baxter,' she was saying. 'His mum was making the train cake from the *Women's Weekly Birthday Cake* book. Baxter wanted five carriages, but Joan said there was only going to be three, one for each year he'd been alive. They were going to use toy ones after that.'

'Sounds cute,' Mia called. The door of a locker slammed, and moments later she appeared in the doorway wearing casual clothes. 'Still, cute and innocent are a farce when it comes to kids.'

Kim laughed. 'Are you speaking from experience? How did your talk go today?'

'Ugh! Disastrous.' Mia put her hands over her eyes.

Dave was still looking at the envelope. Perhaps this needed the band-aid treatment: just rip it off. His first-born daughter, Bec, had been in contact over six months ago to let him know she was getting married. Hearing her voice for the first time in many, many years had brought a flood of different emotions to him, none of which he had wanted nor, as he'd decided after the phone call, needed to experience. Be easier if Bec hadn't rung him, especially with what she'd said: 'We want you to come, Dad, but just you. No one else. I heard you got married?'

'*Melinda and John Bannister along with Carol and David Scott invite David Burrows to the wedding of . . .*' he read aloud, then he hung his head to hide the heat that had found his cheeks.

'What?' Mia asked.

He repeated the words.

'That's just rude.' Mia stared at him before her gaze cut across to Kim.

Kim had been ignored, just as Bec had said she would be. Dave wanted to ring his daughter and demand how dare she be . . . Well, he couldn't say 'just like your mother', but that's exactly how Bec was acting. '*Justin Scott and Rebecca Burrows*,' he finished.

'What date did they choose?' Kim asked. She looked over with a smile, seemingly ignoring the fuss around her.

Astonished and yet not surprised at Kim's response, he answered, 'August.'

Kim at her very best. Kind, loving, understanding. Selfless. Always thinking of others first and certainly always working out what was best for husband rather than herself.

'Better book your ticket,' Kim said. 'Make sure you go and stay for a week or two, so you've got some time with your mum and brother. Maybe you could visit some of your old crew from the Stock Squad. You could go to see Bob in the nursing home.'

Bob Holden was Dave's old boss from too many years ago.

'How could she not invite Kim?' Mia had put down her police-issued belt onto her desk and was taking her gun out of its holster. 'Where's the key for the gun cabinet . . . Don't worry, I've got it.' She unlocked the steel cabinet and put the revolver in its place before emptying the ammunition from her belt.

'How was your day, constable?' Dave asked as he shifted out of Kim's way. She was now unpacking a basket of cheeses and Mia's favourite dip—cheese, chive and bacon cob loaf. There was a bottle of what looked suspiciously like champagne underneath the goodies and Dave pretended he hadn't glimpsed that; if he were in Adelaide or Perth or any other large town, alcohol at a police station would be a serious offence, but out here in the sticks, in a two-officer station, no one would be making a report.

'Oh, formality,' Mia teased. 'Mine was just fine. No problems anywhere, until'—she gave a self-deprecating smile—'I'm not sure Miss Travenski was that thrilled with the start of my talk. I may have mentioned something about dying as a police officer.' She put her hands on her hips. 'I know you gave me that gig so you didn't have to do it, *Detective*.'

'Mia!' Kim's head shot up. 'You didn't.' A pause. 'You did.' Kim sounded resigned now. 'Those poor children!'

'Hey, it's a talk they'll never forget!' Mia ran her fingers through her hair and straightened. 'Still, there are two little girls in that class who are going to come for a ride in the police car with me tomorrow morning, all things being equal.' Perching on the desk, drooling over the spread, she picked up a piece of toasted bread and dipped it straight into the cob loaf. 'What's the occasion?'

'"What's the occasion?" she asks,' Kim said with a small roll of her eyes. 'Seriously, Mia? You don't know?'

The mischief faded from Mia's face and she looked from Kim to Dave and back again. 'Shit! Have I forgotten someone's birthday? What's the date?' Reaching for the desk calendar, she turned it around, searching for what she might have missed.

'No, Mia,' Kim said patiently. 'Not someone's birthday.' Placing three plastic champagne flutes on the desk and extracting the bottle, she handed it to Dave.

'What have I forgotten?' Mia asked again, confused.

'I shouldn't be opening this here,' Dave said. 'Just letting you both know.' He twisted the top and seconds later the loud 'pop' echoed through the office. He emptied the bubbling liquid into the glasses.

The fizz and leaping bubbles caught Mia's attention for a second until she grabbed more bread and swiped it through the dip. Dave inwardly grinned as he watched his constable's mind turn over, her thoughts so clearly written on her face. The habit wasn't a good one for a police officer. The deadpan *I have no emotion and if I did you wouldn't know about it* expression was a much better one. Dave had perfected it, although he'd had many years to practise.

'Well,' she said slowly, 'I'm guessing since there's alcohol involved, you're not pregnant, Kim!'

Kim coughed and Dave looked horrified.

'Not a chance,' Dave answered, handing her a glass. 'Here. Drink up. I'll make a detective of you yet.' His breath caught in his throat. That was something his old partner Bob would have said to him many, many years ago. Bob wasn't dead yet, but he might as well be, stuck in the nursing home he was in, without any family.

After he'd retired from his position in the police force, handing the top job over to Dave, Bob and his wife Betty had traversed all over Australia in a caravan. Years spent seeing all the sights until one afternoon while they were camped in the Streaky Bay Caravan Park, when Betty had gone for a kip and never woken up again.

Bob had packed up the van, driven home and slowly declined until he couldn't look after himself anymore.

Dave still thought of him every day and rang him every Sunday afternoon. Not that the phone calls were long. Bob had trouble following in-depth conversations.

His mate had been there from the start of Dave's marital troubles with Melinda, and would have been elated knowing Bec had been in contact, yet as annoyed about her behaviour as Dave was.

'Not at my time of life, sweetie,' Kim answered, recovering. 'The only babies on my list of priorities these days are ones I can give back. I'll put you out of your misery. Happy twelve months of being at Barker Police Station! Here's to another twelve.' She raised her glass towards Mia.

'Oh . . .' Mia blinked and Dave watched again as she counted back to when she had been given a permanent position at the station. 'You're right! Happy anniversary to me!' Her face cleared and she smiled broadly at them both. 'I didn't even realise.'

'Obviously,' Dave said dryly, holding up his glass. 'Well, Mia, it's certainly been an interesting ride over the last year. And I have to say—'

'Hasn't it? Anyhow,' Mia hurried on.

Perhaps she's worried I'll bring up all the times I've had to save her or reprimand or . . . Yeah, the list is long, he thought. *It* has *been a hell of a ride.*

'Happy one year here with us.' Kim interrupted the two of them by raising her glass.

'Thanks.' Mia took a sip, then put her glass down. 'So, Bec and Justin didn't invite Kim to the engagement and now not the wedding either?'

Dave wasn't going to defend Bec, he was as shocked and embarrassed as Mia sounded. The engagement party was a sore point with his daughter, because it had been on Kim's and his wedding anniversary, and he wasn't not spending that with his wife.

Kim, on the other hand, was calmly putting strawberries next to the carrot sticks, still with a serene expression on her face. 'I was just saying that Dave needs to book his flight. It's March now, so August isn't that far away. You didn't have any plans to take time off around then, did you?' she asked Mia with a smile.

'Um, no, but . . .'

'Well, Dave needs to put in for leave. Maybe a couple of weeks.'

'Henpecked,' Dave murmured again.

The women ignored him.

'But'—Mia frowned and looked at the invitation again, then at Kim—'you're not going?'

'No.' Kim shrugged. 'Dave is her father, and neither Bec nor Alice have met me so . . .'

'But they'll love you when they do,' Mia said.

'Excuse me,' Dave said.

Kim held up her finger, silencing him. 'He needs to go without me.'

'Well, I agree he needs to go to the wedding, but you should be—'

'Mia, it's Bec's wedding, not mine or yours or Adam Ant's. Bec and Justin's. They're going to know what they want.' This time, Kim aimed her dazzling smile at Dave. 'I just think it's wonderful she's been in contact with her dad. Bec is the one who's made the effort and I'm not going to stand in the way of a reunion between him and the girls.

There's plenty of time for us to get to know each other in less'—she paused—'emotional and stressful situations.'

'Ohhh, is Bec the sort who would be a Bridezilla? Can I have a strawberry, please?'

'You're incorrigible!' Kim answered mildly, handing over three.

Dave cleared his throat. 'In case you've both gone blind, I'm still in the room.'

'Of course you are, sweetie.'

'Oh, sorry, I probably spoke—'

'—without thinking,' Dave agreed. 'Nothing unusual there.' Still, Mia was one hundred per cent correct. There was no way Bec should have sent the invitation without Kim's name on it. That was the height of bad manners.

Yet, that was exactly what her mother, Melinda, would have done. Walking to the beat of her own drum, not thinking about anyone except who mattered the most to her. That usually accounted for both daughters, her father and he supposed—or rather hoped, for John's sake—her new husband. Dave had been on the wrong end of that list for a while and he wouldn't wish it on anyone.

In the fifteen-plus years he and Melinda had been divorced, Dave had battled to be allowed to see his children and, in the end, he'd given up. It had only been by chance he'd found out Mel was remarrying, when Bob had mentioned hearing about the society wedding on the police grapevine. He wasn't going to admit that it had hurt like hell to see John's name on the invitation for his daughter's wedding and not his. And that was on Melinda, his ex-wife, and her father, Mark.

There could be no denying the animosity of both people towards Dave.

Kim was more than incredible, he thought, as he listened to her speak. Her love for people shone brightly and, for someone who hadn't trained, her understanding of human psychology was unmistakably high. All of that was what made her beautiful. Happy people are beautiful people, someone had said to him once. Kim was beautiful on the surface and deep inside.

That was also why he couldn't ever vocalise what he was thinking. How did couples who started out loving each other become strangers? Oh, he loved Kim and she was the only woman he wanted, but Melinda? He had so much regret around Melinda. He had loved her once. Loved her enough to have two children with her. Here they were now, however, strangers. So many years had gone by since he'd heard her laugh or watched her shake her hair out. Or caught the wary expression she'd always worn when he'd talked about his job.

You're getting old and thinking far too much, he told himself. *Stop it.*

Bell chimes sounded from the pocket of his shirt. 'Just hang on a sec,' he told Mia and Kim, fishing out the phone. He looked at the screen and took a deep breath through his nose. 'Ah, this doesn't look good,' he said, almost glad of the interruption. 'Burrows.'

Kim and Mia looked at each other as they put their glasses down. They knew what the expression on Dave's face meant. Mia swiped another piece of bread into the dip then chewed, waiting for the information.

Taking the phone away from his ear, Dave punched at the speaker button and put the phone on the desk.

'—deceased male believed to be that of Alex Donaldson.'

Mia stopped chewing and Kim's forehead wrinkled as her hand went to her chest.

Mia grabbed a notebook from her pocket and flipped open to a clean page at the same time as Kim handed her a pen.

'It appears he's fallen at height, from a windmill.' The voice from Dispatch was tinny and echoing through the phone.

'Who called it in?' Dave asked, dragging a map of the area towards him.

'The father. A Mr Rod Donaldson. He and a neighbour are at the scene. The wife, ah, Hallie, is at the house and if you go there, she'll give you directions. An ambulance has been called, although there doesn't appear to be any need, but I haven't stood them down. I'll leave that to you. I'll send you an email with extra information.'

'Right, thanks muchly,' Dave said. 'Contact details?' He scribbled down a phone number and directions. 'We're on it.'

Kim started to pack away the goodies. 'Looks like you're going to have a different one-year celebration to what we planned,' she whispered to Mia.

Mia nodded. Her eyes followed Dave's finger, which was tracing a road north of Barker on the map. He kept going and going until he finally tapped on a spot.

'Way out the back of bum fuck,' he said. 'Come on, we'd better get on the road.' He gave Kim a swift kiss. 'Who knows what time we'll be home,' he told her.

'Be safe.' Kim put her arms around his waist and gave him a brief hug. Dave returned it, before issuing instructions.

'We'll need to take the troopy. When was that refuelled last? And can you give Hamish a call. See if he's the one driving the ambulance tonight. We need the camera and body bag. Make sure we've got everything, because it's a long way to come back to get something we left behind.'

Mia was nodding and, having already changed back into her uniform, reached for her belt again. Kim let herself out silently.

Dave picked up his phone and dialled the number Dispatch had given to him, still on speaker.

'G'day, Rod, is it? This is Detective Dave Burrows from the Barker Police Station. I understand there's been an accident?'

'Yeah, my son. He's fallen from the top of the windmill. Alex, he . . . He was checking the oil . . . He's fallen from the top.' The man's voice was wobbly.

'I'm sorry to hear that. I want you to know we're on our way. I also need to confirm, you've checked for any signs of life?'

Rod cleared his throat before answering. 'He's . . . Alex . . . *ahem*. My son is most definitely dead.'

'I am sorry for your loss. Please don't touch Alex or anything around him until we get there. Do you have anyone with you?'

'Yes. Danny, the next-door neighbour. He came out here with me.'

'Is there anyone with Alex's wife? Her name is'—Dave checked his notes—'Hallie?'

'Yes. Yes, there is. Nicole, she's my wife, is on her way over to be with Hallie and their toddler. Danny's wife, Maggie is driving there as well. They're all close by in terms of the distance out here.' Rod's voice had taken on the practicality of all country blokes.

'That's good. Look, I realise we are going to take a while to get to you, but if you could please stay there until we do, we'd appreciate it. Our ETA is'—he glanced at the clock on the wall—'about two and half hours from now, so it'll be getting close to seven thirty p.m.'

'See you then.'

Mia heard the father's voice break as he ended the call.

'What else do we need? I've texted Hamish and he's going to bring the van, rather than the ambulance. He's checked his body bag supply and is A-okay. Although he doesn't want to start driving out there until we do. Better if we get there first or arrive at the same time,' she said. 'Plus, better to travel in tandem in case he has a problem.'

Dave nodded, checking the battery on his torch. 'Hamish can follow us if he wants, although I'll probably be driving a little quicker than he will want to on those roads out there. We can stay in contact via the radio.'

Mia nodded and tapped out a message on her phone.

Looking at her, Dave raised his eyebrows. 'Right?'

'Yeah, let's do this.'

The door of the police station closed behind them with a loud click and Dave waited while Mia went to get the troopy. Tipping his head back, he looked at the sky. It was a vivid blue now, but by the time he got to the scene, it would be black. The moon was full at this time of the month, rising, spreading an eerie light across the land, casting shadows long and thin as insects flocked to the lights at the front of the troopy. The noise of their bodies hitting the lights made a 'ting' sound. In among the inky black of the sky, pinpricks of silver would twinkle at him, and he remembered how he'd always sung 'Twinkle, Twinkle Little Star' to Bec and Alice when they were tiny. His daughters were warm, living, breathing humans as of this moment.

This morning, a young man with a wife and child was still alive. Maybe he laughed with his daughter and tickled her under the chin before he left the house. Dave had done that to his girls. Perhaps Alex had kissed his wife before he left, patted his dog and got into that ute to go on a normal, everyday bore run. As everyone who lived and worked on stations did every day.

Tonight, he wasn't coming home.

CHAPTER 7

'Shit, bloody hell,' Dave muttered as the troopy hit another deep pothole. 'We've got to get these spotlights looked at. I reckon the bracket on the left-hand side one is broken. Look at where the beam is! Can you hear it hitting against the bullbar?'

Mia didn't answer.

The light had dipped and moved with each corrugation and was now pointing into the treetops and bush, rather than along the track. The other spotlight was picking up the ridges, casting shadows in front of each bump. The road felt as if someone had laid corrugated iron sheets crossways on the road and they were skimming across the top.

'Been a while since the grader was out here, too,' Dave muttered. 'Wouldn't hurt to make a call to the council offices tomorrow. This road is almost unpassable. The wrong sort of caravan out here would snap an axle in a heartbeat.'

Mia was holding on to the Jesus bar, her hair swaying in time with the movement of the troopy. 'I'll ring Kaylee in the morning and see if she can do anything. I bet the Donaldsons and anyone else out here don't come to town very often.'

'Mail still has to be brought out, as do the supplies. My guess would be that this isn't Kurt and Ben's favourite mail run.' He groaned as an extra deep pothole threw him to the right and he hit his shoulder on the window. 'Shit!'

Mia saw the lights from Hamish's refrigerated van bouncing up and down behind them in the side mirror. She peered out into the evening dimness, trying to work out where they were. Silhouettes of gum trees and their branches blocked out some of the sky, yet the evening star shone brightly on the horizon, while the haze of fairy-floss colours stretched out in the distance. Mia didn't recognise the country, and there was nothing to give her a hint of where they were. Her watch told her they'd been travelling for just over two hours, so they shouldn't be too far away from the turnoff.

Sometimes, Mia thought, *our job is terrible*. She really didn't want to think about having to spend any time in the house with a grieving wife and mother. Her nana had impressed upon her that '*People won't always remember what you did, but they'll remember the way you made them feel*.'

Nana had been wise, and Mia wished with all her heart she could have some of that wisdom today. She couldn't think of one damn thing to say that would ease the pain of anyone tonight. Was there even anything that would?

Tears pricked her eyes as she thought of the young woman who might be about her age, perhaps a little older. Mia didn't know what it was like to love someone so much she wanted to marry them, but, if it was anything like losing Nana, she knew what grief felt like. In fact, after the death of her own mum, Nana's passing had felt like she'd lost her mother all over again. Mia imagined this woman—Hallie—had expected to have the rest of her life with Alex. There might have been more kids, laughs and gentle teasing about those first few grey hairs. They would've expected to watch their kids graduate, then one day wake up and realise fifty years had passed and they still loved to sleep in each other's arms and wake up to each other's faces.

That's what Hallie would have pictured, as she'd floated down the aisle towards the love of her life, because that's what every bride thought.

Nice ideals. Life didn't always work like a fairytale. Maybe Alex and Hallie would've made it to ten years and then had a bitter divorce. Or perhaps they wouldn't have bothered with the split, they would've just slowly grown apart, neither interested in the other's life anymore.

But it no longer mattered what the future had been going to hold. The reality was that Hallie was a widow now and her child, fatherless.

Mia's heart gave another heavy, sad thud. She knew what it was like to be without a dad.

'Okay, so there should be a ramp with a buggered motorbike and a steel box strapped onto the back at the entrance to the station. The house is about twenty kilometres in. Dispatch's email said there were reflectors on the seat of the motorbike to show the way.' Dave was leaning forward, looking hard at the beams of light from the headlights.

'Can you see any better with your nose on the windscreen?' Mia asked, her face a picture of pure innocence.

'No different to you turning down the music when you need to look for street names,' Dave hurled back, quick smart.

'Hey! That's called concentration.'

'Ohhh, that's what it is! Concentrate with your ears, do you?'

They fell into a comfortable silence, watching for any sign of a motorbike and a ramp, then a long driveway.

'How are you feeling about this?' Dave asked a few moments later. 'Got any questions? Know what you're going to do?'

Mia felt her stomach tighten for a second, then shook her head. 'Think I'm good. Wouldn't want to be the wife.' She paused. 'Guess there'll be another child growing up without a father.' She was thrust back to the night she found out *her* father had committed suicide after a lifetime battle with mental illness and a personality disorder. That facts had been kept from her, and coming to terms with her grandmother's bombshell, had taken time. According to Nana's friend, Mia had only been tiny—still a bub in arms—when her dad had pulled the trigger.

Then, in her late primary-school years, her mum hadn't survived a car accident, so her grandmother had raised her.

For a short time, Mia had wondered if she'd been so bad as a child that her parents hadn't wanted to be around her, but that idea had been quickly squashed by Nana. Being an orphan hadn't bothered her since then, because she believed what her nana had told her. Not once had Mia questioned whether she was loved or not. That knowledge came easily, because her nana's actions spoke louder than any voices in her head.

Not wanting to linger on the memory, she checked the GPS co-ordinates on the screen, then looked in the direction the spotlight was pointing.

A flash of Hamish's lights again made her focus on the side mirror.

'Did Hamish just flash his lights at us?' she asked.

'You'd never be able to tell on this bloody road,' Dave grumbled.

Mia watched for another flash, but the lights stayed behind them, moving in time with the road.

'He'd call us on the radio if he needed us,' Dave reminded her.

'Mmm.' As she turned to ask him a question a reflection caught her attention. 'Look, there.' Pointing to the right-hand side of the road, she shook her finger. 'Can you see that? I think we're about there.'

'At the turnoff,' Dave agreed. 'Still a bit to go.' He flicked on the blinker and then shot her a glance as the troopy vibrated over the ramp. 'How's Chris? Has he moved stations yet?'

Mia cast her eyes downwards and hid a smile, knowing that was Dave's way of asking, '*What the hell is going on with you and Chris?*'

'He's fine,' she said. 'I can't believe it's been over a year since we left the academy. Constables making our way in the world of policing together. Just not in the same units.' They had been firm friends, both sticking up for each other as they'd gone through their training. Chris had created a fitness schedule for them and spotted Mia as she'd lifted weights at the gym. Mia, being five foot nothing, had been convinced that what she didn't have in height, she'd make up for in strength.

'Did he get the transfer he was looking for?'

Mia turned to him. 'Why don't you just ask me outright if he's moving to Broad River? Not that he'd want to. The three days I spent there was more than enough! Wouldn't wish that misogyny on anyone! And how do you know, anyway?'

'Didn't want to seem nosy,' Dave said.

'I'm sure you didn't.' Mia rolled her eyes, knowing that Dave couldn't see them in the dark.

The troopy shook hard as Dave lifted his foot and they started to slow. Insects pinged against the windshield, distorting their view. The blinker still clicked.

'So?' Dave asked.

'So, nothing,' Mia said. She plucked at the side of her pants, not wanting to have this conversation. 'There really isn't anything to tell you.'

Another sidelong glance and Dave must have seen the look on her face in the dim glow from the radio and computer screen, because he didn't ask anything more.

Mia's memory tossed her back to the bar with Chris in Adelaide last time she'd visited. He'd had something to talk to her about because he'd been fiddling with the collar of his shirt all night. More than once, Mia had slapped his hand away and told him to stop fidgeting. She and Chris knew each other so well, they could hear volumes in their silences and from watching each other's actions. They were best mates. Nothing more.

Chris had ordered four drinks so he didn't have to go back to the bar, and together they'd carried them to the booth in the far corner, right next to the toilet door, where the lighting was low. Once they'd got through each other's news, talking over loud music, Chris had leaned over and taken her hand. '*How would you feel if I asked for a transfer to Broad River Station?*'

Her first reaction had been to squeal and try to throw her arms around him from across the table. '*That would be brilliant! We could hang out on the weekends and muck around.*' Then something in his expression stopped her. Mia withdrew her hands and tucked a strand of dark hair behind her ear. '*Broad River is a pretty shitty station to work at, though. Remember all the crap I went through and I was only there a short while?*'

As Chris drew in a deep breath, a woman had weaved her way around the chairs and tables, hanging on unsteadily until she got to them.

'*Hello, hello,*' she said, leering into Chris's face.

'*And hello back to you. Better move on, all right?*' Even though Chris had used his no-nonsense police officer voice, the woman was too far gone to hear it.

She'd leaned closer to Mia then, as if to share a secret. '*Pretty cute, he is. I'd hold on to him.*' Mia caught the sparkle of drunken tears. '*Wish I hadn't kicked mine out so quick.*' With a wobble, the woman pushed herself off the table and tried to open the toilet door. In the end she hip-and-shouldered it and lurched through to the other side.

Mia had wanted to laugh, but as she looked back to say something funny to Chris, the little alarm bell that had sounded moments before inside her head clanged loudly. She drew back a little and pulled her glass in front of her, then reached for the menu and pretended to read the specials.

'*I thought . . .*' Chris trailed off. '*I thought you might like me to be closer.*' His words had come out in a rush just as Mia's stomach dropped like a stone. Suddenly, the thrum of the band seemed extra loud, the high-pitched voices echoing through Mia's body.

'*Well,*' she'd said carefully, '*of course, that would be nice. It'd be great to have a mate close by to hang out with, have a few—*'

The hope in Chris's face started to seep away. '*Just mates?*' he asked.

'*Well, that's what we are.*'

'Mia! You're not even listening to me!'

She felt Dave push her shoulder gently. 'Sorry, I was thinking. What did you say?'

'House lights. Up ahead.'

CHAPTER 8

'He's here.'

Mia heard the voice before she worked out who was speaking. Dave had turned off the engine only moments ago. After following the instructions from Alex's mother, Nicole, who had been standing at the gate, near the homestead, waited for them. Lights from the ute were highlighting a tarpaulin, which had a man-sized shape underneath it. Mia stepped out of the troopy and took a surprised breath of hot air, despite the fact that the sun had been down for a short time. Brushing away the insects that were crawling over her bare skin, she hoped they would go away, yet knew they wouldn't.

'G'day,' Dave said from the other side of the troopy. 'I'm Detective Dave Burrows. You must be Danny? You're Alex's neighbour? You're the one who sent a text to say Rod had gone back to the homestead?'

'Yeah, that's me.'

The voice lapsed into silence, so Mia walked around and introduced herself. The man who had been squatting next to the tarpaulin struggled to his feet and shook her hand. After the formalities his eyes flicked back to where the body lay. They didn't move again.

'Can you tell me what happened?' Dave asked. He had come to stand beside the man, notebook in hand. Mia took out hers, turning at the sound of another engine. Hamish had followed them to this lonely bush watering hole and was now waiting, out of the way, until Mia or Dave called him over.

'No. I mean, I don't know. Wasn't here. He'd, ah, Alex had asked me to come over around lunchtime for a catch-up. I live over the range on the next-door station. Alex and I went to school together, so we've been mates for ages. When I arrived at the homestead, he hadn't come back from the bore run and then we saw him lying on the ground through the cameras back at the house. Rod and I got out here as quickly as we could, but he—' The young man swallowed hard. 'Alex was a thorough operator so my guess is he would have been checking the oil in the head of the windmill and fallen off. You can see that the platform around the top is only wide enough for one single man up there. It's easy to put a foot over the edge and overbalance.'

The resoluteness and acceptance, yet complete devastation, in his voice made Mia blink away tears.

Danny couldn't have been much older than Mia. He had a twelve o'clock shadow and his thumbs were hooked into his belt loops. In his top pocket, there was the outline of a phone and the tip of a pen protruding out of slit. Even though there were traces of redness around his eyes, she didn't ask if he was okay. The answer to that question was no, because how could anyone be prepared for a tragic death? To Mia's way of thinking, an unexpected death was worse than a long, lingering one. The shock echoed around every part of the body for months and months to come.

'Who's we?'

As Dave asked the questions, Mia went to the back of the troopy and took out the camera bag, becoming aware of the noise of water running somewhere. She took a couple of steps towards the noise, then fished her torch from the loop on her belt. Switching it on, she flashed the strong beam around. Silhouettes appeared, long shadows reaching out past the glow into the darkness, and a shiver ran across her body. There could be anything out there past the torch light and she wouldn't know about it until it was too late. A dingo, a camel, a person. She turned slowly in a circle, listening. The running water, the creak of the windmill head as it turned in the puff of wind that blew every few minutes, and the low hum of the van that Hamish was yet to turn off.

He probably wouldn't, Mia surmised. Hamish wasn't a big fan of summer and heat, even though he loved to run. If there was a choice of turning off the engine and standing outside, getting a bit of sweat underneath those red curls of his, or staying in his seat, listening to music with the cool breeze on his face, he'd always choose the latter. Staying in the background until Mia or Dave waved him over was important while the family was around, too.

On cue, the van's engine changed as the air conditioner kicked in.

A few more steps away from the troopy and Mia found the trough and tank. Water ran like a small waterfall from the overflow outlet into a large pool on the ground below.

Boot imprints in the mud were clear. Taking the camera out, focusing the light on the indentations, she clicked the button. Then with her phone switched to video mode—back tracking—she held the torch in one hand and the phone in the other, walking towards the windmill with the camera rolling. Zooming in, she filmed the ladder then leaned backwards, following it to the top. There wasn't much in her knowledge bank about windmills. She could understand the information that Danny had given them earlier. If that piece of wood around the top was the platform Alex had been standing on, it would be incredibly easy to overstep it and fall. It didn't look more than thirty centimetres wide.

'Rod Donaldson has gone back to the house.'

Dave's voice so very close to her ear made Mia jump. The picture on the screen bounced up and down, the phone shaking in her hand.

'Shit, you gave me a fright!' She looked at Dave. He was hard to see behind the torch light. 'Yeah, I know. Where's old mate off to?'

The red tail-lights of the ute that had been parked out of the way winked at her.

'Back to the house. He doesn't know much. Came over for a catch-up and Alex never showed. There probably isn't much to know, I guess.'

'How high do you think that platform is?' Mia pointed towards the top of the windmill.

'At a guess about ten metres, but we need to ask Rod. He'll know exactly. Ready?' Dave had walked towards the tarp and Mia had gone with him to keep up the conversation. Now she realised what had to happen next.

'Right?'

Readjusting her phone, Mia nodded, and when Dave didn't move, she said, 'Yeah, ten metres is a long way to fall from.'

Dave grunted his acknowledgement.

Slowly, he drew back the tarp. The heavy scrunching noise seemed to echo off the tank and bushes surrounding them. Alex was lying on his stomach, one arm underneath his body and the other twisted backwards, near his rib cage. To Mia, it looked as if he'd tried to break his fall with his right hand, but his shoulder had hit first, crumpling with the force. There were bones sticking out of his hand where his knuckles should have been.

Mia drew in a breath, understanding the carnage she was seeing. A fall from height impacted every part of the body. Even Alex's knees looked as if they'd been forced out the back of his legs.

'Male, deceased,' Dave commentated.

Mia came in closer and brought the phone near to Alex's head, still filming. There was blood on one side, where his skin had split, and his neck was at an angle no one could survive. Thank god it was night and the flies were absent.

Lights flashed through the darkness, illuminating the head of the windmill.

'What? Who's that?' Mia asked. 'Surely no one knows—'

'Reckon that'll be the father,' Dave interrupted, squatting down to look more closely at the body. 'Can you get a photo of this?' He pointed to the fingers, which were unnaturally bent back.

Mia raised the camera from around her neck and clicked. Once, twice, three times until she was satisfied with the photos she'd taken.

'Got enough on video?' Dave asked.

The lights swept around the corner following the track, which meant they were focused on the tank and trough.

'Yep,' Mia said. 'Anything else you want me to capture?'

Dave shook his head. 'What a bloody tragic accident. Did you know farming has one of the highest workplace death rates? Poor Alex is going about his business, checking the oil in the head, and somehow he's taken a misstep or the wind has come along at the wrong time. He could have overbalanced or the tail has swung in the breeze and knocked him off.' Dave was silent for a moment and Mia looked at him. His face seemed older in the dim light. 'I hate windmills,' he said.

There wasn't anything to say to that. 'Have you been to a death like this before?'

Nodding, Dave turned and looked up at the vast piece of equipment. 'Yeah. A couple.'

He didn't elaborate and Mia didn't want to ask. Dave would tell her when he was ready. 'So what do you want to do now?'

'I'll get the father to ID him here and Hamish can collect him after that. Mark around where the body is lying and tomorrow we'll come back and just have another look around and talk to the family. Then we'll have to prepare a report for the coroner, being an unexpected death, not that there is anything unexplained about it.' Dave had the spray can and began outlining where the body lay. 'Quick, grab some video and photos while I'm doing this.'

Mia wanted to groan, because preparing a report for the coroner was a laborious task, but one that had to be done to help the family with closure. Instead, she ran the video over the body, following Dave's progress, then snapped a few final photos with the camera.

'Here, help me shift him,' Dave said, putting his torch on the bullbar of the troopy. He leaned down to adjust the man's legs.

Mia dropped her torch and glanced over her shoulder to see where Rod Donaldson's ute was. The driver had cut the engine and she heard the screech of an old door opening, then footsteps crunching on rocky earth, and a stone skittering from underneath the man's boots.

Dave pulled the tarp up, and Mia and he stood together to greet Rod Donaldson.

Rod stopped as the body came into his view. Jaw clenched, he swallowed before putting his hand out to Dave.

'Rod Donaldson,' he said. He ignored Mia completely.

'I'm sorry for your loss, Rod,' Dave said, shaking his hand. 'I'm Detective Dave Burrows and this is my constable, Mia Worth.'

A small flicker of rage raced through Mia's body as Rod barely glanced in her direction. She took a couple of deep breaths and looked for a way to insert herself into the conversation.

Dave was asking questions and Mia moved towards him so she was standing in Rod's line of sight.

'Hot out here today?' Dave asked.

'Bloody hot. Been that way for the last few weeks. Still, it's nearly the end of summer.'

'Alex had come out here to make sure the stock had enough water?'

'He did a bore run every morning. Because of the distances, he'd check one or two every day so most watering points would be seen at least twice a week.'

'Was there any wind today?'

'Nothing at the homestead, but that doesn't mean there wasn't any out here. The flood plains seem to get a bit more wind than around the hills and gullies. Guess it's more open out here. Or we're more protected. The weather on the plains can be a bit different, see? Get a bit more rain sometimes. The hills seem to make a bit of a rain shadow.'

Dave nodded. 'That's all right, we can get weather reports from the Met office. When did you see Alex last?'

Rod glanced at the bundle on the ground and seemed to deflate before gathering himself. 'Yesterday, at the workshop. We were going over the truck because we'd made a decision to shift some stock around. Feed is getting a bit short in some areas.'

'Servicing it?'

'That's right. Get it ready so we could load sheep into the crate. Easier on the stock to shift them by vehicle than walk them ten or twelve kilometres.'

'And he seemed all right in himself?' Mia asked.

Rod's eyes didn't even move from Dave as he ignored her. In the distance, a mopoke owl hooted.

Silence spun around them as an invisible rope of anger continued on its journey through Mia. She'd come across some chauvinist blokes before, but she wasn't sure if Rod Donaldson was one or if his grief didn't allow him to look at her.

'Mr Donaldson?' Mia said, gently this time, prompting him.

'Yes.' His words were clipped. 'Yes, he was fine. Talking about his daughter and her antics. No different to usual.'

'Thank you,' Mia said, jotting down the information. 'And did you and Alex get along well?'

'Of. Course.' His tone hadn't changed.

'What about Alex and the rest of the family. How many of you live here?'

Rod's eyes swung over to Mia now and she felt the thrill of adrenalin run through her. Rod's eyes were cold.

'What are you asking?'

'Who lives on the station with you?'

'My wife, Alex, his wife and his daughter.'

'No other family?'

'None.'

Dave cleared his throat. 'We understand these questions are distressing for you, Rod. Unfortunately, they're protocol, as is a formal ID. I'm sorry to ask you, but would you mind identifying Alex for us,' Dave said, putting his notebook back in his pocket.

After a short pause, Rod answered, 'Of course.'

Dave nodded to Mia and she pulled at the tarp, only showing Alex's broken face. Rod would have already seen his son's broken body. Still, they would try to shield him now.

Rod's jaw twitched again, this time his hand went out as if to touch Alex, but just as quickly he brought it back to his body.

Dave had warned her when she'd started at Barker that the station men were tough; stoic and stone-faced, these outback blokes rarely gave in to emotion or any kind of weakness. Seemed she'd finally met one.

'Is that your son, Alex, Rod?'

There was a silence long enough for both Dave and Mia to glance at each other, then at Rod.

'Yeah. That's Alex.'

CHAPTER 9

'No,' Hallie whispered. 'Please don't take him.' She grabbed the woman police officer's—Mia's—hand. The contact jolted her, even though she was the one to initiate it. The woman's skin was hot to touch. She was another warm, living, breathing person.

Unlike Alex, who was lying cold and unresponsive in the unmarked, unremarkable van that had driven out of the driveway a few minutes ago. The red tail-lights had propelled her into action. Before that, her body hadn't felt anything she'd ever felt before. She'd been numb and not reacting to the news that her husband was dead. He couldn't be. Only hours before he'd been smiling at her, that lazy smile he'd get that somehow held the full force of his love.

That van was taking away her husband!

'We have to, Hallie. I'm so sorry,' Mia said. 'Alex can't stay out here.'

'Where will he go?'

'Into Barker. Then he'll be transferred to somewhere like Port Augusta or perhaps even Adelaide. There will have to be an autopsy.'

'No! Why?' Hallie put her arms around herself, as if she was giving herself a hug. No one had offered that type of comfort to her yet.

When Maggie had arrived, she'd come into the homestead pale-faced and had held out her arms to Hallie. It had been Nicole who had stepped into them, returning a brief, perfunctory hug, then offered a cup of tea, before asking Hallie to put the kettle on.

'Now listen here!' Rod, who had been standing near the kitchen door, his arms crossed, pushed himself away from the wall. 'There needs to be no such thing. An autopsy? You can't cut up another human being without reason, and there *is no* reason!'

'This is all part of the process, Rod,' Dave, the male detective, said. 'We have to prepare a report for the coroner and that will include an autopsy. This happens whenever there is an unexpected death.' He turned to Hallie. 'We'll let you know when you're able to have Alex taken to a funeral home and you can start organising the service.'

Rod took another step forward. 'You can let me know. I'm head of this family and Alex is my son. The women don't need to be bothered with this sort of thing.'

'Sorry, Rod,' Dave said. 'Hallie is next of kin. She's Alex's wife.'

A tiny victory. Rod had ridden roughshod over her since this had happened, organising Nicole to come over and then Maggie. Hallie had no idea who might walk in her door next. If only it could be Alex.

Danny was leaning against the door frame leading into the passageway, Maggie at his side.

'We can help with anything,' he told Hallie. He nudged his wife. 'Can't we?'

'Of course we can. Oh, Hallie, we're here to help or with anything you need.' Maggie moved towards Hallie and held out her hands. Then tears sprang into her eyes and her shoulders started to shake. Putting her hand over her mouth, she rushed outside to let out her grief.

Hallie watched her go. Not a lot of help to be had there.

Danny moved to the kitchen table. His eyes were trained on the surface, his fingers rubbing over the same knot in the wood, as if he was trying to polish it out.

'He's my husband,' Hallie said, sounding stronger than she felt, trying to secure her place among all these people who were not hers. Her parents were overseas. They'd never been to visit and there was even less likelihood they'd know where she really lived. With no brothers and sisters, Jenna, her best friend and PA, was the closest she had to family and she didn't know yet.

Nicole turned to stare at Hallie, her eyes uncharacteristically bright. 'He's our son, Hallie. We have the right to know all these things as well.'

Mia stepped forward, holding up her hand. 'If I could explain something to you all,' she said quietly.

Hallie marvelled at the small woman's self-confidence. She seemed to have enough energy, assurance and poise to handle anyone. Back in the city, Hallie would've had the exact same stance. But not out here. Not in a place she really didn't understand with people who thought she didn't fit in.

The one person who had wasn't here anymore.

'Hallie is a primary contact because she is Alex's wife. She, of course, can let you know what's happening, but Hallie is the person we will be phoning with any news.' Mia looked seriously at Rod and Nicole. 'You are more than welcome to ring and ask us anything.'

With a kind of satisfaction, Hallie noted that Rod again looked like he was about to explode. Finally, *finally*, after having been stepped all over since she married Alex, she had some standing. She was Alex's wife, his next of kin, and the one whom the police would be talking to. A hollow victory, when all she wanted was for Alex to come home and tell her everything was a mistake. It had been someone else lying at the bottom of the windmill who looked like him.

From her bedroom, Ruby gave a cry. Hallie moved towards the door, but Nicole shot her a look.

'Since you're the primary contact, Hallie, love, you'd better stay here and deal with the police officers. I'll see to Ruby.' Her voice was sweet, but Hallie heard the displeasure. It wasn't a tone Hallie had heard much because, more often than not, she got her own way.

Mia seemed to hear it as well. Hallie noticed she stood back to assess the women.

'Thanks, Nicole,' Hallie said.

'Hallie.' Mia turned to her. 'I'd like to ask you some questions, would you mind? I know this is all so fresh for you, but we really do need to clear a few things up.'

Hallie wanted to scream, 'No!' The minute she started talking about Alex all of this horror, this nightmare would become real.

Yet what option did she have.

Rod was giving her another stern look, so she threw her shoulders back and looked Mia in the eye. 'Sure. Let's go outside.' Without waiting for an answer, Hallie walked past Rod and opened the door, letting herself out into the evening. By the sound of her footsteps, the police officer was following. No one else needed to hear what they had to talk about.

On the verandah around the edge of the house were two cane chairs Hallie had brought with her from Adelaide. The cushions had been white, but she'd recovered them in a deep maroon-coloured fabric when she'd realised they wouldn't stay white for more than thirty seconds. Alex had loved sitting out here of an evening, watching the sprinklers cover the lawn as the day faded and drinking a beer. Hallie had loved it because it had just been the two of them. No in-laws at that time of the night.

Their favourite nights had been when the full moon was rising over the ranges and the pinks and reds of the sunset changed to steel blue, enveloping the moon and highlighting the deep yellow against the darkening sky.

She sank into one of the chairs and indicated for Mia to do the same.

'What happened?' Hallie finally asked. 'I don't understand.'

'We're still gathering information, Hallie. What we can see has happened is Alex has fallen from the top of the windmill. Obviously, that's a long way from the ground, and he's sustained injuries he wasn't able to survive on impact. Do you know how high the windmill is?'

With a snort, Hallie shook her head. 'I wouldn't have a clue. That's not my area. I didn't have anything to do with the outside work. Rod wouldn't have allowed it, even if I'd wanted to . . . Not that I did.

'I'm from the city and all this'—she spread her hand out towards the vastness now closed in by night—'is very foreign to me.'

'You're not local?' Mia sounded surprised.

'No, from Adelaide.' Hallie looked at Mia and saw she had very kind eyes. 'I need to know . . .'

'Yes, of course.' Mia folded her hands in her lap. 'I really don't have much to tell you at this stage. We have to ask questions and some of those won't feel very nice, but they will help us to compile the mandatory report. I hope you understand.'

Hallie appreciated her frankness. She assumed it couldn't be easy, giving this type of news. God knows, it wasn't easy to listen to it being given.

The bubble sitting inside her chest was threatening to burst, but she couldn't let it. Not yet. Not until everyone had gone home and it was just her and Ruby. How often had Nicole told her she was living out in nowhere now and she had to accept that this was her life? That included being hard and not letting your feelings show.

'*Don't let the family name down now, Hallie*,' she could hear Nicole saying.

Alex, she thought, *I think I'm going to break in two*.

Silence.

'Can I get you anything?'

Hallie started as Mia spoke to her again. 'No. No, thanks.' Rearranging herself, she took a breath. 'What questions did you need to ask?'

'I just wanted to have a bit of a chat about Alex. What was he like?' Mia leaned forward and looked expectantly at Hallie.

Through her haze of grief and trying to be tough, Hallie recognised a similar exhaustion and pain in Mia's face.

'Alex . . .' She put her hand to her chest and tapped it against her heart, trying to shift the lump in her throat. Her wedding rings caught the porch light. 'Alex was hard to describe. He was a bit of cliché because I'm going to say he was funny and good-looking and loving. But he was also so much more.'

'How did you meet?'

'Same place as everyone meets these days—on a dating app. He'd been dared to put up a profile by some of his friends and had to come to Adelaide for the annual show. They have ram sales there and he was in town to "buy a ram, not find a wife", as he put it in his wedding speech.' Hallie smiled, lost in her memories. 'We met in the stockman's bar on the showgrounds. I was there covering the fashion parade for my blog. Weird, isn't it? I'd just sat down to take the weight off my feet and was swiping through the app and there he was.'

'Funny guy,' Mia said. 'Buy a ram, not find a wife.'

'He was.' Hallie felt warm affection run through her. 'And he was so laidback, he could have been horizontal! Nothing ever upset Alex. I could have screamed and yelled and hung upside down with nothing on, and he would've only smiled at me. He always would say, "*Now, Hallie, don't lose your rag. It's just not worth the upset.*"' She made quotation marks with her fingers. Usually, the words would come out when she was so angry she could've had a real meltdown, and then he'd disarm her with eleven quick words and have her laughing in seconds. Why? Because every time he said, '*Don't lose your rag*,' she'd imagined a red rag exploding from her head, waving in the wind.

Oh, Alex, she thought. This time her heart felt like there was a hand squeezing it tightly. Any more force, and she was sure it would explode.

'How had Alex been recently? Was he worried about anything?'

Hallie whipped her head around to look at Mia. 'What do you mean?' Her voice had an edge of hysteria to it.

Mia reached out and touched her arm. 'Like I told you, I have to ask these questions to get a picture of Alex. I know this is painful. Was he . . . happy?'

'Yes.' Hallie could hardly get the word out quick enough. 'Yes, we were. There was nothing that would have made him'—she took a breath—'made him . . . jump. Is that what you're meaning?' Her voice had lost all of its bravado now.

The tears were so close and her body felt so out of control. She wanted to run, to leave all of this behind. Pretend it hadn't happened.

Shooting out of the chair, she started to walk, then turned and sat back down. Her knee jiggled instead.

'This is real, isn't it?' she finally said.

Mia nodded sadly and took Hallie's hand. 'Yeah, Hallie. It really is.'

'Okay.' *Breathe, just breathe.* 'Okay. Alex is fine . . .' She paused. 'Was fine. He was fine. There isn't anything in his life that would make him jump.' She indicated, again to the expansive land outside the homestead's boundaries. 'Out here, you can't hide anything. Alex, Rod and Nicole are the only people around unless Danny and Maggie or the stock agent call in. And more often than not, they ring to make sure we're home. Make sure we're not out on a bore run or something. No point in coming all this way to an empty house.

'So, I know that Alex is feeling fine. He loves Ruby, he loves me. Occasionally he gets annoyed with his mother but that's only when she's smothering him more than normal, because he's so damn patient. His health is fine. Everything is just fine!'

'Okay, that's really good information. Does he get along with his father?'

Hallie exhaled. 'Yes.'

'And Alex doesn't owe any money?'

'No. Everything is tied up here.'

'I know you said your marriage is strong. What about you? Are you happy?'

'If I wasn't, I wouldn't be here, I can promise you.' Her words tasted bitter as she said them. 'Living out here was never in my plans. I'm a city girl through and through, but Alex . . . he made it sound like paradise. And it is to him. This bloody heap of nothingness! It's his paradise.'

'But not yours.' Mia said.

'It's only mine because Alex is here.'

'What did you do before you moved out here?'

'I was—well, still am—in fashion. My podcast *The Threads Code* is classed as influential in the industry.'

'Fashion? Out here? How do you do the interviews?'

'Over Zoom. I know, I know, we're all over Zoom since Covid, but it does work well and the sound quality is great. I have a YouTube channel as well, and any designs we talk about I upload there so people can see.'

Mia laughed, then sobered. 'I'm sorry, but what you've just told me is so surprising out here.'

'I know, right? I don't think my in-laws have any idea about what I do, nor do they care. I'm just Alex's wife, expected to'—she made quotation marks again—'"toe the company, or family in this case, line".'

'Rod seems as if he needs to be in charge. Have they ever listened to your podcast?'

This time Hallie laughed, except it sounded harsh and bitter. 'They wouldn't even know the name of it. I love my work,' Hallie said, surprising herself. 'I really do. My opinion matters in the fashion world, and I have sway. Influence. And here? I'm a bottom feeder.'

'Did Alex support you?'

'Absolutely.'

Mia nodded. 'Thanks for being so honest.' Standing now, she said gently, 'Did you want to come back in?'

'No. I'll stay here for a while.'

CHAPTER 10

Hallie climbed into bed and curled her body around Ruby. She'd never let her little girl sleep in their bed before, but tonight was different. Tonight was the first of god knew how many nights alone. For the rest of her life maybe.

She didn't close her eyes, only stared into the blackness, trying to make sense of what had happened. There had been nothing amiss with Alex. Hallie had told herself that time and time again, since she'd seen him lying broken on the ground through the camera. Not that she'd really seen him, only enough to know his body would have been damaged beyond repair.

No, Alex had been fine in every aspect of the word.

Hadn't he?

Hallie leaned her head against Ruby's and breathed her in. She smelled like . . . innocence.

When Ruby had been born, Alex had been frightened he'd hurt her. '*She's so small,*' he'd said. '*I might accidentally break her fingers or something awful.*'

'*You won't do that,*' the nurse had told him as she'd touched Ruby's cheek. '*Mostly, these incredible, tiny creatures are a lot more robust than they look, and your little one is the same.*'

Hallie remembered how her heart had felt back then, as she lay in the hospital bed, too tired and sweaty to do anything but watch her husband and their new daughter. The feeling was almost as it was now: her heart swelling, fit to burst. Except back then, her emotions had been high with love, pride and gratefulness. Now they were grief, anguish and plain, simple sadness. How did two very different feelings manifest the same way in her body?

Her eyes had mostly stayed dry. She imagined that was the shock. There wasn't one person Hallie knew who had gone to work and hadn't come home. How did that even happen?

What was next for her and Ruby? Were there government agencies who would have to be involved? A soft, involuntary moan slipped through her lips as she thought about the prenuptial agreement Rod had put in front of her that day.

'*I'm not signing that,*' Hallie had told him, with a bemused look on her face. She'd pushed the paper back towards him. '*Alex wouldn't ask me to and it's him I'm marrying, not you and Nicole.*'

Rod had nodded, his face serious. '*Of course that's true, Hallie, but you see, out here the land is never owned by any person. It's a living, breathing, pulsating thing and we are only custodians of it and that's why, out here, we get you blow-ins to sign these bits of paper. Not because we're protecting the assets that past generations have built up, but because this land can't go into the hands of someone who wouldn't love it and can't care for it the way that people who have been brought up on it can.*'

Hallie remembered the shock that had electrified her as he spoke.

Blow-ins? Her eyes had widened and were about to pop out of her head, when he said something else.

'*This isn't between you and Alex. This agreement has nothing to do with your relationship. You won't see my son's name on that piece of paper anywhere. At this stage, Alex isn't included in our partnership and won't be for some time. It is between you and me and Nicole, and our business.*'

Looking back at the paperwork, Hallie had realised he was right.

She had shrugged at the time. '*So it won't matter if I don't sign it then. I'm marrying Alex, not you two, nor your business.*' *Thank god*, she'd wanted to mutter.

'*You're mistaken, there*,' Rod had said. His smile was anything but nice. In fact, it could have been classified as a sneer. '*When you marry, you marry the whole family. I'm afraid that if you don't sign this, then I can't allow you to marry my son.*'

Hallie remembered how she'd snorted . . . Until she realised how serious Rod was.

'I'm sorry?'

'Neither Nicole nor I can allow you to go ahead with the wedding if you don't sign our agreement.'

'Did you make Nicole sign it when you were first married?' The words, coupled with fury, were out before she could stop them.

Rod hadn't answered her, only held the pen towards her.

It was strange, she thought, holding Ruby tightly, *he was so sure I would sign. His hand hadn't even been shaking.*

And you did! a little voice screamed inside her head. *You dissolved like an ice cube melting in the heat.*

About five months ago, Alex had found out.

'Hallie . . .' he'd started when he came into the kitchen. His face was red, but that could have been from the dust, because he and Rod had been tagging sheep in the yards and they always came back with dirt in every crevice of their bodies. She'd been planning another interview and updating her website and YouTube channel when he'd put his hands on her shoulders.

'Hi, honey.' She placed her hand over his but didn't take her eyes from the screen. 'Good day?'

'Not bad.' He pulled a chair alongside her and swivelled hers so he could look her in the face.

'Hello, you,' she said, smiling.

'Did Dad ask you to sign something before we got married?' Alex's expression was grim.

Her lips had parted in an 'oh' and she tipped her head to the side. *'Why are you asking?'*

'It's a yes or no question,' he prompted.

'*Yes*,' Hallie answered. She'd searched his face for anger or indignation. Instead she saw resignation.

'*You did that for me?*'

'*What do you mean?*'

He'd shrugged. '*My brother, Sam, he's not here, is he? He won't have anything to do with Mum and Dad.*'

'*Yeah, I know*,' Hallie said. She remembered frowning and putting a hand into his while her other thumb smoothed the lines on his forehead. Her thumb had come away dirty.

'*I've never told you why, because I never believed what he told me.*' Alex had taken a breath and let the words rush out. '*Sam said that Dad asked Jan to sign a type of binding financial agreement between them, the station and Jan.*' He paused. '*And Dad did that to you, too.*'

There hadn't been anything to say, so Hallie had only nodded.

'*Well, that's shit*,' Alex had finally said, after a long pause. '*And wrong.*'

'*But I signed it, Alex. And I'm here with you.*'

'*There is no way you should have even been asked to do that.*' Alex stood up and took a few steps towards the door, then returned to Hallie. '*I was hoping you were going to say no. That Sam got it all mixed up, or Jan was trying to cause problems. God knows, they've never got along anyway.*' He turned away and then back again, as if he couldn't quite work out what he should be doing. '*What the bloody hell?*' His broad Australian accent seemed even more laidback and casual than usual, yet his actions were all distress.

'It doesn't matter,' Hallie said, getting to her feet. She'd put her arms around Alex's waist and hugged him to her. *'I'm happy. You're happy. Isn't that all that matters?'* Not believing she was saying this sort of thing. Hallie was an independent woman, one who'd earned her stripes in the fashion world not by rolling over, but by standing with her head high, saying *'come at me'*, then tossing off whatever was hurled her way. Men didn't frighten her; she had no problem standing up to them. But she loved Alex and would do anything for him. Rod had caught her off guard, in a society she didn't know or understand. The thought of losing Alex had been too much.

'But, Hallie, I'm not sure if you appreciate the situation. If something ever happens to me, they can do anything to you. Ask you to leave or—'

'Nothing's going to happen to you. Why would you say that?'

'Who knows? Nothing is a given.' His whole face and neck had been bright red, though not from the dust.

'What's done is done. And if anything happens to you, I'm perfectly capable of looking after myself and Ruby. Plus'—Hallie pulled away and gave him a sassy grin—*'I can't see them getting rid of me while I've got their granddaughter. Can you?'* She'd given him a quick kiss. *'I've got to finish doing these updates before dinner. Can you bath Ruby for me, please?'*

Alex had looked unhappy, not at her request, but at the situation, which seemed to have knocked him off centre.

'If they have done something like this, I can't be sure of what they wouldn't do to protect Tirranah.'

Those words had left Hallie with lumps of cold discomfort in her stomach for a while. And now they were back.

Over the next few months, she'd found Alex had been reading law websites and googling information on binding financial agreements, but she was sure nothing had changed between him and his parents. They seemed as blasé about the situation as ever and nothing caused Nicole to hold her tongue.

'Hallie, the garden is looking untidy. When do you think you might mow the lawn?' she'd asked one visit.

Alex had been sitting at the table with a cup of tea and his head had jerked up. *'Mum, this is Hallie's home, not yours. Let her be.'*

The warmth of gratitude had washed through Hallie, but Nicole hadn't taken any notice.

'You forget, Alex, first impressions are important and Hallie is holding up our family name. Everything around here must be spick and span all the time, in case there's a visitor we aren't expecting.'

'You have to give over on this "family name" crap. This isn't the 1960s, you realise?' Alex had risen from the table and paced the floor.

'Doesn't matter what the date is, Alex. What's the matter with you? The house and grounds are the responsibility of the woman of the house, and the homestead is what is seen first. The area needs to be neat and tidy'—her glance had slid sideways to Hallie—*'as per our agreement. Much better*

to do something useful than always be playing around on the computer.'

'*Your agreement!*' Alex exploded. '*Your agreement shouldn't exist! It's bullshit, Mum, and you know it.*'

Heavy boots had sounded on the verandah at that moment and the door had sprung open with force. Rod's face held the same colour as Alex's. '*What seems to be the problem*?' he growled.

Hallie had walked to Alex and put her hand on his arm, giving it a light squeeze. *It's okay*, she was telling him. *Don't worry.*

'*I'm going to make you tear that piece of paper up*,' Alex had said quietly, fire blazing in his eyes.

'*You'll do no such thing, my boy*,' Rod said. '*No such thing. Do you want the land to fall into the hands of someone who has no idea how to care for it?*'

'*Is the land all you give a shit about? What about us? Hallie and me? And Ruby? What gives you the right—*'

'*What gives me the right*'—Rod's determined tone broke through Alex's rant—'*is that this land is* mine. *We're five generations in, and now it seems that marriage doesn't mean what it used to, we have to protect the assets, which is exactly what I've done. It's tradition, and tradition is not made to be broken!*'

'*Danny's family never asked Maggie to sign any bullshit agreement.*'

'*They are not our concern and more fool them when something happens.*'

Hallie had watched Nicole while the furious exchange was going on, hoping for some type of secret smile or wink. An action that said: *What we women have to put up with!* Yet it didn't come. Her head nodded up and down in agreement with Rod.

'*What about moving with the times, Dad? Haven't you seen what Hallie is capable of online? Go and have a look! She could put us on the map. Help pay some of the bills by telling our story. Marketing. Let her be a part of this, not keep her on the outside. How do you think she'll settle in if you keep seeing her as an outsider?*' The words shot from Alex as if he had a loaded cannon inside him.

Nicole stood and picked up her cup. '*Alex, it appears you are overwrought. Can I suggest you have a rest this afternoon and turn up to work tomorrow with a much calmer state of mind?*' She placed the cup on the sink and moved to the door. Because good manners dictated she should, she stopped, turned and smiled at both Hallie and Alex. '*We'll see you tomorrow. Thank you for the cup of tea and*'—her tone became critical—'*the piece of . . . cake. That was what it was, wasn't it? Don't forget to mow the lawn.*'

Rod turned as well, then as an afterthought, looked back, his eyes locking with Hallie's. '*Out here a person is judged by their ability to keep an agreement. Spoken, handshake or otherwise.*' Then he and Nicole left.

But Hallie didn't know what was in the agreement, because as soon as she'd put her signature on the paper, Rod had whipped it away with a great smile.

'You won't regret this, Hallie. It will mean that everyone is protected.'

She'd bitten back the words, *Even me?* because she was one hundred per cent sure her wellbeing and protection didn't enter Rod and Nicole's thinking.

'I'll fix this,' Alex promised. *'I won't let them get away with it.'*

'It doesn't matter.'

And it hadn't because Alex would always be here to protect her and Ruby.

Now it did matter. A great deal.

Ruby whimpered in her sleep and Hallie pulled her closer, stroking her hair. 'Shh, Ruby-girl.'

What would become of them? Would Rod and Nicole ask her to leave? More than likely.

Still, she told herself, that wouldn't matter. Wouldn't hurt to head back to the city. Ruby would get to play with other kids and socialise more. Hallie could go to more fashion events and be at the meetings that Jenna had been going to on her behalf.

Despite her gaping hole of sadness, she felt a glimmer of excitement. Then a deep hole of desolation at the thought of leaving the place that Alex loved so much revealed itself inside her, too.

'I won't let them get away with this.'

CHAPTER 11

'Hallie, what a godawful thing to happen. I'm sorry to hear about Alex.'

Tucking the phone between her shoulder and ear, Hallie listened to the rich voice of Alex's friend, Mick.

'Anything we can do to help, you know we will. Just ring one of us. We're all here for you. The whole group.'

Three days had passed since Alex's accident and Hallie was trying to hold everything together. To be practical and not let anyone see her devastation. Because that's what everyone did out here, wasn't it? Held everything together?

'Thanks, Mick, I will.' She drew in a breath and checked the emails that were coming through at a snail's pace. There was supposed to be one from the funeral director with bank account details, and she'd just finished looking online at casket sprays, though nothing had caught her attention. Alex loved gum trees and she had been trying to find an arrangement using their green-grey leaves. 'I'm going to rely on you all to tell Ruby about her dad when she's old enough to hear those stories. You're all such a massive part of his life.'

'And we'll all do just that, don't worry. Promise not to tell her all the really bad things he used to get up to at ag college. Just the minor ones.'

Hallie gave a laugh. 'There were plenty, I guess.'

'For all of us. I can't believe this, Hallie. I just . . .' Mick's voice trailed off. He would be shaking his mop of shiny black hair, the fringe falling over his eyes. Then he'd swipe his fingers through the locks like a comb and push them back over his forehead. Hallie had seen him do it a thousand times before. Alex, Danny and Tom had always taken the piss out of Mick when he did it. '*Got that girly twitch down pat, mate,*' Tom would say, whenever they were together.

'Everyone from the group is coming to the funeral. Even Tom. He's back in Australia already. Kaylah is flying in from Singapore today.'

Emotion welled in her chest. How could these blokes who went to agricultural college with Alex be kinder to her and Ruby than his own family? Or her parents for that matter.

'Thanks, Mick. How are you going to get away from Canberra? Isn't parliament sitting?'

'Told them all I've got a personal emergency and I'm unavailable for at least a week. If it takes longer to have the funeral I'll use personal leave. No question. You know we wouldn't not be there. We're closer than brothers.' The hissing sound of the landline was the only noise and then he asked, 'Is there any indication on how long before you can have the funeral?'

'Thank you,' she whispered, then cleared her throat. 'Not at this stage. I'm trying to organise as much as I can without having a date. The lady police officer, Mia, she said it might be weeks.' Her voice dropped in despair.

'Well, don't worry. We'll all be here for as long as it takes. I'm sure there are things you need help with.'

'Do you, um, would you . . . all be pallbearers?'

She heard a swift intake of breath before Mick cleared his throat. 'Of course. How many do you need?'

'All three of you. Danny, Tom and you. I guess I should ask Rod, but I don't want to. And maybe he wouldn't want to be in the spotlight, having just lost his son. Is there someone else you can think of? I haven't heard anything from Alex's brother Sam. Or even about him.' As she said the words, it was Hallie's turn to draw in a breath. 'Do you think Sam knows, Mick? He hasn't spoken to his parents for years and Alex was never the best communicator.'

'No need to worry about that, Hallie. I've been in contact with him. Sam is devastated, as we all are, but he won't be back for the funeral, said the differences between him and Rod and Nicole are too great. I don't understand his thinking, but each to their own.'

'He's not coming?' Hallie was dumbfounded. 'He didn't come to our wedding, but Alex's funeral, surely that's different?'

'His anger towards Rod and Nicole far outweighs sensible thinking at this stage, I'm afraid.'

Hallie bit her tongue. She couldn't be seen to be bad-mouthing her in-laws, but by hell, she wanted to. They were all about how they were perceived in the public eye, yet their family life, which was far more important, was in disarray.

'Fuck's sake,' she muttered, against her better judgement. Ruby stirred in the pram and Hallie stuck her foot out to rock it in the hope that she wouldn't wake.

'Ah, Hallie, are you having any trouble? With Rod and Nicole, I mean.'

Mick was good at compassion. Hallie'd seen him on TV many times, hugging children who had lost their parents in road accidents as he launched a road awareness campaign. Then there were the terminally ill people who greeted Mick as if their lives were dependent on him being with them, and he would sit and listen and gravely nod or shake his head then announce funding towards trauma units or cancer wards. And he never let a chance go by to thank the women of his electorate for shaping communities. Mick Fowllis was the best politician Hallie had ever seen. And he was another of Alex's best friends. Blood brothers.

'It's been a bit'—she paused—'prickly.'

'Rod and Nicole won't mean anything by their attitude, Hallie. You know that. They're just very old school. Don't forget where you're living. There is nowhere more conservative than the people out bush. They don't have to move with the times or keep up to speed with what's going on in the real world, because they're so isolated and none of this politically correct caper comes knocking at their door.

Life just plods on as it did for the generation before this and the generation before that.'

'I know, I know,' Hallie said, the fury from her last conversation with Rod still sitting in the pit of her stomach. 'But they're wrong, Mick. Shouldn't I be the one to organise Alex's funeral? He's my husband. Rod seems to think it's his responsibility. The police told him otherwise and there's all the other stuff—the *agreement*.'

An email pinged and Hallie leaned over to check the screen. Not the funeral director; Jenna had copied her in on the email rescheduling Anthea Crawford's interview due to unforeseen personal reasons. *Would Anthea have availability in April or May?*

'Only because he wants to protect you from all of this . . . reality. To his way of thinking, he's doing the right thing by you.'

That statement hung in the air between them. Again, Hallie wanted to rant and rage against the ridiculousness of everyone's thoughts out in this backwards hellhole; thank god, Alex had never held those beliefs and neither had Danny. He'd always supported Maggie in what she had wanted to do and neither man had ever considered their wives were less than they were. Mick and Tom were of the same view as Danny, but they didn't live here. Young women didn't let young men get away with thinking that way anymore.

Neither should they, Hallie huffed. She shuffled through the newspapers and documents spread across the surface of the table. The kitchen had become her office after the snake incident. There was no way she was heading back into that bloody office without someone else in the house. Danny had helped her shift the computer and all the equipment she would need after Rod and Nicole had left the night Alex had died, much to their disgust. An office out in the entertaining and eating area was not on.

'*Sympathy to Rod, Nicole, Hallie and Ruby on the death of their much-loved son, husband and father. May your memories sustain you*,' she read aloud.

'Who's that from? Sounds pretty formal.'

'The local branch of the Farmer's Faction. Another bunch of old guys who need a shake-up. Did you notice the order? Son, husband, father.'

There was a pause. 'Hallie, I don't want to cause any trouble, but that's the order he lived his life in. Not saying that you and Ruby shouldn't have been put first, but it's a bit like alphabetical order. Alex was a son first, then a husband and then a dad.'

Groaning, she dropped her head into her hand. 'I know, I know. Sorry. Rod's just giving me the shits and normally it's Alex who defuses everything. I'll take a breath.'

'Excellent idea. I've known Rod and Nicole for a fair few years now and . . .'

Ruby gave another little murmur and this time Hallie got up from her chair and pushed the pram towards the window, only half listening to Mick. Her daughter should probably be in her cot, but Hallie didn't want her away from her side. She needed to be near Ruby every waking moment to protect her, love her and get comfort from her warm body and funny, toothy smiles. Because that's the only place any affection was coming from right now. Outside, the world glistened in the moonlight and the temperature was much cooler. Hallie wanted to sit outside in the chilled air and enjoy the peace. To try to ground herself. Alex was the calm one. He'd sit next to her with his heavy hand on her knee, or stand next to her, his hand on her shoulder. Sometimes he would pull her to him and give her a quick hug. Knowing he was right alongside of her, not in front, or behind, as the well-known quote had said. Beside her; her friend as well as her lover.

Was.

Past tense.

Oh, Alex.

The phone on the kitchen table dinged and Hallie started, thinking he had walked through the door with his phone in his pocket. That notification was his WhatsApp messages.

'Alex!' His name left her lips involuntarily and stopped Mick mid-sentence.

'What?'

Hallie was still looking for her husband when reality kicked her in the stomach. The pain was so physical she gasped and put her hand on the table to steady herself.

'Hallie, are you all right? Can I call someone for you?' Mick's voice had taken on the first sound of panic.

'Um, yeah, sorry. Just got a fright.' She reached for the phone, looked at the screen, then held it to her chest. She closed her eyes wearily. Who didn't know what had happened to her husband? Who did she still have to let know?

I miss you.

Taking a breath, she drew herself upright and pulled her shoulders back. 'Sorry, Mick, can you say that all again?' She had to make Alex proud of her. He always said she was made of much sturdier stuff than anyone around here thought. She'd made the move to live out in nowhere, hadn't she? Yep, Hallie would prove him right. Even if just to spite Rod and Nicole.

'Rod only wants to protect you from any nastiness. It's what we blokes do.'

Hallie put the phone on the table, still deep breathing.

'Are you sure you're okay?'

'I'm not that fragile, Mick. I don't need protecting.'

Another ping from Alex's phone. Both messages were from his Blood Brothers WhatsApp group. All the blokes who went to ag college together. She covered the screen with her hand, guessing they were organising how to get to Barker and perhaps accommodation. Perhaps they should stay with her, but she couldn't face other people in her house for any length of time.

'I realise that, and the rest of us who know you recognise that you're not, but sometimes these older blokes, well, it's a bit hard for them to understand. They've spent their lives protecting their wives and daughters from things that are supposed to be "secret men's business".' He changed the subject. 'So, tell me, what's happening with the funeral? We've all got accommodation in Barker, I'm sure you don't need the trouble of us staying with you. Is there anything special you want us to wear?'

Relief flooded through her.

'I've been wondering if you guys had old rugby jumpers or t-shirts or something with the college logo on it? It'll be too hot for a coat or jacket.'

'Leave it with me, I'll get the boys sorted. We'll wear the same thing, like a guard of honour.' This time Mick's voice sounded a bit blurry as if he'd covered the phone with a hankie. It took him a few seconds to say anything else. 'What would you say if we put an ag college logo on the coffin? Would that be okay?'

'Like a sticker?'

'Yeah, something like that. Just something small on the end? He loved his time at ag college with our group of friends. We all did. I've been talking to the principal there, and he's also offered anything that you might need.'

'That would be nice, Mick. Thanks so much.' She stopped, her throat closing over again. 'Thanks.'

'Just ring if you need anything. Doesn't matter how small.'

Hallie put down her phone just as a text message came through from Maggie.

Just checking in, how are you doing? Do you feel up to company tomorrow?

Exhausted, Hallie couldn't think what to answer, so she left the phone and bent over Ruby, wishing she could sleep like her daughter was at the moment.

An email pinged on the computer. Hoping it might finally be the funeral director, she went back to the table and wiggled the mouse to life, realising it was probably too long past business closing.

Scanning the inbox, she was disappointed to see the new message was from Rod Donaldson. There was no way she was opening that email now. Who knew what it contained.

'What do you think he wants?' Hallie muttered to Ruby. She rubbed her eyes. They were gritty, dry and achingly tired. Someone had thrown sand in them, she was sure. Knowing there were some eye drops in the bathroom cabinet, she headed down the hallway to get them.

Once in the bathroom, she automatically checked the washing basket and saw three of Alex's shirts. She got them out to wash. The scent of sweat and his deodorant rose to meet her. Longing took her off guard. With the shirts clutched to her chest, she stood still, her face buried in them. These wouldn't be washed any time soon. They were her last tangible link to her beautiful man. His smell so familiar, made Hallie feel like he was right next to her.

If only that were true.

Hallie tucked the shirts under her arm and went to the cabinet. A short search later and she hadn't found the eye drops. Taking the dirty shirts with her, she went into the bedroom and placed them on her pillow. She would sleep with them every night until they didn't have Alex all over them. But logic told Hallie that as soon as she started to do that, the shirts would lose his smell and take on hers, so it would have to be one at a time.

Picking up a photo that Alex had on his bedside table, she looked at the group of men for a long time: Alex, Mick, Danny and Tom. The four blood brothers.

There had been five, Alex had told her. Five friends, but Charlie had ended up in gaol as they were finishing college. None of them spoke of or to Charlie. His name wasn't ever mentioned. Alex had said it was a pact they'd made. '*He goes against everything we stand for,*' Alex told Hallie. '*Everything.*'

The four young men in the photo looked excited and happy. They were holding beers, slightly bleary-eyed from maybe only half too many. They were on the dance floor at Hallie and Alex's wedding and Mick was pointing to someone out of the shot, while Alex and Tom were unbuckling their belts.

Hallie smiled, remembering what happened next. The first bars of 'Eagle Rock' had started to play and the four of them had yelled, '*Eagle* drop!' Mick had pointed at the DJ, and seconds later, all four men had their pants around their ankles, arms linked, and were yell-singing, '*Doin' the Eagle* drop!'

She'd been so shocked. '*What are they doing?*' she'd gasped to her PA, Jenna, who was also her bridesmaid.

'*Haven't you seen this before? All the Aussie fellas do it, apparently.*' Jenna's English lilt was more pronounced, most likely because of the champagne in her hand. Normally, she tried to sound Australian. '*How've you not seen it and your English friend is telling you about this phenomenon?*' Jenna raised her eyebrows. '*Anyhow, it's all about shaggin', isn't it?*' Then she burst out laughing at Hallie's expression. '*I heard that Ross Wilson interviewed once and he said he was trying to create a dance craze and then, somehow, all these blokes just started dropping their trousers every time the song came on. Nice boxers.*' Jenna took a sip of her champagne and moved in time to the music.

Hallie had stared. Each bloke had a letter printed on plain white boxers: *B. R. O. S.* They wiggled their arses and started doing some kind of strange dance that didn't even match the rhythm of the song. Tom held a beer over his head and whooped, manoeuvring the line in the opposite direction.

Hallie took a sip of wine to try to stop from laughing.

On the back of each of their boxers was a hand, making it look like every bloke was feeling up the one next to him.

'*Wouldn't mind taking home that Thomas*,' Jenna said, with a wink.

Hallie didn't know if that had happened, but what she did know was that straight afterwards, Alex had found her and swept her away to the waiting car and the hotel for their wedding night.

From the kitchen came a whimper then a full-blown sob. 'Muuuummmaaaa!'

Hallie put the photo down and went into the kitchen in time to hear Alex's phone beep again. This time it didn't shock her.

'Hey, hey,' she said to Ruby, unclipping the straps of the pram and lifting her daughter into her arms. 'Hey, it's okay. Mummy's here.'

'Dadda. I want Dadda.' Ruby's cheeks were red and she banged her little fists on Hallie's back. Hallie jiggled her around.

'Me too, Ruby-girl, me too.'

Another ding and another.

Picking up Alex's phone to put it on silent, she saw the first line of the message from Mick on the screen to the rest of the Blood Brothers.

College shirts, lads.

Ruby gave another loud cry and Hallie shoved the phone in her back pocket and rocked her hard.

'S'okay, s'okay. Here, let's put on the TV. Want to watch *Play School*?' She started to hum the opening music and hoped that she could find it on iView.

Ruby hiccupped and put her head on Hallie's shoulder while Hallie found the remote and fell onto the couch with her daughter resting on her stomach. They'd spent many hours like this when Ruby had been a colicky, hard-to-settle baby. She'd always hoped it would create a deep bond between the two of them, but Ruby was Alex's girl. How was she going to explain all of this to her?

That was when the tears hit her cheeks. Her little girl was going to grow up not remembering her dad. Ruby would never have a brother or sister and she would never be able to understand what a funny, warm, kind and deeply mischievous man Alex was.

His phone was digging into her back. Rolling a little without upsetting Ruby, she got it out from her pocket and looked at the screen again. The wallpaper photo was of Alex, Ruby and Hallie from about six months ago, on Father's Day. All three were smiling. None of them could have known what was going to happen to their little family.

Another message flashed up on the screen.

Tom: *Charlie's been in contact. He wants to come to the funeral.*

CHAPTER 12

'Here,' Dave said, holding out a manila folder to Mia. 'It's Alex Donaldson's autopsy report. You'll need this to put with the information for the coroner. Have you uploaded the photos and videos you took?'

Mia took the file. She scanned the first page. 'Mmm, probably nothing we didn't already know there. Broken neck, ribs, knee, shoulder. Geez, the poor bugger. He was totally mangled. I'm not sure what would have been worse, knowing he was falling, thinking he was going to die or the seconds of pain he would have had.'

'Better not to think about it. Those type of thoughts will twist your head into all sorts of problems. Just focus on the big picture.' Dave leaned back in his chair, his glasses perched on the end of his nose. 'So, have you?'

'What?' Mia was still reading.

'Uploaded the photos and videos?'

'Oh, yeah, I did that the next day, but I've made a note there will be more coming. We did say that we'd go back and take more photos and look at the scene during the day.' She looked up at him. They hadn't done that yet.

'Yeah, the day after the death would have been better, but that traffic accident held us up. That's the trouble being such a small station—not enough resources and such vast distances to cover.'

'Here we go again,' Mia said, with a roll of her eyes. 'You know you can't fix it, so why keep complaining?'

Taking off his glasses, Dave rubbed his eyes. 'Because,' he said patiently, 'you and I can't work like this forever. I've put in for leave for Bec's wedding, and Steve, my long-suffering boss, rang me this morning, saying he can't get anyone to cover the dates I want to have off. At this stage, he's still hoping he can find someone, but there's only a select few who want to come this far from the city lights.'

Mia shrugged as she stuck a pen behind her ear and used the 'Received' stamp to mark the document then entered the evidence number in the log. 'Nothing new there. Last time I had a week off you were by yourself. And when your last senior constable Jack Higgins was working with you, it was the same.'

'Which is fine if everything is quiet and Mr Grafton doesn't run his car into the IGA. Or if Deena Foy doesn't let herself out of the nursing home and go missing like she did last week. If there's no action in Barker, one police officer is more than enough. But all it needs is for something small to pop up and then it's not.'

'Hmm, I know what you're saying.' She swung her chair around and started the computer. Suddenly, her head snapped up. 'Wait, did you say you've put in for leave?'

Dave nodded. 'Yeah, for Bec's wedding.'

Mia regarded him for a moment, then leaned back in her chair. 'That's great. You excited?'

Dave shrugged. 'Long way off yet.'

'Kim going, too?' Mia fired off the second question so quickly, it sounded as if she was interviewing a suspect and was about to break them.

'No.' Dave avoided her eyes. 'Talk about understaffing. Catering Angels is a one-woman band and she's got clients coming out of her ears. She can't take any time off either.'

Mia held her eyes on him, not saying anything, just waiting.

'And Bernie, the new manager in the roadhouse, has decided country life isn't for her and resigned yesterday. We're trying to find another manager, but people who want to work roadhouse hours, let alone in the country, are few and far between. Kim and I were joking last night that I might have to resign and take over the roadhouse.' There was a pause. 'Not the cooking, though!'

'Oh.' Mia didn't say another word. She was practising the tactic Dave had taught her while interviewing the last driver she had pulled over. '*Stay quiet. What do people do when there's a long silence? They want to fill it, so in turn they normally ramble. Best way to get them to confess. Stay quiet. It puts pressure on them to talk.*'

Dave would be pretty well versed in silence, too, so she wasn't convinced it would work, but nothing ventured, nothing gained.

He seemed to be taking an extra-long time to find what he needed from his desk drawer. Five minutes, then another five passed, and finally Mia couldn't stand it anymore.

'What the hell? You're not taking Kim just because Bec said she couldn't go? Do you know how five-year-old-ish your daughter is sounding? Not that I've met her, but seriously? Thank god Kim is a saint, because if that was me and you weren't sticking up for me, I'd be telling you exactly what I thought.'

Dave looked up, mild amusement on his face. 'How unlike you to be at all lippy and opinionated, Mia,' he said.

'What?' Then she laughed. 'Yeah, well, I wouldn't want you to be surprised by an unusual reaction.'

'Unlikely,' Dave said, crossing his arms, eyes crinkling. 'Look, I know this isn't ideal, but Kim has been the one pushing for me to go by myself. If I had my way, she'd be coming with me. And yes, you're right, she *is* a saint, which is why she's saying that it's important that I meet the girls without any outside influences. That part I understand and agree with. But meeting with the girls for the first time in over fifteen years, I think it should just be me, Bec and Alice. We've got to get to know each other again. Talk. And I guess some of those conversations mightn't be that comfortable.'

'Yeah, yeah, totally,' Mia said. 'But still take Kim to Perth with you. She doesn't have to go to any of the catch-ups or anything to do with the wedding, if it gets to that, but Dave'—Mia leaned towards him, urgency on her face—'have her there so if the moment is right, she can meet the girls.'

Indecision crossed Dave's face. 'Guess there isn't any manual for this type of thing. I'll think about it a bit more. Talk to Kim again.'

'You know what I reckon you should do?'

'You're going to tell me anyway,' Dave said, adjusting his glasses.

'Just take her. At the risk of upsetting your male ego—'

Dave feigned a heart attack, hands flying to his chest. 'No!'

'*You* might need her. Have you thought about that?'

Again, an uncertain silence. 'Let's see what the next few days are going to bring,' he finally said.

Sensing that she wouldn't get anything more out of Dave on that subject, Mia switched to a different tack. 'I hope you can get some time off. You need a break.'

'Do I? Getting cranky or something, huh?'

'No, I just mean . . . Have you even had any holidays since I started?'

'Did I have holidays before you started?'

'How am I supposed to know that?'

'Doesn't matter, Mia. Yes, I'll see if I can get a couple of weeks.' His tone was patient but held an edge. She was treading a fine line. 'I've got a Teams meeting with Steve this afternoon, see what comes of that. He was going to approach a few people directly.'

'I'm only being bossy because I care.'

She expected him to say something like: '*Well, don't care too much*,' but instead Dave said two words that completely spun her out.

'Thank you.'

Mia reached under her desk to pull out the rubbish bin for no reason other than to hide her flushed face. Considering they spent most of their time giving each other shit, his heartfelt words meant an awful lot to her.

The phone rang out in the main area, and Mia heard Joan answer it, then the phone beeped at her desk.

'I've got Ruben Forrester on the phone,' Joan said. 'He's wanting to report a stranger hanging around.'

Mia rolled her eyes as she picked up the phone.

'A stranger? Here in Barker? Probably a local that he hasn't seen properly.' She pressed the button to take the call off hold. 'Constable Worth speaking, Barker Police.'

'Mia, Ruben Forrester here. Just wanted to let you know that I've noticed a man hanging around in the parking bay near the cemetery the last few days.'

'That sounds a bit uncomfortable. When have you seen him there?'

'Mid-morning, today and yesterday.'

'Okay, so what worried you about him? You must be suspicious, yeah? Otherwise, you wouldn't have called.'

'Oh no, only thought it was odd. He was just sitting in the little shed there that's got the seat in it, and only because I've seen him twice and didn't know who he was.'

'Righto, Mr Forrester. We'll swing by and have a look.'

'He wasn't there when I went home for lunch.'

'Okay, don't worry about this anymore, we'll keep an eye out.' She paused. 'Did he have anything with him? Bags or the sort?'

'Not that I could see.'

She thanked him and hung up, shaking her head. 'That bloke is such an old busybody. I wish he'd just concentrate on the finances for the council, rather than trying to create something that's not there.'

'That was the council CFO?' Dave groaned. 'You're right, I reckon he's made seven or eight reports over the last six months of unusual happenings in town. None of which have come to anything. Sometimes I think his life of figures and accounts must be so boring that he tries to spice things up.'

Mia scribbled a note in the daybook, then flicked the page to see the next day's date. 'We don't have anything on tomorrow as yet, so we could head out to Alex Donaldson's then.'

'Yeah, if we don't go soon, anything of note will be affected by the elements. Probably already is. Doesn't really matter with an open and shut case of non-suspicious death.'

'What I want to know is why you are sure it's accidental. How can you rule out suicide?'

Dave seemed to be weighing up what he was going to say. 'Look, we're police officers and we've sworn to uphold the law, right?'

Mia nodded and drew her notebook to her.

'You don't need to take notes on this. It's common sense. Did you get the impression that Alex was unhappy in any way?'

'No, but we haven't dug very far. Only asked a few basic questions.'

'Right. Alex has got a little girl, a wife and what seems to be a happy home life. Certainly a happy family life. A young daughter, loving wife, et cetera, et cetera. That's a tick in the no-suicide box.' Dave checked one finger off. 'He's not in the average age range of suicide. I know there is always the exception to the rule, but at thirty, Alex falls outside of that average.' Another finger pointed upwards. 'We've not found a message to indicate that's what he's done and neither have Hallie, Rod and Danny, nor do any of them think he was depressed or unhappy in any way. Agreed?'

'Yes.'

'You videoed me looking through Alex's phone on the night. There was nothing of note there. No text message to his wife, parents or friends to say goodbye, no video, nothing at all that caught my attention.' He raised his eyebrows at Mia. 'You haven't mentioned any concerns either.'

'Not every suicide leaves a note.' Mia wanted to play the devil's advocate here. Hadn't Dave taught her to question everything?

'True.'

'Do you know the family at all?'

'Not overly. I know they've been in the district for a few generations and I've seen them all around town to say g'day to, but I haven't got an intimate knowledge. Long way from their place to Barker. But see, this bloke has climbed up a windmill. Alex had a reason to check the water and then make sure the windmill was operational. Yes, it's a long way to fall. That's unfortunate. There're no witnesses and nothing to cause me any concern, which is why I'll sign it off as an accidental death. You saw how narrow the platform is at the top of the windmill. When we go back out, we'll check that and make sure the wood hasn't rotted through and look for other matters of concern, but I would bet my badge there aren't any. Have you seen something in the autopsy that might make you think otherwise?'

'Ah, no. But we haven't been back out to the scene. There might be more to find. Like you say, rotten wood.'

'Which still makes it accidental. Even if Alex did decide to jump, does it do any good in trying to prove that? Is causing the family so much extra trauma on top of their grief going to change anything? I think it'll make it worse,' Dave said quietly.

Mia gaped at him. 'What? Are you serious? You don't want to look any further?'

His face was grim. 'I am serious and it's not about *not* looking any further—I don't have enough reason to *warrant* looking beyond what we've already done. If I had even an inkling that Alex's death was a suicide, rather than an accident, I would have followed it through on the night. Questioned everyone out there. The autopsy hasn't shown any abnormalities, so my gut is saying it's non-suspicious, and if by some tiny percentage it wasn't, I'll still sleep at night. Sometimes saving the family even the smallest amount of pain is good policing.'

Mia remained still, staring at him in shock.

'Think about it,' Dave continued. 'I'm sure you'll realise I'm right. Life isn't black and white, Mia. As I've got older, I've learned there are many, many grey areas. People are hurting from all types of unseen, unrecognised trauma. Why make their time here on earth any more difficult for them if there isn't a reason to?'

'Insurance companies don't pay out on suicides,' she said, searching for all the consequences from a wrong conclusion.

'I'll repeat myself. The scene doesn't tell me it was a suicide. As it stands, the coroner will make the final decision and we'll give him or her the information to help with that verdict.'

Leaning back in his chair, he held her eyes and steepled his fingers. 'If you don't agree, now is your opportunity. Did you see something different to me?'

Not able to think of anything to say, Mia blinked. She ran through the scenario. A young mum whose husband wasn't coming home. A child who would always have the stigma of her dad committing suicide attached to her. Questions that couldn't be answered. Always living with the why.

'I suppose I can see your point,' she said finally, although the words didn't sit well with her.

CHAPTER 13

'I need to talk to you.' Nicole was standing at the door, her hands clasped in front of her.

Hallie looked over her mother-in-law's shoulder to see if Rod was there, too. Pushing the door open and waving her hands to shift the flies, she said, 'Of course. Come in.'

'Thank you.' Nicole closed the door and followed Hallie inside, only to pull up short when she saw Ruby sitting with her feet in the sink, hands in the bubbly water, and more bubbles on her nose. 'Good lord!'

'Nanny,' Ruby said and held out her arms. 'Nanny, Nanny!'

Privately, Hallie thought the name 'Nanny' sounded like a goat, but to be fair, she also thought it suited Nicole. She was a goat. And that was a generous assessment of this tough, hard-faced woman.

Alex told her he had called his maternal grandmother Nanny and the name had been passed down. '*There's something gentle about it*,' he said and grinned when she rolled her eyes. '*Well, I've got good memories of my nanny*.'

'*Gentle? You think of your mother as gentle?*'

'*My nanny was*,' he told her. Hallie noticed he refrained from commenting on Nicole.

She'd smiled. '*Well, Ruby can call her whatever you want*,' she'd said.

'Good lord, Hallie! What are you thinking, leaving Ruby unattended on the bench? She could have fallen off and hurt herself!' Nicole snatched up Ruby and put her on her hip, rubbing a hand softly over her head.

In her defence, Hallie wanted to say, '*Well, you knocked on the door!*' But what was the point? She was aware there was very little that Nicole would approve of.

'Nanny, 'ook, bubooles.' Ruby laughed and tried to reach back to the frothy white suds.

'If there weren't snakes in the house, I'd be able to have her on the floor,' Hallie retorted. 'No one has been over to help me search the house for where they're getting in. When I get up in the middle of the night for Ruby, or to go to the loo, I turn on every light in case there's one around. I hate living like this.' As she said the words, her stomach dropped a little. Shit, had she just played into Nicole's hands with those last words?

Her mother-in-law turned towards her. 'I guess we've all had things on our mind, with Alex's passing. And really, you are going to have to let this go,' she said calmly. 'A once- or twice-off occurrence doesn't make it an always thing. As I've told you before, anything can happen out here and snakes are a part of life. Yes, granted, uncomfortable to have them inside, but these are old houses. Of course there will be cracks and holes in places. Don't forget, this house was built back in the early nineteen hundreds, so it's over one hundred years old. Quite understandable if a few little visitors get in now and again.'

Hallie glared at Nicole, fury rushing through her. As far as she was concerned, the gloves were off. Hallie didn't have to be one iota of nice now.

'Would you have put Alex on the floor?' she challenged. 'Or Sam? When they were babies?'

Nicole rubbed foreheads with Ruby. 'Look at your bubbly nose! Aren't you the cutest?' Without looking up, she said, 'I'd rather mice than snakes, but we have to accept what happens.'

The windows rattled as an extra strong breeze picked up and the lighting changed for a moment as the single cloud in the sky hid the sun. But during the summer months and beyond, wishing for a cool change had become a pipe dream. Hallie understood the weather better these days. It was hot. Hotter. Stinking hot or cold.

Hallie rubbed her eyes and sank into a chair. 'What do you want, Nicole?' Easier to get whatever it was out of the way.

'Well, Rod thought I should have a talk to you about the future now that Alex isn't here.'

'Of course he did. Hell, your son isn't even cold and—'

'Do you think you are the only one who is sad?' Nicole broke in. 'Let's get this straight, you do not have a monopoly on grief here. Alex was our son.' Nicole stood tall, bouncing Ruby on her hip. 'The fact of the matter is we are all sad, but again, this is life. People live and then they have to die, because that is just life. Alex's accident isn't unique and I, more than anyone, wish it didn't happen. Still, there is no changing this. We must get on and not wallow. The Donaldsons face problems and misfortune head-on.'

That brought Hallie up short. Of course she knew her in-laws were suffering, too, but she hadn't wanted to give Rod and Nicole the privilege of recognising their anguish after everything they'd done to her. The loss of Alex was her burden alone to bear.

Yet myriad emotions exploded inside: was Alex only a 'problem and misfortune' to them?

Running her fingers through her hair, she waited.

'There is a saying: *Tonight, we cry, we despair, we fear. Tomorrow, we get back to trying to build the world we want.* A moment of pain, reflection and sadness is acceptable, Hallie. However, facing problems head-on builds character. You'll have to trust me when I say I know.' Nicole looked hard at Hallie now. 'I *know*.'

Silence spun around them until Hallie felt the unspoken words, choking her. What was Nicole telling her?

'The funeral.' Nicole pulled out a chair and sat down, settling Ruby on her lap. 'We need to talk about the funeral. Alex will be buried in the family plot here on the station.'

Hallie thought about the lonely graves at the base of the ranges. White headstones with a layer of red dust. Carved black writing against the marble. A history lesson about all who have gone before. Not just a history lesson, a past that needed honouring. Hallie did understand, because Alex had told her the stories passed down from each generation about everyone who lay under that cracked, dry earth.

'That's where he'd want to be,' she said.

'Every generation since the Donaldsons bought Tirranah has a child in that cemetery.' Nicole sounded lost in her memories.

There was a sadness around her words that made Hallie look more closely at her mother-in-law. She saw old heart-ache sitting heavily on her shoulders, a grief different to losing Alex. Had Nicole lost someone else? A baby, maybe? Alex had never spoken of another sibling.

Hallie swallowed. She had lost a husband, yes, but that didn't give her exclusiveness to sorrow.

Alex was about to become history. Once Rod and Nicole were gone, and Hallie was too old to remember, her husband would be nothing but a name to those who came after him.

And now he was gone, who would carry on the station? His parents, though fit and active, wouldn't last forever. Sam wouldn't come home. Without Alex, there wasn't family to carry on the legacy.

'And our family chaplain will conduct the service.' Nicole interrupted her thoughts.

Hallie bristled. 'Considering I'm organising the funeral, it seems as if a lot has already been done,' she said.

'Mumma, go to Mumma!' Ruby cried, holding out her arms.

Nicole let Ruby lean over to her mother, who took her, kissing the child on the forehead and tucking her into her hip.

'Family tradition, and that is important to the Donaldsons. We hope you can understand that also.' Nicole's voice was softer than before, tremulous.

What would it be like to lose Ruby? Perhaps *two* of Ruby. This warm, squiggling little bundle. Ah, there was that heart explosion feeling again.

'Yes, of course,' she said. 'Alex would want that. He believed in tradition, even if he didn't agree with the way it was enforced.'

Another score for her, as Nicole narrowed her eyes.

'Good, I'll make those arrangements then. Now, the eulogy. We would like—'

'My domain.' Hallie stood her ground. 'He might have been your son, but he was my husband and we shared . . . different things.'

Nicole seemed about to argue, then changed her mind. 'Sure.'

They stood there, avoiding each other's gaze. Hallie nuzzled Ruby.

'Was there anything else?' She was wary, still pretending to be occupied entertaining Ruby. It would be great to think that the funeral was all that her mother-in-law was here to talk about, but Hallie was sure that wasn't the case.

Nerves weren't usually obvious with Nicole, but Hallie was picking up on them as she took a breath.

'The future needs to be discussed.'

Bouncing Ruby up and down, Hallie walked over to the bench and sat her daughter down. Dipping her hands into the bubbles, Hallie blew gently towards Ruby, who giggled as the cold froth landed on her face.

'More, Mumma.'

Hallie repeated the motion, waiting for Nicole to continue. The risk of losing her home should have caused fear to course through her. But Hallie stood calmly and waited.

Instead of continuing the conversation, Nicole was looking at Hallie and Alex's wedding photo, which hung near the door. Only one set of parents with the bride and groom.

As soon as the borders had opened after Covid, Hallie's parents, Jonathan and Selena, had packed their suitcases and passports and left Australia. They were running out of time to travel to the countries they had always wanted to, Selena had said. '*We want to spend months in Italy and Greece, see the northern lights! There are so many castles and so much history to absorb. We need to go while we're still young enough to not trip over those cobbled stones of Italy after a few drinks! You'll be okay, won't you, darling? You understand?*'

Hallie did understand, but not enough when Jonathan had been given the task of ringing her and saying they wouldn't make it home for her wedding. Nicole's mouth had actually hung open for a few seconds when Hallie passed on the news.

Despite her own disbelief over their decision, Hallie had, in a small way, been glad. The two sets of parents were miles apart in attitude and life and could have caused a few slip-ups if they'd both been there on the day. Instead of being on her father's arm, she'd been on her husband-to-be's and they had walked down the aisle together.

Now, Hallie continued to observe Nicole discreetly. The strong, straight-backed woman with a no-nonsense bob. Her hair was streaked with lines of grey and her thin frame told of hard work in a hard landscape.

Selena, on the other hand, had a pixie cut, dyed blonde. The style suited her sharp nose and slender face. Like Nicole's, her hands and nails were sensibly cut and moisturised, but the difference between the two women was that Selena had always tapped at a computer or pored over numbers as an accountant. She'd only worked part-time, not from dawn until after dark.

Hallie wondered how she'd ended up with two aloof women in her life. The same, but different.

'Where are your parents right now?' Nicole finally asked. 'They're not here to support you?'

'They're coming,' Hallie told her. 'It takes a while to get back from overseas. Actually, getting in contact with them took a couple of days. They'll be here.'

Pivoting, Nicole looked from Ruby to Hallie. 'They are coming out here? To the station?'

'That's the plan, but I guess it depends on when we can hold the funeral and how long it takes them to get back to Australia.' Hallie twirled a strand of Ruby's hair around her fingers.

'If that's the case, then you should start to pack up the house. Go back to Adelaide with them.'

Hallie froze. 'Sorry?'

'You should go back with them, so you have someone to travel with. Make sure you're okay. Help you get set up when you get back to Adelaide. That's where you'd like to live, isn't it?'

'You're really going to kick us out?' Hallie spoke quietly, knowing it had been coming but still unable to believe her in-laws could be so cold. 'I can't believe—'

'Our agreement states that if you and Alex should separate, you need to leave the station. You have no reason to be here.'

'But we haven't . . . I'm not . . .' Hallie looked around wildly as the force of Nicole's words hit her. 'Why? What about Ruby?'

'We are going to need to employ a workman and we don't have another house, so he will have to live here. As for Ruby, we will visit her often enough when we come to Adelaide and maybe, when she's a little older, you might be comfortable for her to come and stay with us.' Her eyes were weary.

'You want me to pack up the last years of my life in a few days, go to my husband's funeral and then leave, with nowhere to go?' Panic in the way of multiple waves of butterflies in her stomach rolled at Nicole's words.

'It's part of the agreement you signed. I would also imagine we've got another week or so to wait until we hear from the police before we can set a date for the funeral.

Autopsies take time and the funeral home won't let us set a date until they have a body—'

'No, but we can still organise the whole service, which I've been doing,' Hallie said, but Nicole didn't break stride.

'—that will give you some more time and I assume your parents will help you.'

The coldness from this woman was unbelievable. Hallie hugged Ruby to her, her heart beating wildly. This was crazy. Unrealistic.

'Alex would hate what you're doing.'

'Alex,' Nicole answered, her eyes flashing, 'never knew what was good for him.'

CHAPTER 14

Mia got out of the troopy, Dave's advice ringing in her ears. '*Sometimes the area will tell you more about a scene than anything.*'

What did that mean? she wondered as she looked at the windmill, standing tall against the blue sky. Flies buzzed and bombed her face and occasionally there was an annoyed flap of wings and a cry from one of the white cockatoos in the large gum trees on the creek. Mia could hear them tearing at the leaves and bark.

Considering there were no humans around other than Dave, who was still sitting in the troopy, writing up some notes, it was incredible how much noise there was. When the wind blew, the trees' leaves rustled against each other. The automatic filler in the trough kicked in when the stock drank and the sound of water running filtered through. In the distance, sheep bleated, and every so often dust would rise on the horizon. No noise, just a long dirty cloud indicating there was a car on the public road.

Today, the blue sky had puffs of white fluffy clouds drifting lazily across it and there was talk of a cyclone coming down from Queensland, which could mean rain. Pretty late in the season, she'd been told by Hopper from the pub, but '*by hell, I hope it happens*'.

'*This has been one of the longest, hottest summers I can remember since I moved here. Need something to break the cycle.*' He'd waggled his finger at her. '*And none of that "you're getting old, Hopper, and feeling the heat" crap, okay*?'

Mia had opened her eyes in mock shock. '*I wouldn't say that!*'

Snorting, Hopper had continued to dry the glasses under the cool breeze of the air conditioner.

Mia adjusted her hat and opened the back door of the troopy to get out the sunscreen. Heat swirled around her, making her feel as if she was in an oven, baking. Smearing the cream on her arms and face, she handed it through the window to Dave, then approached the windmill with trepidation. What could this massive piece of equipment tell her if it were able to talk? Well, that was up to her to find out.

Putting one foot on the ladder, Mia swung herself upwards and climbed steadily to halfway, before looping her arms around the steel frame and turning to look across the countryside for a bird's-eye view. She wanted to know what Alex had seen moments before he'd died.

Flat land stretched out until the horizon blurred into a hazy mixture of blue, and Mia couldn't tell if she was looking at land or sky. Dotted over the country were scrubby acacia bushes, stones and large swathes of bare red dirt. She couldn't understand how anyone could make a decent living from this dry, baked earth, let alone want to live out here.

Mia brushed her cheek, swiping away the sweat that was tickling her as it ran down the side of her face. Surprisingly, the flies were still annoying her. Not once had she ever wondered how high flies could . . . well, fly. Obviously, it was as high as the top of the windmill and probably higher.

Across the creek—probably two kilometres away, she judged—was a line of ranges. The map had told her these were Chambers Ranges, which ran for about thirty kilometres in a winding north-west direction. The tall hills threw out long shadows and shaded the creek from the midday sun.

A willy-willy of dust kicked up across the flats and twirled and curled towards the creek before it blew itself out.

'Careful up there,' Dave called as he shut off the engine and slammed the car door.

'What?' The wind blew around Mia's ears, blurring any voices or noise.

'See anything of interest?' His voice was louder.

'Not really. Other than the ranges, the land is as flat as a tack. You can see how this would flood in really wet years. The water would spill over from the creek, because that's not very deep, then just run out onto the land.'

'That's when the best seasons are,' Dave answered. 'The map says there's a public road directly to the south. Can you see it?'

'The bush is too high for me to see the actual road, but I can tell where it is.' Surveying the rest of the land, Mia frowned. 'Have you got the map there? It almost looks like there is an access road or something coming across in that direction.' She cast her arm out towards the south-east to indicate where there was another long line break in the bush.

'Might just be stock tracks. They always walk the path of least resistance through the bush and make their own routes. Rod mentioned to me the other night there were sheep in this paddock—the whole reason Alex was out here checking the water. I'll make a note to google the satellite view and see what we can see that way.'

'Okay.'

Mia continued to climb higher.

Above her head, the fan continually circled slowly in the breeze, a large, obvious presence. Reaching the wooden platform, she pushed up on it and it wobbled.

'This is pretty loose!' she yelled at Dave.

He indicated she should take photos, but Mia was one step ahead of him. The bodycam she wore was already recording.

Pushing again, the platform splintered in her hands, pieces tumbling to the ground.

'Look out!' she called.

There was no way the wood could have held a man of Alex's size and weight.

Dave was right, Mia realised. Accidental or non-suspicious death. Poor bastard.

Mia climbed down and picked up the pieces for evidence. Inspecting the edges, she ran her hands over the small part of the break that was smooth and clean, then gave way to the jagged edges of the rot.

Dave poked around at the trough and tank area. 'You got a record of this boot print?' Dave asked, pointing at a clear imprint in the damp earth near the tank.

Mia dropped the evidence into the plastic box in the back of the troopy and flipped through the photos she'd printed off. 'Yep. I guess we should match that to Alex's boot, shouldn't we? Although with the state of the platform, it doesn't seem worth it.' She took a step back and looked up at the steel head. 'There is something incredibly eerie about that piece of equipment. I feel like it's got its own personality. A very dark one.'

Dave raised a shoulder. 'You can if you like. It will be good practice in processing a scene for you.'

Mia made an entry in her notebook not to forget and then wandered off towards the track. Her eyes flicked back and forth across the ground, looking for anything of interest. Ants scurried, carrying pieces of . . . Mia wasn't sure, but whatever it was, they were huge titbits; almost bigger than the insects' bodies. Following the trail of ants, she saw a large built-up nest.

'Nana always used to say that, when it's going to rain, the ants build their nests high,' she told Dave, who had joined her.

'I've never really worked out if that's true or not,' he said. 'Ants are always so busy and they seem to be building nests all the time. Probably to cope with the population explosions they're always having.'

Mia laughed softly, before following the ants further towards a cluster of bushes. They ran up the branches and across the spindly leaves, gathering nectar and food, before swinging around and heading back to the nest.

'They all seem to have one speed,' she said, 'and they never seem to get tired! I wish I had their energy. Oh—' Mia stopped and squatted down. 'Dave? Look at this.'

With phone in hand, she pointed towards two boot prints behind the bushes. 'What do you think these are?'

Dave bent over and looked, then straightened up and checked where the windmill was. 'Might've come over here to have a piss,' he said. His eyes were casting around, and she could tell he was checking everything he knew about the scene in his head. She walked on a bit further, eyes on the ground. The soil hadn't been disturbed in any other areas, but neither were there footprints leading to where she'd found the two prints.

'That's probably the case,' he decided. 'Look, the prints are about thirty centimetres apart, and they're pointing towards the windmill, so—'

'Why would he move all the way over here to take a leak when there was no one else around?' Mia asked as she snapped some photos. 'But they do look the same as the other one near the trough,' she conceded.

'There's a camera pointed at the trough,' Dave reminded her. He reached for her folder and flicked through until he found the angle of the image that he'd taken the night they'd been at the homestead. 'See? You can't see this part of the landscape. Maybe he was getting out of the way so Hallie and Ruby couldn't see him.'

'Hmm.' Mia cast around again. 'But there aren't any more. How did these even get here?'

'His death would've been instantaneous.' Dave's attention was on the autopsy report and he didn't seem to hear her question. 'You can't get head trauma the way Alex had and a broken neck and not die. A blessing that he wouldn't have known anything about it.'

'But he would have,' Mia said. 'He would have known he was falling.'

'Did you ask if the video had any recording? If the images were saved?' Dave asked suddenly.

'Yeah. If any movement sets the camera recording, they're saved for a couple of weeks then deleted from the server. The camera only recognises movement within a three-metre radius. Do you want me to ask Hallie for the footage?'

'Yeah, let's get it.' His mobile phone rang, causing them both to jump.

'What the hell?' Mia asked.

'Starlink,' Dave said, pointing to the satellite dish on top of the tank. 'How do you think the images are streamed back to the homestead computer? I asked for the password. Hello? Burrows.'

Seeing something at the base of a bush, Mia leaned in and used her fingers to dig around the object, careful not to touch it. When she realised what it was, she rested back on her haunches and waited until Dave was off the phone.

'Check this out,' she said, pointing.

Over her shoulder, Dave gave a laugh. 'A horseshoe! Plenty of them to be found around here. For a long while, before motorbikes, horses were used to muster this land. You'll find heaps of them scattered about, the stones played havoc with their hooves.'

Mia stood up and dusted her hands and knees. 'So really, there's nothing extra here of concern? Except how these prints got here without someone walking to this spot.'

Dave walked away, not answering.

Mia watched him inspect the base of the windmill and look back to where she was standing. Then he walked towards her, his eyes downwards.

'I have no idea how they've come to be here,' he said. 'I don't think there's been enough wind to cover them with sand, but like Rob said, there's different weather out here on the flats to elsewhere. Plus, there's nothing across the ground that indicates someone has swept them away with a branch or the like. Maybe they've been protected because of the bush. Anyhow, you're right. Doesn't look like there's anything to worry about.' He paused and walked a bit further, in the other direction, still looking at the ground. 'That was Hamish on the phone. He's brought Alex's body back to the hospital morgue, so the funeral can go ahead as planned.'

A heavy sadness settled inside Mia's body. Twelve months had passed but she still remembered how final it had been when her nana had taken her last breath and how quiet the hospital room had been afterwards. Later, when she'd walked into the church and seen her coffin at the front, there had been no turning back. That day, she'd railed against going to the church because that would make it real, but Chris and Dave and Kim had all arrived on her doorstep and taken her hand, guiding her, standing with her as she had entered the church and given the eulogy, and then as the coffin had been lowered into the ground.

Her grandmother wasn't coming back. Neither was Alex. Sadder still was the fact that Alex hadn't lived the same full life as Nana.

'Well, that's that, then,' Mia said.

'Let's call into the house and let Hallie know,' Dave said, heading back towards the troopy.

~

The first thing Mia noticed about the homestead was how many cars were parked under the trees. The visitors obviously knew how hot it got out here and were finding shade for the vehicles. There were four unfamiliar vehicles and Alex's ute. In the daylight was the expanse of green lawn and the trees around the edge of the yard. A mixture of mature pepper and gum trees and a large wall of bright purple bougainvillea hemmed the yard in. To the west of the house were a couple of sheds and one had the back end of a tractor poking out. Sheep yards were under another roof and what looked like a sea container was plonked in the middle of the yard with nothing next to it.

Dave found a free tree next to the gate and poked the nose of the troopy into the shade.

'Hello!' A young woman came onto the verandah and waved. 'We heard you arrive. I'm Maggie. Hallie's inside.' She kept the door closed until Dave and Mia had taken off their boots and were ready to run the gauntlet of flies and heat to the inside of the house.

The kitchen was dim, the curtains closed, trying to keep the heat out. Cardboard boxes lined one wall, and there was newspaper spread across the floor. Mia squinted at one of the men sitting at the table, recognising his face, but unsure as to who he was. He had a long fringe, which he swept off his forehead every few minutes. Mia knew the action, but she couldn't place him. Not from the pub in Barker.

Danny was there, too, along with another man and woman whom Mia didn't know.

'Hi,' she said to the group. 'I'm Constable Mia Worth and this is Detective Dave Burrows.'

'I'm Tom,' one of the men said. 'And my wife, Kaylah.' He held out his hand and Mia shook it, nodding at Kaylah.

While Tom was speaking, the other man stood up and held out his hand. 'I'm Mick. Thanks for supporting Hallie, Rod and Nicole as you are,' he said. 'Terrible, terrible business. We're here to help, too, of course. Old mates from ag college. Been friends with Alex for as long as we can remember. This is all so awful.'

'Mick? Have I met you before? You seem—'

'Familiar. Yep, get that all the time. I'm a federal minister for the government.'

'Ah, that's right, you're the, um . . .' She thought hard. 'Health minister, aren't you? Sorry, I should have realised.' Mia wanted the floor to open up and swallow her.

'No bother,' Mick answered, sitting back down. 'I'm out of context and that always makes it difficult to recognise people.'

'Nice to meet you, Tom and Kaylah. Danny.' Dave acknowledged the other man, who was sitting at the head of the table, looking miserable. 'Sorry to meet you all under these circumstances.'

'Tea or coffee?' asked Maggie, hovering near the stove.

'We're fine, thanks,' Dave answered. 'Is Hallie here?'

'Yes, I am,' a tired voice said from the hallway. Hallie appeared wearing shorts and a singlet. Her face was grey and she looked like she needed a long sleep.

'Hi, Hallie. How are you and Ruby getting on? How come you're packing?' Dave gave a nod towards the boxes.

With a half-hearted grimace, Hallie looked around the room as if realising for the first time she had visitors. 'Fine. Yep, all okay.'

'I've just managed to get Ruby down for a sleep,' Maggie chimed in. 'Poor little mite keeps asking for her dad.' She paused. 'I wish Hallie would have a rest.' Maggie looked sternly at her friend. 'Hallie isn't too great at following instructions and now this . . .' She swept her hand over the boxes. 'It's all a bit much.'

'There are things to do,' Hallie answered as if on automatic pilot. 'I have to be out of here as soon as the funeral is over.'

'Be out of here?' Mia asked. 'Why's that?'

'It's Nicole and Rod,' Danny answered. 'They've told her she has to go so they can put a workman in here, now they don't have Alex.'

Mia's head spun at the surprising words. 'A workman?'

'Rod and Nicole have always been exceptionally organised,' Mick said. 'They would already be thinking of the future.'

'That's a lot of pressure to be under,' Dave said kindly.

Mia could tell he wanted to ask a lot more about the move, but this wasn't the time.

'Well, we wanted to let you know we've finished what we needed to do at Red Dirt Bore,' he continued.

'Thanks.' Hallie moved slowly and carefully, sitting down at the table and pulling a sheet of paper to her. 'Do I need to get anything more for you?'

'Nothing that's urgent. We wouldn't mind seeing the footage from the camera on Red Dirt Bore when you're able to send it through, but there isn't any rush.'

'Okay.'

Mia watched Hallie write 'footage' on her notes.

'We also wanted to let you know Alex is back in Barker, so you can finish off organising the funeral . . .' Mia paused. 'Do you think you know when it might be?'

Hallie looked at her as if the words didn't make any sense. 'Sorry?'

Mia crouched at Hallie's side and took her hand. 'Do you know when the funeral is going to be?'

'Hallie has done a lot of the organising already,' Mick said. 'Now we know that information, we'll make sure the funeral director is free, but Saturday would be Hallie's preferred day, wouldn't it?'

Hallie looked at Mia. It seemed as if there was a switch inside her. 'Yes. Saturday. My parents won't be here by then. Doesn't matter, though.'

Maggie put a glass of water in front of Hallie. Tom and Kaylah leaned into each other. Everyone at the table had the shell-shocked look that Mia had seen before when tragedy hit. Knowing they had to continue on, but not sure how that was going to be possible since their world had slipped off its axis.

'Yeah, I think Saturday,' Hallie repeated. Her smile at Mia barely reached her lips, though, and her eyes were full of grief. 'That will give the people who need to travel time enough to get here.'

'Okay.'

'Rod and Nicole want the funeral out here. To bury him in the family plot. There's so much history and heritage on this station. Did you know it's been in Alex's family for five generations?'

Dave nodded. 'Like a lot of this country, it takes a special type of person to be able to work this kind of land. Easy to farm when it rains, not so much when it's a low rainfall season.'

Danny nodded. 'Alex loved it out here. I know, Hallie, you'd rather have the funeral in Barker and, yeah, it would be nicer and probably a whole lot less work, but I've got to back Rod here. This is where Alex would want to be buried. This land was his life.'

'I'm not arguing that point, Danny,' Hallie said, twisting the glass of water in her hands. 'Although, I'm not sure Tirranah was completely his life. There were things that annoyed him about being here. It's just . . . it's just I don't want to bury him at all. I want him alive and this'—she waved her arms around, indicating the boxes and the empty hook on the wall, where Alex's hat used to sit—'this is shit.'

Maggie put her arms around Hallie's neck and gave her a gentle hug. 'You're not wrong. Really, Nicole and Rod shouldn't have asked you to move on quite so quickly.'

'Certainly a bit rich,' Danny said with a frown.

'That's life,' Hallie said.

'I don't know,' Mick said. 'As forward thinking as they are, it seems unusual for Rod and Nicole to want everything wrapped up so quickly and so neatly.'

'Unusual? How so?' Dave pulled out a chair and sat down.

'Hallie, what do you think?' Mick turned to her. 'Did you feel the tension I did between Alex and his folks recently? I haven't seen them together for a while, but when I spoke with Alex he mentioned that he was really annoyed with them.'

'There was always some kind of antsiness between them. They were close, but then they'd get upset with each other . . . often,' Hallie said.

'Same as with any father and son relationship,' Tom put in. 'Nothing more than normal, though, was there? Geez, I used to argue with my father all the bloody time until I got out from under his feet and went and did my own thing.'

Mick tipped one shoulder. 'I thought there might have been.'

Hallie shook her head. 'No. Not recently. They had a bit of a problem a few months ago, but that all settled down.'

'What was that over?' Mia asked.

Hallie clasped her hands together on the table. 'His parents asked me to sign a binding financial agreement before we married. I'm not one hundred per cent sure what was in it, because I was so shocked when I realised what it was, I didn't take it in, but Alex was pretty annoyed when he found out.'

'Did you sign it?'

'Yeah.'

'Happens a bit out here,' Maggie said as if she saw the look of horror that had crossed Mia's face.

'Why?'

'Because,' Danny said, 'these places have been in families for generations. If a partner comes in and then divorces the son, they could claim part of the land in the divorce.'

'In turn,' Mick picked up the thread, 'no one wants to lose a station or even have to front up with a payout to an outsider. There's not enough profit out here.'

'Outsider?' Mia said.

'In-laws will always be outsiders here. No matter how much they're loved or part of the family.'

To Mia, the inside workings of family businesses, like this one, were hard to comprehend.

'Since I have you all here,' Dave said, gently changing the subject, 'would you mind telling me a bit about Alex? How you all knew him, what he was like, that sort of thing?'

There was a collective intake of breath around the table.

Tom leaned forward, his fists holding his chin up. He looked uncertain, then started to speak. 'When someone dies unexpectedly, it seems to me everyone wants to make out they were perfect.'

Mia brought her eyes up to meet Tom's. He had a few days' worth of stubble on his chin and large bags under his bloodshot eyes. He was either tired or hungover, Mia wasn't sure which, but thanks to his grief, he looked older than his friends at the table.

'I'm not going to do that with Alex. He was a top-shelf fella, but like the rest of us, he had his faults.' He gave Hallie a lopsided smile as he said, 'I'm sure you can attest to that. Always used to drive too fast, didn't he?'

Mick let out a soft laugh. 'Yeah, remember that time he bought that Mini for a song and decided we were going to go bush? We packed that little car up with as much beer and food as we could, sat on our swags—' He turned to Dave. 'Sorry, everything about this story is illegal.'

Dave raised his hands. 'No problem here.'

'That's right,' Danny said. 'We went out to Woolly camp, where it's all pretty flat, and put the Mini through its paces. Ended up rolling it. Alex was driving.'

Tom laughed. 'Yeah, and all we did was rock it until we could turn it back over onto its wheels.'

'What about you, Maggie, Kaylah? What are your memories?'

Kaylah looked uncomfortable. 'I'm sorry,' she said in an accent Mia couldn't place. 'I didn't get to meet him. Tom and I only met twelve months ago in Singapore and we eloped, so no one came to our wedding. I didn't want a fuss. This is my first visit to Australia. First time meeting everyone Tom has talked so fondly about.'

Maggie reached out her hand to Kaylah. 'And we're glad to have you here,' she said.

'Yeah, that's right,' Hallie said. She looked at everyone sitting at the table. 'You guys have always been so welcoming to whomever you've brought into the fold. Doesn't matter who we are, what our jobs were. Obviously, I've never had anything to do with agriculture before now, yet you were all so accepting of me. Even if I do ask stupid questions at times.'

'Why wouldn't we be?' Danny asked, looking perplexed. 'We're all the best of mates. If we didn't get along with our mates' better halves, then we wouldn't have the opportunity to see each other. Bit like in-laws. Gotta love them, because the alternative isn't that good.'

'Great outlook,' Dave said. 'There're probably a few people who could learn from you fellas.'

'What I remember most about Alex is his ability to work hard and play hard. He's a bit of a larrikin, isn't he?' Maggie said with a smile. 'Both Dan and Alex are.'

'Was,' Mick said softly.

There was another collective breath.

'He was. Loved a drink, was pretty keen on the footy. We always argued about which code we followed because here in SA it's AFL, yet Tom's from Queensland, so for him it was rugby league.'

'Charlie was from New South Wales,' Tom said. 'And he and I agreed on what footy was. It was the rest of you who didn't.'

A hush fell around the table and Mia searched each face. Tom, Danny and Mick shared a glance, then looked at the table.

'And Charlie is?' Dave asked.

Mick cleared his throat. 'Charlie was our other blood brother at agricultural college. There were five of us, but he ended up in gaol just as we were finishing. We haven't had anything to do with him since then.'

'Oh.' Kaylah looked at Tom. 'I thought you said he wanted to come to Alex's funeral . . .' Her voice trailed off as her cheeks flamed red. Tom wriggled in his seat.

'Yeah, I thought I'd seen that, too,' Hallie said.

'Well, yeah. But that's only been in the last few days. We've had nothing to do with him before then,' Danny said.

Maggie glanced at her husband with a frown. 'You never told me that.'

'Nothing to tell,' he answered. 'Just because he got in contact doesn't mean he's going to do what he says. Charlie's always walked to the beat of his own drum.'

CHAPTER 15

Hallie fell into bed after everyone left, glad that Maggie had offered to take Ruby for the night. She needed one whole night's worth of sleep. Would that make her feel normal again? Probably not, but it had to help. At least she hoped it would.

Of the friends who had been there, Danny had left first. He had to catch up with someone, he'd said, then Mick's phone hadn't stopped beeping and he'd excused himself to get back into better range so he could deal with whatever was going on in his office.

A little while later, Tom had said he was going to see Nicole and Rod, organising for Kaylah to hitch a ride back to Barker with Mick.

Maggie had stayed to help her pack the spare room.

There wasn't much in there, only a few books in the shelves and linen in the cupboard that Hallie hadn't had room to store anywhere else.

Some special trinkets, which her grandmother had given her, had been arranged next to the bed, and as Maggie had gone to pull the doona back from the bed, a mouse had run out from underneath and they'd both screamed and leaped onto the bed.

After a few seconds they had looked at each other and laughed, before a few tears had arrived.

After hitting the pillow to try to puff it up, she leaned back, staring at the ceiling, then at the empty boxes Maggie had dumped into her bedroom so Hallie could start unpacking the drawers. This would be the first night she'd ever spent at Tirranah Station by herself. Alex had hardly ever stayed away overnight and if he did, she'd always been with him.

The knot in her stomach wasn't fear, though. Holding Alex's shirt to her face, she closed her eyes and breathed in his scent, pretending he was lying next to her for one last time. She rolled over to hug the shirt between herself and Alex's pillow.

Her husband's body had been solid and toned. Years of hard work meant there wasn't an ounce of fat anywhere on him, and she'd loved to run her hands up and down his arms as he pulled her to him at night. They'd lie together, talking about their day. Sometimes, if she was facing him her head resting on his breast, chest hair tickling her nose, she'd sneeze.

Outside was silent and the whole house and landscape were engulfed in darkness. She assumed the dingo they'd been hearing over the last week or so would turn up again.

The dog had become braver and braver as he came in closer to the buildings. Hallie half expected to find him inside the house yard one morning.

The first time Hallie had ever heard a dingo howl, she'd just about shit herself. It was a low moan that went higher and higher and reached a crescendo of moaning, sighing and keening. 'OoooOOOOHHHH!'

'*What the hell is that?*' she'd asked Alex, sitting upright in bed, pulling the covers to her chest.

He'd continued to snore gently alongside her without moving.

'*Alex!*' She reached out and shook his shoulder. '*What the hell was that?*'

'*What?*' he'd asked sleepily.

'*That noise, what is it?*'

As if on cue the howling started again. Hallie shook him again.

'*Hear that?*'

'*Oh, yeah. Mmm.*' Alex pulled her to him, tucking her body in around his. '*It's a dingo. That's all. Go back to sleep.*'

'*A dingo? Are you sure it's not a banshee or some type of spirit? It sounds like it should be in a Halloween movie.*'

'*Mmm. It's a dingo. Settle down.*'

He'd gone back to sleep within seconds, and Hallie had lain awake all night, waiting, listening, to see if it came back. But just as wild dogs did, it slipped away into the inky night to hunt somewhere else.

A muffled ding from Alex's side of the bed made Hallie jump. She'd wanted to turn the phone off, but instead, she'd put it on charge that morning. After everyone had left that afternoon, she had scrolled through the photos in his album, looking at the pictures he'd taken over their time together. Every second one was of a piece of machinery or a part that he needed for fencing or a windmill, or the solar pump he'd put on the new bore. Vin and chassis numbers of utes. Batch numbers and expiry dates of drenches, chemicals and sprays. What farmers did before the invention of the phone in their pocket, Hallie wasn't sure. Perhaps they used the little stock agent book that was always in their top shirt pocket.

There had been a photo of Nicole and Rod on their fortieth wedding anniversary. That day had been special.

Well, the day had been special for the Donaldson family, Hallie supposed. If you were an in-law of the Donaldsons it was a normal day. '*I hope you and Alex last as long as we have*,' Nicole had said to her. '*There's something wonderful about being able to give your all to your husband*.'

The implication that Hallie was not doing that was clear.

A rush of anger towards Nicole and Rod made Hallie throw off the top sheet and get out of bed. She yanked open the top drawer of the tallboy and started to throw her knickers, bras and socks into the open box. What had Nicole meant when she'd said earlier, '*Alex didn't know what was good for him?*'

'I don't know how you can sleep at night,' she hissed through her teeth.

But as quickly as the anger appeared, her body lost the adrenalin and all Hallie felt was exhausted. *Why are you doing this?*

Back in bed, tucking the sheet around her, she put a pillow on her knees and hung Alex's shirt on her shoulders. Propping up his phone on the pillow. What was she going to do when she couldn't smell him anymore?

The phone lit up with her movement and she picked it up again. Photos Alex had taken of Ruby were next in the camera roll. Ruby lying on Hallie's chest as a small baby. Both asleep. Hallie had asked Alex to send her the one he'd snapped in the shearing shed: Ruby sound asleep, curled up in a fleece. That one now graced the wall in their sitting room.

Alex and Hallie in many different poses; her favourite was from the day they had walked to the top of Mount Clayden and had a picnic. They'd eaten cheese, dips and biscuits and drunk wine and beer, sitting on the granite and overlooking the land as the sun set. They had been able to see for miles up there: a large hill on the horizon in one direction and flat station land in the other. The drive to get there had been a bit of a slog. The track was overgrown and they'd walked the last thirty metres or so up a steep incline. When they made it to the top, they'd explored first, looking for wildflowers and finding old tyres and rubbish instead. Even the remnants of an early phone tower.

Just before the sunlight had completely disappeared, they'd made love on the blanket Hallie had brought.

Alex had the longest of arms to take selfies. Not that he'd ever wanted to, thought they were ridiculous things, but Hallie had always asked, and he'd always complied. Now that photo of them, curled together on the blanket, sat on the windowsill in the bedroom, for their eyes only.

Her next favourite photo was in her natural habitat, the city. They had been dining at a restaurant on the River Torrens, the deck hanging over the water, with swans and ducks swimming underneath. She'd worn an aqua, abstract-print Sacha Drake dress, and Alex had worn chinos and a shirt the same shade of blue as her dress. They looked as if they could have walked down a red carpet together.

A powerhouse couple, Jenna had called them.

Alex didn't mind the city and he made sure they went back often.

'*I don't want you hating the station because you can't visit where you love*,' he'd told her one night as they walked down a street, looking for an out-of-the-way bar. His face had been lit by a streetlight and she'd stopped him and looked up into his face. Placing her hand on his cheek, she'd kissed him.

'*Thank you for being so thoughtful*,' she'd told him.

Another beep from the phone.

The Blood Brothers had forgotten to remove Alex from their group chat—or maybe they didn't want to. She touched the WhatsApp icon. They'd probably realise that she was reading Alex's messages over time.

Tom: *Anyone heard from Charlie again?*

Mick: *Not me. No.*

Tom: *Do we need to be worried?*

There were three little dots as someone was typing.

Mick: *Why would we need to worry?*

Tom: *What if he makes a scene?*

Mick: *Unlikely.*

Hallie put the phone down, wondering why they would be worried about Charlie causing a scene. Maybe because they hadn't seen each other for so long.

She rolled over and opened the top drawer of Alex's bedside table, looking for something of his she might be able to hang off her necklace and have with her all the time. The wedding ring she'd given him, which he very rarely wore.

'*It's too dangerous to wear a ring around machinery and out on the station. I might catch it on a piece of wire or something and bugger my finger up completely,*' he'd told her not long after their honeymoon as he'd put the ring back in the box and stored it in his drawer.

If she could find his ring, she'd put it on her necklace and then it would always be close to her heart.

Pushing aside the name badges, random pieces of paper and band-aids Alex kept there, she looked for the ring box.

She couldn't find it.

Going through the drawer again, this time more slowly, Hallie made sure she looked under every piece of paper and shifted even the tiny portable radio he had. Alex was an ABC listener when he couldn't sleep at night and often Hallie would wake to Philip Clark or Pav asking quiz questions or talking to special midnight and early morning guests.

Hallie had never gone through Alex's drawers, because there'd never been a reason to. His jocks and socks were kept in the tallboy and she'd hardly seen him open any of the other drawers.

The ring box wasn't in the top drawer.

Opening the second one, she rifled through old year books and journals. Cut-out newspaper articles that showed Alex and four other boys in a boat, rowing for Head of the River. A cursory glance told Hallie she didn't know any of the team members except Alex. That was taken at boarding school.

Another article celebrating the time Alex had won the Young Farmer's Challenge at the local show. He'd had to up-end tractor tyres, strain up a few wires of a fence, unroll a hay bale and complete other activities to win. Danny had come second and their fresh, excited faces, still glistening with sweat, stared back at her from the black and white photograph.

A display folder was at the bottom of the drawer, and Hallie pulled it out, flicking open the cover.

The headline screamed at her: STUDENT ACCUSED OF RAPE.

'Oh,' Hallie started. Then she ran her finger down the smooth plastic, finding the name in the article: *Charles Dynner.*

Charles. This was Charlie? Rape was the reason Charlie had gone to gaol?

Hallie had never thought to ask harder questions about why Charlie was in gaol. Alex had shut down every conversation about him, only repeating: '*He didn't stand for the same things we did.*'

An Australian College of Agriculture student has appeared in court charged with rape. Charles Dwain Dynner, 24, is accused of raping an eighteen-year-old woman at a party at the college three days ago. The woman was later hit by a car and is in hospital in a critical condition.

The accused was denied bail and the matter has been referred to the Crown.

Mr Dynner, who has yet to enter a plea, will be remanded in gaol until his hearing in April.

Hallie's eyes flew to the date and saw it was exactly as Alex had told her: as they were all finishing their last year of college in 2017.

No wonder Alex had distanced her from what Charlie had done. She guessed the boys had been there on that night, since they were always together, and knowing Alex the way she did, she suspected Alex blamed himself for somehow not being able to help the woman involved.

She turned the page.

CHARGES UPGRADED TO MANSLAUGHTER.

'What?' Hallie's hand flew to her mouth as she read.

A woman involved in an alleged rape four days ago has died in hospital without regaining consciousness.

Police have upgraded the charges against Mr Charles Dwain Dynner, 24, to manslaughter.

More to come.

'Shit!' Hallie couldn't believe what she was reading.

The next report told of the trial and then Charlie's sentencing. Alex had collected a few more articles on the parole hearing as Charlie's release date came nearer.

A loud ringing from outside made her jump.

Alex had rigged up an outside phone bell so she'd been able to hear the landline when she was outside. Was it only out here in nowhere that landlines were still in existence? Mobile towers were few and far between. Starlink and wifi calling were a godsend when rain came through and the lines went down.

'Hello? This is Hallie?' As she spoke, the clock showed it was nearly 9 p.m. Late for a phone call.

'Hallie?' A tiny, strained voice came down the line. It was laced with tears.

Hallie stood straight up. 'Maggie? What's wrong? Is it Ruby? What's happened?'

'Can you come and get Ruby please? It's Dan. There's been an accident.'

CHAPTER 16

'Bec?' Dave lifted the phone to his ear. The dial tone hadn't even rung before he'd heard her voice. 'Bec, it's, um—' He'd been about to say Detective Dave Burrows and stumbled over the word. 'Dad.'

'Dad, hi, how are you?' Her voice was hurried and business-like. Dave smiled as she used the word *Dad*. The first few times they'd spoken, Bec had steered away from calling him anything and then had tried it out tentatively.

In the background, Dave could hear traffic and the clip-clop of high-heeled shoes. He looked at his watch, thinking it was late for her to be still working.

'Fine, how are you? How are the plans going for the wedding?'

'Everything is on track, thanks. Have you booked flights? I've made sure you have accommodation at the hotel where the reception is being held.'

'Not yet. I was hoping to talk to you about that.'

The clip-clop stopped. 'You are coming, aren't you?' There was a challenge in her voice.

'I am coming,' he told her firmly. 'I'm trying to organise a couple of weeks' leave.' He paused. 'Bec, I wanted to talk to you about Kim.'

The clip-clop started again, and Dave imagined his daughter striding down the street, briefcase in hand, long hair flowing over her shoulders and bouncing in time to her gait.

'We've already talked about Kim. What more is there to say?'

Anger flared through Dave's body. *Little upstart,* he thought. *If she was my daughter . . .*

She is *your daughter.*

'Bec, I'd really like to bring Kim. Now I understand that it isn't approp—'

'No, Dad—'

'If you would just hear me out.'

Silence except for the clip-clop.

'Kim is my wife, and we all agree that meeting her for the first time at the wedding isn't best for anyone. What I'd like to propose is that Kim and I come for the long weekend, later this month. If we all went to Margaret River for the weekend, then we could spend time with each other and when you were ready—if you were ready—Kim would be there and you could meet her. Perhaps given the chance you'd have to see her beforehand, you'd feel happier to have her at your wedding.' He spoke quickly so she couldn't interrupt. 'Kim is very respectful of your decision, so this is coming from me as your father, and Kim's husband, rather than from her. It would mean a lot to me if you would at least think about this option.'

Heavy breathing now as the clip-clop changed to a climbing-stairs beat.

'When's the long weekend? What are the dates? Hang on.'

Dave waited as he was told, hearing tapping on her phone screen.

'No, sorry, Dad. No can do. We have Justin's work dinner that Friday night and then it's Mum's birthday. I guess you'd forgotten that.'

I haven't had to think about Melinda's birthday for a fair while; sorry if it wasn't at the top of my thought process, he wanted to say but reined himself in. This wasn't an easy situation for anyone and, if he wanted to reconnect with the girls, he would have to give a little, just as Bec would.

'Ah, so it is. It slipped my mind. Look, maybe check your diary and see if you've got a spare weekend. We can juggle things here to make it work with whatever suits you and Justin.' He paused. 'And Alice. She needs to be there, too.'

'You're right,' Bec said, 'Alice needs to be there. Have you talked to her yet?'

He felt his spirit lift. She hadn't given a flat-out no, like he'd thought she might.

'I've left a couple of messages, and she sent a text to say she'd ring when she could, but I haven't heard from her yet.'

'Hmm, she'll call you when she's able. The last time we spoke, Alice was heading out to the back of beyond. She could still be there. Leave it with me.' Another lot of clip-clops.

'I know she's keen to talk to you, Dad. But Alice really does do what she wants, when she wants, and nothing gets in the way of that.'

'I'll be happy to hear from her when she's ready,' Dave said. He took a breath and turned back to the skyline, where the sun was setting. 'Alice must really love her job.'

'Being a tour guide in the north isn't for everyone,' Bec agreed. 'Yet she seems to thrive on it.' There was a pause. 'Mum always says she must have got a lot of your genes to love the bush as much as she does. She always gravitated towards it.'

Dave felt a rush of satisfaction. At least he was acknowledged somewhere in his children's lives. It was on the tip of his tongue to tell Bec he'd always written to her and Alice, and for so long he'd tried to call, but he'd been met with a stone wall from Melinda and Mark.

Oh, how he wanted to tell her. He couldn't, though. Dave had made a pact with himself never to cast any blame towards either his ex-wife or ex-father-in-law. They had provided his girls with a secure, happy upbringing, even if that hadn't included him. He wouldn't be the bitter, twisted father. He'd spent too many years doing that when he was younger.

'The bush is a great place. Very soul restoring,' Dave said.

'Not my cup of tea, but each to their own,' Bec replied. Her voice faded a little as she spoke to someone else for a second, then she came back clearly. 'Oh, and Dad, Mum asked me to check with you about Bulldust. You know, making sure he can't cause us any trouble.'

The air left Dave's lungs. 'Check with me about Bulldust . . .' he repeated slowly.

'Yeah, she got a phone call a while back to say he'd been released from gaol. Do you know where he is or has he been in contact?'

Mel knew. Mark, of course, would have his ways to find out and sometimes the parole officers let the victims of crime know their perpetrator had been let out. Dave hadn't been told. In fact, he wouldn't even know his nemesis had been released from gaol if it hadn't been for the one time he decided to check on his status.

Seven or eight months ago, Dave had made a bad decision—he'd never call it a mistake, because he had knowingly opened Bulldust's file. That same day he had received the letter from his mother, enclosing the newspaper clipping about Bec's engagement to Justin. Dave had been all sorts of angry, sad and frightened, and had wanted to check out Justin. Make sure he didn't have any convictions against him, for his own peace of mind. Didn't matter that what he was about to do was against the code of conduct for police officers.

Instead, he'd brought up Bulldust's file and found out he had been released from gaol a few months before.

'Dad, can you hear me?'

Clip-clop. This time the footsteps echoed down the line, and he thought Bec was probably in a building with high ceilings and tiled floors.

'Ah, yes. No. No, I don't know where Bulldust is. There's been no contact. You can assure your mother of that.' This part was true. 'And look, he's an old man now. I don't think he's at all a risk to anyone.' He couldn't be sure about the risk part, but the old was true. Bulldust had a good ten years on Dave and, if he was feeling the way Dave was these days, he'd probably be happy to set up camp on the edge of a creek with an esky full of beer and stay there.

'Right. I'll let her know. Well, let me talk to Justin and Alice. See if we can work something out. Bye now.'

Before Dave had a chance to move the phone away from his ear, the call ended.

'"Bye now"?' he muttered to himself. 'Who says that? Your daughter, obviously.' Dave shook his head. 'Wow.' His daughter was so different from how he'd imagined she would have grown up. He'd always pegged her as soft and kind. Gentle. But there didn't seem to be too much of that in Bec. Her self-confidence was right up there. Along with a few other traits that, for Dave, weren't that desirable. He remembered that someone had told him once that, when they divorced their partner, they had started to see in their children the traits they'd never liked in their ex.

'*No one ever warns you about that*,' whoever it was had said. '*We're supposed to love them no matter what, then they start acting like your ex and you can want to divorce them, too. Well, not quite divorce, but you know what I mean*.'

Dave hadn't, until now. Although divorce was probably too strong a word, especially since he was just trying to get to know Bec and Alice.

Kim came out onto the patio and put a beer on the table for him before pulling out her chair. 'What's happening, my love?' she asked.

'Very quick phone call with Bec,' he told her, then talked about his idea.

When he'd finished, Kim reached across and took his hand, squeezing it. 'That was really kind, honey. Thank you.'

'Let's see how we go.' He took the lid off the stubbie and drank deeply. 'Be nice to talk to Alice some time. Sounds like she's often out of range.'

'It will happen at the right time, I'm sure.'

The air had cooled and the voices of kids playing on the oval rose on the breeze and drifted towards them.

'Joan rang me a little while ago to say that she'd driven past the cemetery on her way home, and there wasn't any sign of the man who Ruben Forrester rang about. The shed was empty and nothing in there to look like anyone was sleeping rough.'

Dave frowned. 'Why was Joan doing that sort of thing? That's not in her job description.'

'It's been ten years since Harry died. Remember, her husband? She was visiting his grave.'

'Ten years?' Dave couldn't believe time had passed so quickly. 'You know, honey, we're going to be in a grave before we know it. Where have all the years gone?' Did he still have time to do everything he wanted to? Perhaps not. Who knew what the future held.

Maybe he should be thinking about his bucket list and Kim a little more, rather than wrestling with drunk, disorderly locals.

'I think you're being a bit dramatic there, love. Three

score and ten remember. We've still got ages to go. Speaking of funerals, has Alex's been organised?' Kim asked.

'Mmm, they thought it would be this Saturday.' Dave flicked through the newspaper he'd been reading, then closed it and put it on the table. He rubbed a hand across his creased forehead. 'Bec asked me about Bulldust. I hate that she even knows his name.'

'Did she? What did you tell her? There hasn't been any noise from higher up about the breach last year, so you didn't have anything to say, did you?'

Kim had been the first person Dave had told when he'd looked up Bulldust's file. He'd get the sack if anyone inside the police department ever found out and although he'd been confident that wouldn't happen, he could never be one hundred per cent certain. Even after eight or so months.

'Not yet. Hopefully the risk factor has gone now. I thought it might only happen if that bloke . . . what was his name? The one who headbutted Mia?'

'Nathan.' Kim took a sip of her wine.

'Yeah, that tosser. If he had decided to put in a complaint about me after I belted him, then I could've been in real trouble. So far, so good.'

It had felt good to punch that Nathan. Totally out of character for Dave these days—not so much when he'd been young—but all those horrible whirling feelings about Bec and Justin being engaged without anywhere to put them, along with Nathan's terrible attitude towards Mia, had been enough for him to let fly. He'd broken two code of conduct laws within the space of about half an hour that day. Something he never wanted to do again.

Kim swiped at a mozzie before lighting the candle sitting in the middle of the table. She took the glass jar and placed it on the ground near their feet.

Dave wrinkled his nose at the scent of the citronella. 'Why is it that something so useful has to stink?' he asked.

'I quite like it.'

'I know you do. Anyhow, let's hope that Bec comes back with a date and we can all go somewhere to get to know each other again.'

'Your mum and brother could come, too,' Kim suggested. 'Why don't you ask them?'

'If we're going to do it, I probably will. It will be the almost-inaugural meeting of the Burrows Family.'

Dave's mobile phone vibrated on the table. 'Mia,' he said, picking up the phone. 'Hi.' He listened, then frowned. 'Are you joking?'

Pause.

'Jesus Christ.'

Pause.

'Okay, I'll meet you out the front of my place.'

Dave stood up, then sat down again. He took Kim's hand. 'I'm getting too old for this shit,' he said.

Calmly, Kim ran her thumb over his. 'What's happened?'

'Danny Betts, Alex Donaldson's mate, was changing a flat tyre and the vehicle has fallen off the jack.'

CHAPTER 17

'What the hell happened?' Dave asked Mia as she pulled up in front of his house and he climbed into the troopy. 'And how did you get the call?'

'Hamish,' Mia answered shortly, flicking the blinker on and pulling back out onto the street. 'He got the call from triple zero. It's happened out on the Tanaram Road. I think that's one-lane bitumen isn't it? It branches off from the road that goes out to Alex and Hallie Donaldson's place.'

'Yeah, it is. But that's almost a dead end. There's stuff-all out there a local would want to see. Where was he off to?'

'Not sure. I haven't spoken to Maggie. Hamish just said the call came in from a couple of caravanners. They were about to park up for the night and they saw something in the distance. Decided to get a bit closer in case someone needed a hand and found the ute crushing Danny. They rang for an ambulance before they realised there was nothing to be done.'

'Fuck, this must've only just happened. We haven't been back from the Donaldsons' for very long. He's dead?'

'Wish it was still daylight.' Mia flicked the lights to high beam and activated the spotlights, which were still broken. 'Yeah, Hamish says it's messy.'

'Where's Hamish now?'

'Waiting for us.'

'Fuck,' Dave repeated. Then added: 'No doubt about the messiness. Anything more?'

'Not really. I'm about to ring Maggie. Unless you want to?'

Dave rubbed his forehead. 'We should get out there and see what we're looking at before we ring.'

'Maggie took Ruby home with her this afternoon. I heard Maggie and Hallie organising that before we left. She'll have a child with her.'

Grunting, Dave thought about the situation.

His phone rang. Looking at the screen, he grunted again, then held it up for Mia to see. Maggie's name showed clearly.

He swiped the screen and answered. 'Maggie, how are you?'

'What's going on, Dave?' Maggie sounded panicked. 'I've had a phone call from a local telling me something has happened with Dan. I know there's been an accident. What is it?'

He mustered his most calming voice, wanting to curse the bush telegraph. 'Yes, we understand there's been an accident, Maggie, and we're en route to Danny now.'

'Well, I'm coming. He's not answering his phone.' Terror and panic mixed in her voice.

Dave could imagine her running around the house, gathering the things she might need and tearing out to the car.

'No need to come yet, Maggie. Let us get there and assess everything first.'

'Is he . . . is he okay, Dave?' Her voice dropped to a low pleading.

'Like I said, we're en route.' He paused. 'I promise I will ring you as soon as I know.'

'Well, I'm coming.' The phone went dead.

'Shit, bugger, hell!' Dave threw the phone onto the dash and looked over at Mia. 'She's on her way. Danny must've told her where he was headed.'

Mia didn't answer.

'We should get him to the morgue and cleaned up before we get a formal ID.' Dave ran his hand over his face, trying to soothe the distress in his chest.

'Hamish says once we get there and do our part, it won't take long for him to get Danny into the ambulance.'

They drove in silence, Dave checking the pin drop that Mia had sent to his phone. 'You need to take a left here,' he said, 'then a right. We should almost be on it.'

Around the corner, Dave saw the reflections of the number plates from two caravans parked off in a gravel pit. Chairs were set up outside and the spotlights from one of the vans highlighted a table. Two women were sitting there with drinks in their hands.

Further up, Hamish had the lights of the ambulance flashing and witch's hats set out across the road.

'We need to close the road,' Mia said.

'There're signs in the back. Get onto Comms and let them know. Wish we had some decent lights,' muttered Dave. 'Righto, park here and let's get cracking.'

Hamish was waiting for them. 'We have to stop meeting like this,' he said, his face pale. The joke fell flat. There was nothing funny about what they were seeing tonight.

'Bloody awful. Deceased?'

'Yes. No question. Looks like the axle has him pinned to the ground. It's across his chest. I suspect he'd have broken ribs to boot. The jack is underneath here.' Hamish pointed and Dave bent down, flashing his torch. Then he went to the front, got down on his hands and knees and looked from a different angle. 'I guess he's put the jack under and got the tyre off, but why he'd go back under the vehicle once it was only held up by the jack . . . I'm buggered if I know.'

'Sometimes when the ground is uneven you have to make sure the jack is solid. Obviously shouldn't do this when the tyre is off. Makes it heaps more dangerous,' Mia spoke up. 'I guess Danny mightn't have been thinking clearly with Alex's death causing him so much distress.'

'Fuck,' Dave whispered. 'Fuck this. How do we lose two young men in the space of a week? Accidents happen all the time, but this is ridiculous.'

The town was already in shock after losing Alex Donaldson. It was easy to tell when a country town had a tragedy. The streets become quieter, and disbelief bounces through the community, hitting each person in a different way. The smell of casseroles and stews radiates from houses, and plastic and foil containers sell out from the shelves of the IGA, because everyone is cooking for the family.

Hopper in the pub once told Dave that one of his best trading times is after a tragedy. 'Most people come in for a drink, even the ones who don't usually. I think everybody is looking for a shoulder or ear. Companionship. Even if it's only mine. That's what we do when someone dies. The ones left behind need each other.'

Dave could already feel the heaviness of the town's second lot of grief enveloping his body.

'Dammit,' he said. He checked to see where Mia was, then walked out of the light to stand in the dark, rocking on his heels, head back, looking at the stars. 'Dammit, dammit, dammit.' Dragging in a deep breath, he wished he could have a drink. He hadn't been joking when he'd told Kim he was getting too old for this shit.

Hamish held the torch and Mia directed him where to shine the beam as she took photos.

'Check this out,' she said, when Dave came back and got down on his hands and knees next to her. 'Looks like the jack has slipped off the piece of wood he had it on.'

'Like all good farm kids, he would have been taught to put the jack on the most stable piece of ground,' Dave said heavily. 'See where he's scraped the dirt away to make the block more stable than just placing it on the uneven surface? Ironic after all his preparations.'

'I was wondering what that was,' Hamish said.

'Where's the tyre?'

'Over here.' Hamish flashed his torch towards the bush. 'He's rolled it out of the way while he's got the spare out, by the looks. I can't see why it's gone flat, if it's a tiny hole, it can be pretty difficult to see without a good light, air compressor and a bottle of dishwashing liquid.'

'True.' Dave went over and photographed the tyre in situ, then tucked the torch under his chin and ran his hands over the wall of the tyre.

Ah, there it was. He kept one finger where he could feel something protruding from the tyre and grabbed at his torch, before flashing the beam over it.

'A bolt,' he said. 'A bloody bolt. Look at that, on the inside of the tyre wall.'

'What's that?'

A voice he didn't know came from behind him and Dave dropped the tyre and stood up.

An elderly gentleman, wearing a t-shirt and shorts, looked at him seriously. His glasses had slipped to the end of his nose and even though it was dark, a white cap sat on his head.

'Detective Dave Burrows,' Dave said. 'And you are?'

'Ted, Ted Mundary. I called triple zero.'

'Well, Ted, we're very glad you did. Thanks.'

'Pretty awful sight. Glad the women folk stayed in the camp.'

'Nothing about these types of accidents is nice,' Dave agreed. 'I need to ask you a few questions, if you don't mind?' He pulled out his notebook.

'I thought you might. Go your hardest.'

'Can you remember what time you pulled up?'

'Oh, yes, about five p.m. It's a lot later than we normally set up camp, but we couldn't find anywhere that suited us. This road, there's not much room either side to be able to pull off.'

'No, the bush grows right to the edge, doesn't it?'

'That's right. Not easy to see kangaroos when it's like it is. Someone should have a word to the council about clearing it away.'

'Yes, I should. But you found a spot to pull off into?'

'Yeah, we kept going, in the hope that we'd find something, and then just back there'—he jerked his thumb over his shoulder—'was a small gravel pit, so we pulled in. While the ladies were getting the dinner ready, Darren and I came for a walk and found this.'

'Oh, so you just went out to stretch your legs. And found this by accident?' Inside, Dave cringed at his choice of words.

'No, no, we saw something reflecting in the sun, so we went to investigate. Our wives think we're like magpies. Find something shiny and have to have a look—' He paused. 'Unfortunately, we found this poor lad.' He glanced over to where Hamish and Mia were working and Dave followed his glance.

Mia had the camera out, taking photos and videos while Hamish held the torch for her.

Ted sighed and took his hat from his head. 'Bad show.'

'Awful. There isn't any mobile range out here. How'd you phone it in?'

'I've got a Starlink satellite in my caravan so we can call with wifi from anywhere once it's set up.'

Dave gave a smile. 'All these mod cons. How bizarre it is. When I used to go out bush with the Stock Squad, we didn't have anything except a radio. That's when I first started my career.'

'Doesn't look like it could be that long ago. You're still a whippersnapper compared to Darren and me.'

'Feels like a long time ago.'

'Well, my boy, I guess it is if you see a lot of this sort of thing.' He nodded towards the ute.

Dave wanted to agree, but professionalism stopped him. 'What did you do once you called triple zero?'

'They told me to wait until the ambulance arrived. And they said you blokes wouldn't be far behind.'

'Okay. Do you have any idea how long the ute might have been like this for?'

'The engine was still warm—I know because I put my hand on it. Don't rightly know how long it takes for an engine to cool down in this sort of weather, but I reckon it would be a long time.' Ted looked at the sky. 'Last few days have been pretty hot and the bonnet would hold the heat for a while. Obviously I'm no expert in that area, but common sense tells me that the air temperature would have an impact on the heat of the bonnet. We didn't lift it to feel the engine. Thought we shouldn't touch anything. Although'—he cleared his throat—'if we thought the young lad could have been saved, we would have tried to lift the car from him. Seemed futile, unfortunately. We only realised that after calling for an ambulance.'

Dave looked at his watch. He and Mia had left the Donaldsons' at about 2 p.m., and it had taken them two and half hours to get home—4.30 p.m. The group sitting around Hallie's kitchen table hadn't looked like moving when Mia and he had left.

He jotted a note in his book to remind himself to ask Maggie what time the others left the Donaldsons'. With a quick calculation, Danny must've left at least by 3 p.m. to get back to his place and then to here.

Danny couldn't have been here long. Not that it mattered, because the life had gone out of that lad the minute the ute had fallen. Like with Alex, Dave was sure that death would have been instantaneous. A crushed chest, pressure on the heart and it was lights out.

'Dave?' Hamish called.

'Coming.' Dave asked Ted to stay where he was and walked back to the ute.

'Ready to move him,' Mia said, standing back up and brushing dirt from her hands. She glanced at her watch. 'We need to do this quickly, because Maggie might be along at any moment. Going to be hard to keep her away by the sounds of the phone call you took.'

It only took a few moments to get the kangaroo jack under the front and stabilise everything before the ute was gently lifted from Danny's body.

Once on the gurney, Hamish strapped his crushed body in and covered it with a sheet just as headlights came around the corner.

'And here's Maggie now,' Mia said, as a Prado pulled up and the driver tumbled out of the driver's door, crying.

'Dan? Where's Dan? My god!'

Dave moved forward and stopped her, by holding her arms gently.

'We've got him here, Maggie,' he told her quietly. 'Unfortunately, Danny has passed away, but we have him.'

Maggie let out a guttural moan as her knees gave way.

Dave caught her and helped her towards the ambulance, and Hamish grabbed the oxygen mask and put it over her face, despite Maggie's insistence she go to Dan.

Discreetly, Mia shifted the gurney out past the lights, so it wasn't obvious until Maggie had recovered slightly.

'Did you bring anyone with you, Maggie?' Dave asked. She shouldn't have been driving in the state she was in.

Another set of lights came around the corner, this time more sedately than Maggie's driving had been.

'Hallie,' Maggie said from behind the mask. She pulled it off. In only seconds, her eyes had gone from clear to haunted. 'Sorry, it's a shock, I'm fine. I want to see him.'

Dave closed his eyes. They were the same words he'd heard from Hallie only days before.

'And you can,' he promised her, 'in a minute. Hi, Hallie,' he said quietly. She had Ruby tucked on her hip. Hallie looked like a little lost lamb, not old enough to be looking after a toddler.

'Is Danny . . .' She didn't appear to be able to finish her sentence.

Dave nodded. 'Unfortunately, there's been an accident and Danny has sustained fatal injuries. I'm so sorry.'

Standing in the half-light, Hallie looked stuck until Ruby started to cry. That seemed to give her mother permission to sob, too, and Maggie joined in.

Hamish comforted Maggie while Mia went to Hallie and Ruby, putting her arms around them both.

Looking at the broken women, Dave clenched his jaw and took a few steps back into the darkness again, wondering why he had ever become a police officer.

CHAPTER 18

Alex's funeral would be first.

After Danny's death, Rod had come in and taken over the organising of everything. In consultation with Maggie and Danny's parents, Rod had told Hallie, they would postpone Alex's funeral until they could hold both on the same day. They would likely be mid next week.

Hallie hadn't even cared. The quiet, deep shock and bottomless grief had rendered her incapable of anything except the day-to-day care of Ruby.

Two incomprehensible accidents with far-reaching consequences.

Coping with Alex's death had been hard enough, but to have a friend taken so close after Alex was indescribable. Different love for each man, but she *had* loved both. Danny had been very kind to her since she'd moved out here.

Every morning since Danny's death, she'd got up, drunk coffee, fed Ruby and turned on the TV. Ruby had watched every children's program known to man, while Hallie had lain on the couch and stared into nothing. She didn't think or feel and was only functioning on automatic pilot. Maggie would be the same.

Mick had rung, but Hallie hadn't answered the phone, nor had she when Jenna, then Tom had tried. Her parents hadn't arrived yet and if they'd left a message on either the answering machine or mobile saying when they would, Hallie hadn't checked.

The packing boxes taunted her. Needing to clean out her home so a stranger could move in was urgent, according to Nicole.

The phone call she'd received the day after Danny had died had reminded her that this tragedy wouldn't change what Nicole and Rod were asking of their daughter-in-law.

'Please make sure you're ready to leave the day after the funeral. You've got a few extra days now, because we won't be holding it until Wednesday next week, but we are going to start interviewing prospective employees, and they'll need to see the house.'

Again, Hallie didn't give a toss.

The dogs barking alerted her that someone was coming up the driveway. She hoped it was Rod. He'd texted to say he'd come and collect the dogs and look after them at his place. One less thing for her to think or worry about.

Good. There was nothing about adulting that she wanted to do right now. Lying on the couch and staring into space held more appeal than anything else. Except having Ruby alongside her.

A rap on the door and Hallie waited for the sound of it opening.

A female voice called, 'Hello?'

Still Hallie didn't move.

'Hallie, are you there? It's Constable Mia Worth. Hello?'

Ruby was staring at the TV screen, watching the mindless colours and music whirling past her. She didn't move either, mesmerised.

There didn't seem to be a choice about answering the door, so Hallie swung her legs over the side of the couch and walked gingerly out to the kitchen. She gave it a once-over glance and decided it wasn't too bad, even though there were a few dishes in the sink. Even so, Nicole would have had a pink fit, knowing there was washing up that hadn't been done and a visitor at the door. But Nicole wasn't here. Hallie didn't care about bringing the Donaldson name down to gutter level, as Nicole might think she was doing, opening the door to Mia with the kitchen as it was.

Mia didn't hide her shock at Hallie's appearance very well, but she recovered quickly. Her expression made Hallie touch her face and then her hair self-consciously.

'Hi, Hallie. I was just passing. Thought I'd call in and see how you were coping.'

Leaning against the door frame, Hallie answered, 'Sure you were. Everyone who turns up out here is "just passing".'

Mia grinned. 'I guess you're a little out of the way for that. Could I come in?'

'If you like.'

Leading the way into the kitchen, she heard Mia close the door as she put the kettle on.

'Cup of tea?'

'Thanks, I can make it if you're . . . busy?'

'It's okay—I can do it. I'm fine.'

Mia didn't answer. Instead, she looked around for a place to sit, picking up a pile of papers from a chair and putting them on the table. 'Are you?' she asked.

Staring at her blankly, Hallie tried to remember what they had been talking about. 'Sorry, I missed what you said.' She ran her tongue over her dry lips and realised her teeth hadn't been cleaned in a few days. More self-awareness started to filter through. When had she washed her hair last? The better question was when had she showered last? Discreetly, Hallie tried to sniff under her arms. Did she smell?

'Are you okay?' Mia asked with such concern that Hallie blinked, swayed, then crumpled onto the closest chair.

Mia was alongside her in an instant. 'Ah, Hallie, what a shit time for you.'

Hallie found herself leaning into this woman's comfort. There were no tears. Why wouldn't they come? 'I'm fine,' she said again. Why did she feel so numb? Surely it would be better if she could cry and rage, like Maggie had.

For Maggie the grief of Danny had come straightaway. Hallie, however, still was having trouble understanding that Alex wasn't coming home. She looked for him each night, found herself getting that second coffee cup out at smoko, or putting two steaks on the bench to defrost instead of one that she'd share with Ruby.

The empty space on his side of the bed felt like a chasm. Reality was that Alex was never walking in through the door again and that wasn't something Hallie's brain or heart could understand.

The injustice, the awfulness. The empty space Alex had left was enormous and yet she couldn't feel sadness and grief. Only nothingness.

'I'm fine.'

Mia didn't answer, only continued to hold her tightly.

It took Ruby coming into the kitchen for them to break apart.

'Hello there,' Mia said, getting up to switch off the boiling kettle. 'How are you, Ruby?'

Ruby went to Hallie and hid behind the chair, her head peeking out. What Hallie wanted to say was, '*Say hello, Ruby*,' but she couldn't be bothered. Speaking took too much energy.

'I've got an idea. Why don't you have a shower and climb into bed. I'll take Ruby for a walk and maybe we could do some cooking when we come back. When you've woken up, we can have a chat. Sound okay?'

'But . . .' Hallie felt lost at her kindness.

Mia smiled. 'No buts, as my nana used to say. I'm on my day off so you won't be holding me up. Off you go.' Then Mia bent down and whispered to Ruby, 'Do you like hedgehog slice? It's my favourite. Wanna help me make it? I'm sure your pantry is fully stocked like every good country woman's is, but just in case, I've brought everything we need.'

Ruby gave an excited squeal and clapped her hands. 'Cooking!'

'Yes, cooking,' Mia said. 'Come on, Hallie, you head off to the shower. I've got Ruby.'

'But I can't,' Hallie said, still not moving. 'If I go, something might happen to her.'

And there it was. The secret fear that maybe wasn't so secret to everyone else. When people went out of Hallie's care, they died. That was the truth. She couldn't let Ruby out of her sight.

Ruby had left her mother and was now holding her arms up to Mia. 'Cooking!' she said again.

'Come here, Ruby,' Hallie said. 'Come back to Mummy.'

Ruby turned her innocent face towards her mother. 'No, cooking.'

Mia put her hand on Ruby's head. Then she went to Hallie, squatting down to look her in the eye. 'I swear on my life that I will allow nothing, *nothing*, to happen to Ruby while you are in the shower or asleep.'

'But accidents happen.' Her words were slow, her tongue heavy inside her mouth.

'Yes, they do,' Mia said. 'And you've had two awful ones in very short succession, which is enough for your brain and body to be highly traumatised. But I promise there won't be any mishaps today.'

Uncertain, Hallie got up and kissed Ruby. Then she sat back down. 'I love you, Ruby-rubes.'

'Lub you, Mumma.' Ruby was busy watching Mia.

This time, when Hallie stood, she headed towards the shower.

Standing under the hot, steamy water, she lathered her hair and then tipped her head underneath the stream. The suds flowed over her shoulders and down her back. Months ago, Alex had got into the shower with her and washed her hair. If she thought hard enough now, she could feel his heavy fingertips massaging her scalp, then gently tilting her head back to rinse her hair.

Now her tears mingled with the water. That day, Alex had hugged her close.

'*I'll make this right between Mum and Dad and you,*' he'd said. '*I've been talking to them about that agreement, but I wasn't getting anywhere, so I'm going to ring a lawyer.*'

'*A lawyer?*' Hallie had been shocked. '*Alex, there's no need to be so heavy-handed. What's done is done. I'm not worried about it and I'm not sure why you are.*'

'*I need to protect you,*' he said.

'*But we're all family, even if your folks are a bit over the top at times. They're never going to cause me any trouble.*' She'd given him a cheeky smile. '*I've got their granddaughter.*'

Alex hadn't smiled back, only her hugged her closer. '*You don't know them like I do.*'

Now, those words sounded ominous. Out of the shower and dried off, Hallie brushed her hair, not caring that it was still wet when she pulled the covers back. Climbing into bed in the middle of the day seemed too luxurious for everything that was going on. Perhaps she should be with Rod, learning how to check water and stock. Maybe that was the way to stay here—learn to do what Alex had been doing. Did she want to stay? Maybe not, but Tirranah would be Ruby's in time, wouldn't it? There weren't any other grandchildren. The land was her heritage, so she should be allowed to stay and learn. Love the land the way Alex had. Half her mind screamed a very loud *No!* to that thought. Ruby should be comfortable, in a town at the very least, if not the city. She could go to the best schools, play sport, work out what she loved and what career she was going to choose, not have it chosen for her.

You don't know them like I do.

Realistically, Hallie was sure that Ruby wouldn't ever be welcomed on the station like a grandson would have been. Perhaps that's what Alex had meant when he'd said that strange sentence.

Surely, she should try.

A conversation was needed. Perhaps Hallie shouldn't just accept what Nicole had said about employing a workman.

This is too hard! her mind screamed.

Hallie closed her eyes. She didn't want to think about any of that. The future was too uncertain to even contemplate. She lay there not moving and trying to keep her mind blank.

Except she was sure she could feel Alex in the bed with her. That his side had an Alex-sized dip in it.

Her fingers snaked out, in the hope that this was all a bad dream.

They were met with cold sheets.

~

Hallie woke with a start and sat up. 'Shit! Ruby!' She flung the covers off just as Ruby's giggle reached her ears. Mia was talking softly and her daughter was laughing.

Her heart fluttered with relief. Nothing had happened in the few hours she had been asleep. Hallie relaxed against her pillow and took a few deep breaths like she always had in the city. '*Breathing helps everything*,' her yoga instructor had told her. '*Slows your heart rate, helps shift anxiety . . . deep breaths, now.*'

The instructor would always hold her hands to her chest, turned inwards, and act as if she was scooping water when she breathed in; then, when she wanted the class to breathe out, she let her arms move slowly outwards as if she was conducting an orchestra.

A dark heaviness sat in Hallie's chest, but had it shifted a little with the deep breaths? She wasn't sure, but she felt more in control.

'Show Mumma,' Ruby called out.

'Mummy is still asleep,' Mia said from the kitchen.

But Ruby was off and running, her feet thumping on the wooden passage floor. 'Mumma, Mumma. Look!'

Tumbling into the room, Ruby climbed up onto the bed and shoved a piece of chocolate something in her face.

'Hello, Ruby-rubes,' Hallie said, pushing her hand gently away. 'Come and give me a cuddle.' She wrapped her arms around her little girl and breathed deeply again. Then she pulled back.

'Did Mia give you a bath? Your hair is so clean.'

Ruby grinned and put her hand under her hair to flick it. 'Pwetty.'

'It's very pretty. We should go and see Mia.' Pulling on a pair of shorts, Hallie ran her fingers through her own hair and shook herself a little.

'Come on.' Ruby tugged at her hand.

'Sorry,' Mia said as they came into the kitchen. 'She got away from me.'

'It's okay, I was awake,' Hallie said. 'Good god, what have you been doing?'

Piles of biscuits and cakes were cooling on racks and there was a bowl of chocolate icing next to the hedgehog slice.

'My nana used to cook a lot when I was little and she let me help,' Mia said. 'Ruby is the best helper ever, aren't you?' She reached out and tousled the little girl's hair.

Ruby giggled again. 'Yummy chocolate,' she said.

'What am I going to do with all of this?' As the words came out, Hallie realised she sounded ungrateful. 'Sorry, I didn't—'

'No, it's fine, I know what you mean. I came prepared! Brought a heap of freezing containers with me, because I thought Ruby might like to cook. It's my happy place. Makes me feel useful and kids love to make mess! Cooking fixes both those needs. I left everything in the car until you'd gone to bed—didn't want to put pressure on you or Ruby until I knew it was something she wanted to do.' She grinned and wagged a finger. 'But don't tell anyone, because when I'm a police officer, I'm tough and get annoyed whenever anyone questions my authority because I'm a girl. Don't need them thinking I'm a pushover, hey, Rubes?'

'Your secret is safe with me,' Hallie said. 'I'm terrible at baking. Alex did most of the cooking here. Not that anyone knows that either. His mother would hunt me out of the house and send Alex to find another wife, if she knew.'

Laughing, Mia finished wiping down the bench and put the kettle on. 'It must be cup of tea time now?'

Hallie was surprised to feel her tummy rumble and checked what the time was. 'Gosh, it's so late. I've slept right through lunch. I think there's some cold meat in the fridge.'

Mia poured a cup of tea and placed it in front of Hallie. 'Does Ruby have an afternoon sleep?' she asked, seeing the little girl yawning.

'Not every day, but it looks like she might need one now. All that work must have tired her out.'

'You eat, I'll read her a story and pop her into bed.'

'Watch for snakes.'

Mia turned back, uncertainty crossing her face. 'Snakes? In the house?'

'Hopefully not, but they've been known to visit before. You just need to keep an eye out.'

Mia looked doubtfully towards the passageway. 'Right,' she said.

Sipping her tea, Hallie got up and went to look out of the window. In the few days since Danny had died, it seemed that everything had shrivelled to a crisp. The heat had been more intense, like the hell they'd all been living in. Mother Nature had gone out in sympathy.

Hallie pushed the button to turn on the computer and was rewarded with the low hum of the motor starting up and the fan whirring. She clicked into emails and waited for them to download while she helped herself to a melting moment. The biscuit crumbled in her mouth perfectly.

'You're right,' she told Mia as the police officer came back into the room. 'You're a great cook. These are delicious! I can't even believe I want to eat something. Food hasn't been high on my priority list lately.'

'Like I said, my grandmother was good at making yummy things. Not that she had many people to cook for—just me, mostly. But I'd bring friends home occasionally and they'd always get the benefit of Nana's culinary skills.'

Normally Hallie would ask Mia more about herself, but not today. Even though she was feeling better, she was aware that could change at any second.

'Alex sounded like a lovely bloke,' Mia said, finally sitting down, a cup of tea in front of her.

'He was. We were married for five years.' Hallie turned her wedding rings on her fingers as she spoke. In time, she would have to take them off and that made her feel sick.

'I'm so sorry, Hallie. There aren't words to give you any sort of relief from what you're feeling. But I know, from experience, that sometimes just talking about the person helps. So, if you want to chat, I'm here.'

Picking at another biscuit, Hallie thought about that. Sharing Alex with someone who didn't know him would help keep him alive in another person's memory, not just her own.

'Thanks, Mia. I keep thinking about Maggie in all this awfulness, too. It's pretty hard to believe we're both in the same situation only days apart. How does this stuff happen?'

'I don't know,' Mia answered honestly. 'It's pretty hard to get your head around.' She waited until Hallie had finished sipping at her tea, then asked, 'Did Alex and his parents get on well?'

'Yeah, they did. Like any family, there were always differences of opinions, and Rod rules with an iron fist.' She rested her chin on her palm. 'Alex always seemed very accepting of that, as if he knew there was a protocol he had to go through before he would ever be in Rod's position or at least be seen as an equal. I don't know why that never bothered him, but it didn't.' Hallie gave a soft smile. 'He had the patience of a saint and I do very much mean that, despite Tom saying that all who die are made out to be saints!'

Mia smiled sadly. 'What is with that, I wonder?'

Shrugging, Hallie smiled. 'I guess we all have to make ourselves feel better . . . and that does. When we talk about them, we only remember the good memories, and so the bad ones fade. Suddenly they're nothing but flawless.'

'When Nana died, I already knew she was pretty much perfect, so I didn't have to make anything up!'

Unexpectedly, a giggle started in Hallie's chest. It felt nice. 'What was she like? I've never known anyone to be perfect.'

'Kind, selfless.' Mia took a biscuit and chewed thoughtfully. 'The best mum I could have had.'

'Mum?' Hallie's tone raised in surprise.

'Uh-huh. My dad died by suicide when I was very young and Mum was killed in a crash when I was in late primary school. Nana looked after me from then on. She was the best, even if I do say so.'

'She sounds wonderful. I wish Alex and I had relationships with our parents like that.'

'So there *was* angst between Alex, Rod and Nicole?'

'I don't know,' Hallie answered tiredly. 'Sometimes I thought there was and other times everyone seemed to get on really well.' She looked over at Mia.

'Do you think there's anything strange?'

'Why? Do you think there is?' Hallie asked.

Mia smiled. 'I'm asking for your take. Only for my own curiosity. Even though I grew up here, I didn't have a lot to do with the stations and I've heard some comments that made me uncomfortable, that's all. Just trying to understand it.'

This time, Hallie laughed loudly. 'I am the wrong person to ask. Didn't you know I'm a blow-in?'

'Where are you from originally?'

'Adelaide. I'm a fashion reporter.'

Pressing her lips together, then pursing them, Mia looked as if she was trying not to laugh.

'I know, the sheep really don't have much of an idea of who Anthea Crawford or David Lawrence are,' Hallie said.

'Gives a whole new meaning to fashion in the field,' Mia said.

This time Hallie laughed properly. 'True. From the time I moved out here, I've very much been on the outer. Never really fitted the bill Nicole and Rod had envisioned for their son.'

'Dare I ask about the binding financial agreement they had you sign? What was Alex's take on that?'

'He didn't like it. Not at all.'

'Could he do anything about it?'

'He said to me once he was going to get a lawyer to look at the agreement, but I never heard anything more about it, only gave my approval to the lawyer.'

'Must've been awful. You know, to feel like you're not welcome, or your wife isn't welcome.'

'Alex wanted to speak to his parents before he contacted the lawyer but it didn't seem to do any good.' Hallie brought her head up to look at Mia. 'What I do know about this area is land is king and everyone seems to do their best to keep whatever they have in the family.'

'Hmm, I thought as much.' Mia picked up a piece of hedgehog slice.

Hallie drew herself a glass of water and turned it around in her hands, fixing Mia with her gaze.

'What is it, Hallie?'

'Look, it's so small, but there are two things that are worrying me and I can't even tell you why. Yes, Alex hated the agreement and we had done lots of talking about it. Usually, it was me trying to calm the situation, because

I never thought . . .' Her voice trailed off. 'Well, I didn't think anything like Alex dying would happen. But one day I said it didn't matter, and he told me I had no idea what they were capable of.'

'They being . . .'

'Rod and Nicole.'

'Interesting,' Mia said. She licked her fingers. 'And the second?'

'Nicole said to me that Alex never knew what was good for him.'

Mia cocked her head to one side. 'In what context?'

'It was said at the time I told Nicole that Alex would hate what she was doing. She'd been over here telling me what the future was going to hold. Asking me to move out.'

'So difficult,' Mia said, picking up another piece of hedgehog. 'Oh my god! Someone take this away from me otherwise I'm going to eat it all!'

Hallie reached over and grabbed the slice, depositing it into a container and sealing the lid. She was grateful for Mia's change in subject, deliberate or not. Bagging out her in-laws didn't come naturally.

'I wonder how Maggie is today. I'll try to go and see her over the next few days, too.'

'Probably pretty shit,' Hallie said.

'Alex and Danny were pretty tight?'

'Oh, yeah. And Mick and Tom. Alex and Danny went through their school years together and then they met Mick, Tom and Charlie at the Australian College of Agriculture when they studied farm management. The five of them were so close, they did that weird blood brother thing where they all had to prick their fingers and touch their blood together.' Hallie shuddered. 'Sounded yuck to me, but they did it.'

'Charlie. I haven't met him yet. He's coming to the funeral?'

'Supposed to be. I haven't met him yet either. Wait here and I'll show you something.' Hallie got up and went back into her bedroom, stopping at Ruby's room to listen for any noise.

Pulling open the second drawer, she took out the display folder and carried it back into the kitchen.

'This is Charlie. Up until Alex died, none of the boys had spoken or even talked about him.'

Mia took the file Hallie offered and opened the front cover. 'Oh,' she said. 'That's intense.'

'I know, right? Mick and Tom said that he wants to come to the funeral, just out of the blue like that. They haven't heard from him since he got out of gaol. Nothing more has been said to me about him coming, though.'

'Well, I guess it can't hurt for an old friend to pay their respects, can it?' Mia said.

'Guess not.' Hallie cast her eyes down, as she realised the funeral was in four days' time. 'Just so long as there's no trouble.'

'Trouble?' Mia looked up. 'You think there'll be trouble?'

Now Hallie looked sheepish. 'I'm sure there won't be. I'm probably overreacting. But these blokes haven't seen each other in a while and knowing that Mick and Tom don't like Charlie . . . A funeral is a pretty emotional place to suddenly all reconnect again, isn't it? I'm not sure . . .'

Hallie took a breath. 'I'm not sure Alex would be pleased that Charlie wants to be there.'

'Hmm, I see your point.'

'I know Mick is a great bloke, and such a people person, but he does have a bad temper. I can't have anything go wrong during the funeral because it's going to be hard enough.'

'Of course. If it puts your mind at rest, Dave and I will be there. We'd always intended to go. But tell me about Mick . . . He's got a bad temper? Anything usually set him off?'

'I've heard him talking to reporters when they've caught him off guard.'

'Hmm, reporters could set anyone off, I think,' Mia said.

'If Charlie makes a scene, Mick and Tom will be really pissed off.

'And then it's Danny's funeral straight afterwards. His body is being brought back in a couple of days, and I know Maggie and his parents have been talking to the funeral director. They felt it was the right thing with so many people here for Alex's who would want to go to Danny's.'

'Yes, I understand the thinking there. Look, I'm sure everything will go smoothly. I'm glad you told me about Charlie, though. With a history like he's got, a heads-up is always a good thing.' Mia took a sip of her tea. 'Forewarned is forearmed and all that. No one likes a rapist in their town.'

CHAPTER 19

Mia couldn't shake the feeling of impending disaster. Never in her life had she been one to have *feelings*. Her grandmother had occasionally, and she'd been correct mostly, but not Mia. But the thought of Charlie coming to town during a highly emotional time, as Hallie had pointed out, could have consequences.

Rod and Nicole's behaviour wasn't sitting well with Mia either. Everything she was hearing about out there on the station sounded controlling and unsettling.

'I'm off for the rest of the day,' Dave said, popping his head into the office. 'You good?'

'Yeah,' she glanced up at the clock and saw it was nearly midday. 'I won't be long behind you.' Today they had both started on an early shift, meaning the station would be unattended until 8 a.m. tomorrow, although their mobile numbers would be on the answering machine and taped to the door, while the station number would transfer to Mia in case they were needed.

'Right, see you tomorrow.'

'Dave?' Mia tapped the information she was reading. 'I think we need to talk to Rod and Nicole Donaldson.'

'About what?'

Dave looked at his watch, then back at Mia.

'About Alex. Sorry, I know you're ready to head off. I should have spoken up earlier.'

'You've got concerns? About what?' Pulling out a chair, Dave sat down.

'It was just a feeling I had yesterday when I was talking with Hallie. You've always told me to trust my gut.' She quickly ran through the couple of sentences that Hallie had mentioned. 'I know it's not much but, in the overall scheme of things, do you think it's worth asking them about it?'

'*You don't know what they're capable of* and *Alex didn't know what was good for him*,' Dave repeated. 'Looking at the words in context, it's a bit of a long stretch, don't you think?'

'"You don't know what they're capable of" is what's raised my antenna.'

Crossing his arms, Dave leaned back in the chair. 'Are you telling me you think the Donaldsons did away with their own son?'

'What? No! Well . . .'

'That's what it sounds like to me.'

'Don't you think those two statements sound at least threatening?' Mia leaned forward and put her elbows on the table. 'Rod and Nicole obviously saw Hallie as a threat to their business and their assets, which is why they asked her to sign that agreement. You must agree with that?'

'My opinion is that any family business is difficult for in-laws, farming especially, when where people live and work are one and the same.'

'How about this for an hypothesis? What if they realised that Alex wasn't going to take this lying down—which obviously he wasn't because he'd engaged a lawyer. Perhaps the lawyer had some type of advice that made the agreement obsolete.'

'Engaged might be too strong a word. But yes, let's run with your hypothesis for a moment,' Dave said. 'How could they be sure Hallie knew what that advice was? I imagine that taking Alex out of the picture wouldn't stop Hallie from starting proceedings if she had the information required.'

Mia didn't answer.

'You think that Alex challenged Nicole and Rod over the agreement, however he did that, and then they decided to kill him because they *might* lose their land if Alex and Hallie ever divorced?'

Mia held his eyes.

'You're telling me that's not a long bow to draw?'

She raised a shoulder. 'Maybe, but shouldn't we at least talk to Nicole and Rod?'

'If you want to talk to Alex's parents, you go for it, Mia, but before you do, go over the evidence you have and what the scene showed. Don't forget the platform at the top of the windmill was rotten, not tampered with in any way.' He paused. 'And Mia, be very careful with how you phrase your questions.'

'Nana told me once that land was the root of all evil.'

'So is money.'

'Hmm, money and land, can't see anything that would go wrong there,' Mia said with a wry smile.

'So cynical for one so young.'

Mia laughed this time. 'Okay, so I can give Rod and Nicole a call?'

'How about you go out there? I think these types of questions might be better in person.'

'Okay, I'll tee up a time with them.'

'You could ring on the pretence of finding out when Alex's funeral is. I heard they're changing it so Danny's can be held on the same day.'

'Two birds with one stone.'

'Jesus, Mia, really? I know what you're saying but let's not say that aloud to anyone other than me, okay?' Dave stood up, a deep frown crossing his face. 'God, I wish you'd think before you open your mouth sometimes.'

'Don't see anyone else here other than you.'

Dave laughed. 'Fuck me dead, sometimes you are unbelievable! Right, anything else before I go?'

'Actually, there is.' Mia brought up the report she'd run and swivelled the computer screen for Dave to read.

'Charles Dynner? He's the other friend of the men?' he asked.

'Yeah. Check out his rap sheet.'

'Excellent,' Dave said heavily, after a few moments of silence. 'Excellent.'

'I asked Hallie if there'd been any word from him, but there's been nothing more than we heard about when we were out there the morning before Danny was killed.'

'He was in contact with Mick, Tom and Danny, wasn't he?' Dave sat down in the chair again. 'I remember them talking about it.'

'Yeah, from what I can gather. Hallie mentioned there were a few messages on the group chat. Seemed that Tom was a bit nervous about him causing a scene, but Mick said he didn't think there'd be any problems.'

Rubbing his eyes, Dave rested his head on his palm. 'Mmm.'

'Do you think we should make some enquiries through the motel and caravan park? See if they have a booking for this Charlie? We could pay him a visit. Have a quiet chat.'

'I don't know, Mia. There's a bit to be said for a bloke having done his time and police harassment. We would be checking in with the best intentions, but how he'd take it could be a different matter. Not sure we need to stir up any problems when there mightn't be any.' Another sigh. 'Still, we could do that. Those two poor families don't need any extra trouble getting through the funerals.'

'Can I throw something very random out there?' Mia asked, sitting back in her chair and running her fingers through her hair.

'Other than you already have? Sure. Shoot.'

'Well, this goes along with what I was saying before. I'm concerned there is something about the way that Rod and Nicole have been treating Alex, but mostly Hallie, which is worrying. The "it's my way or the highway" attitude is very controlling, don't you think?'

Dave raised one shoulder.

'So, I'd like to talk to the lawyers, too. I mean, let's mix it up. I don't just have to talk to Nicole and Rod.'

'Jesus, Mia, you're jumping from this Charlie Dynner to Rod and Nicole, to the lawyers. I've already told you, these two deaths are accidental. There was nothing else to say otherwise at either scene. And I've processed many, many homicide scenes. Neither of these were homicide, which therefore means, no Charlie, no Rod and Nicole. Nothing but accidents. What could possibly link Alex's and Danny's deaths?'

'I'm not saying they are, but Alex was in conflict with his parents when he died. When you take Danny's incident into account, well, I can see how both deaths could be seen as accidental. I'm just going to start by saying that. But two mates' deaths, in such chance circumstances, about a week apart? Doesn't that have alarm bells ringing in your ears?'

Dave didn't say anything for a while, just tapped his fingers on the desk. Mia could see he was running through all the information he had, sifting through details, trying to find links.

'So, which is it? Alex's parents or some mysterious perp we know nothing of?' Dave asked.

'And what would Alex's parents have against Danny?' Mia forged on.

'Links between the two deaths?' Dave repeated.

'None that I can I find.'

'So why are we having this conversation?'

'I don't know.' Her frustration was teetering towards annoyance.

Dave's lips twitched. Mia knew he wouldn't laugh at her, though.

'Look, I understand why you are questioning this and I'm glad you are. You're thinking like a police officer should,' he said. 'It's the coincidence that's causing you to think like this, but as we've just discussed, these are two accidental deaths without a link between them.'

Shaking her head, Mia got up and paced the room. 'But there has to be . . .' Stopping to look at Dave, she gave a small smile. 'Ah, don't worry about it. I'm obviously seeing things that aren't there.'

'No, let's keep working through it. I agree this is a highly unusual week, and if I hadn't examined the scenes with my own eyes, I'd be having similar thoughts. Alex: windmill, falling, sustained non-survivable injuries. Dan: ute, changing a tyre, ute falls from the jack and he sustained non-survivable injuries. Now when we processed the scene where Danny died, again there was nothing. The only person who was there that day was Danny.

'Yes, he was under the vehicle, which could be classed as odd, but it can still be explained. The jack was wobbling and he needed to stabilise it, Maybe be thought there was something wrong with the steering arms and he wriggled under to check while the vehicle was jacked up enough to get easier access. Do you disagree with anything I've said there?'

Mia shook her head. She got the photos out from another file sitting on her desk and spread them across her desk.

'Hamish was careful at the scene,' she said. 'He and I chatted afterwards, while you were talking to the two men in the caravans. Once he'd established there wasn't any hope for Danny, he stayed in the ambulance until we got there, other than setting up the witch's hats around the accident.'

'Right, and the two fellas who called it in told me they walked up the bitumen, so we wouldn't have seen their footprints.'

'But that's a problem right there,' Mia said. 'It's a single-lane bitumen road, so if someone had been there, we may not have known. No prints can be seen on the bitumen.'

'Hmm.' Dave picked up a photo and looked at it carefully.

'Both Alex and Danny have wives,' Mia added. 'Both involved in the family businesses, both close mates.'

Dave was quiet. Then he said, 'Don't suppose we've looked into those businesses? Any chance that Dan and Alex were partners in something that we haven't heard about? Doesn't have to be a farming business.'

'I can check. If they were making money on the side to their normal work, would that upset Nicole and Rod?'

'Nah,' Dave said, shaking his head. 'To both of those. Can't work. Not unless there was a third business partner who had a grievance. And neither Hallie nor Maggie have mentioned a partnership. Still, maybe make a note to ask them.' He looked at Mia. 'If, and it's only a very small if, you are right, and these two men were murdered—which is really what you're getting at, isn't it?—then somehow, they are linked. Friends, business partners, whatever. They're in something together and that's what we need to establish.'

'The wives may not know anything, if it's something illegal.'

'More than likely they don't.'

'I'll ask now,' Mia said, picking up the phone.

'Not yet,' Dave cautioned. 'Let's do a bit more investigation. Business partners and what else?'

'Hellooo? Dave? Mia?' Joan's voice called through the walls. 'You're here late. You should have knocked off an hour ago!'

Joan let herself through the locked front desk and out to where Dave and Mia were sitting.

'God, look at that! We've been discussing this for an hour already,' Dave said, looking at his watch. 'How come you've come in?'

'I didn't finish that paperwork to release Danny Betts's body, so I thought I'd better come in and do that.' Joan gave a little grimace. 'He'll be back in the morgue tomorrow. Those young lads lying next to each other on a cold slab gives me the heebie-jeebies.'

'We're just talking about that,' Dave told her. He pushed a chair out with his foot, sending it towards Joan. 'Take a seat.'

Mia was tapping at the keyboard and swung the screen around to show Dave and Joan. 'There's nothing to show Alex and Danny were business partners on the ATO ABN search records. Not that it had to be a formal arrangement.'

'Gosh, Mia,' Joan said, her brow wrinkling with concern. 'Are you thinking there's something more to their deaths?'

'I don't know,' Mia answered. 'I can't help but feel we're missing something.'

Joan crossed her ankles and sat quietly waiting.

'Look,' Dave finally said, 'I don't believe there is any more to this than we have already noted. It's been a worthwhile exercise to think it through and look at it from different angles, but unless you can come up with a concrete link between the two incidents, then I don't think we've got anything to work with.'

'What about Charlie? Do we need to check him out?'

'Who's Charlie?' Joan asked.

'Another bloke Alex and Danny went to ag college with. He's done time for rape.'

'Oh.' Joan's face was still impassive, but Mia could feel her shock. 'Oh, while I think of it, Ruben Forrester came in again. He's still bemoaning the fact that there's someone living out at the cemetery. I've been past a few times and haven't seen anyone. Have you been out there?'

'No,' Dave said. 'Kim told me you had, though. Thanks for keeping an eye out. I don't know what's got into that bloke. Talk about a pain in the arse.'

The silence in the station stretched out until finally Joan stood. 'I'll go and finish the release paperwork and let you know when it's done,' she said.

'Thanks, Joan.'

Mia looked at Dave. 'You still going to head off?'

'I think I will. What about you?'

Mia looked at her watch. 'I might make a couple of phone calls. See if I can tee up a time to talk to Rod and Nicole, perhaps ring the caravan park and then go home. There was supposed to be tennis tonight, but they've called it off because of the heat.'

Dave stood. 'I'll be glad when summer's finished.'

'Will you? I thought you'd start bemoaning the fact that it's cold.'

'What else are you supposed to do during each season?' he quipped. 'Oh, and I had that meeting with bossman Steve. He's managed to get someone to cover for me while I'm away for Bec's wedding.'

'Great!' Mia's face lit up. 'That's fantastic. Do you know who it is?'

'He didn't say. But look, Mia, Kim and I might try to take a few days over a weekend in the next month or so as well. I'm hoping we can go to WA and see Bec and Justin and Alice before the wedding. Get the meet and greets well and truly out the way beforehand, and then Bec might be happy for Kim to come on the day.'

'That's a great idea.' Mia stood and put her notebook in her pocket. 'Pity she didn't offer you that first.'

'Mia,' Dave sighed, 'this is a complicated situation.'

'Not really,' Mia told him in her usual forthright way. 'But don't worry, I'll keep my thoughts to myself.'

'That would make me very happy,' Dave said. He patted her on the shoulder and left the room.

Mia sank into her chair and put her head in her hands. God, she was tired. After babysitting and cooking today, all she'd wanted to do was go home and fall into bed, even though it was only early afternoon. Yet, Hallie's information about Charlie had worried her so much on the drive home, she'd needed to check on his record.

Mia had grown to love Barker and the townsfolk in the year she'd been here. These days, as she walked down the street, most people smiled and stopped to talk to her. Their inclusiveness made her feel like she was home. Dave had said there would come a time when she'd feel as if she needed to protect the whole town and everyone in it. Tonight it had finally happened and that need was going to take over her life. It was her purpose now.

Shutting down the computer, she turned off the lights and said goodbye to Joan. Then she stopped at the door as she was about to head out into the sunshine.

'Do you know much about Alex's and Danny's families, Joan?'

'Not really, Mia. They live a fair way from Barker. Obviously, everyone knows the surnames—they've been locals for generations—but as for knowing the ins and outs, no.' She stopped typing and looked up. 'Although the Donaldson family is well known for keeping to themselves and making sure their business is the same. When

Sam left it caused a bit of a ruckus . . . and gossip. There was some talk that he'd been kicked out of the family but no one seemed to know why.

'I talked to Nicole once after Alex brought Hallie home. She said Hallie didn't have the right sort of grit it took to live out here. I didn't take any notice because I'd heard it before from other families, who, might I point out, are usually proved wrong by the young women. But really, that's about all.'

'Why does land and succession seem to bring out the worst in people?' Mia shook herself. 'Right, I'll see you later, Joan.'

'See you later, Mia. Don't worry yourself sick about this. These types of things have a way of rising to the surface without too much help.'

'All good. Bye.' Mia closed the door behind her and walked across the street to the pub.

A puddle from the drip of the air conditioner next to the entrance spread out under her feet and, as she pushed open the door to the bar, the moist, humid air hit her in the face.

Surprisingly, the front bar was almost empty.

'Hey, Hopper, you've upset everyone, have you? Been boycotted?'

'Keep those sassy ideas of yours to yourself, miss,' Hopper said with a grin. 'It's good to see you, Mia. How are you? Been a tough week?'

Climbing onto a bar stool, she nodded. 'One of those ones I'd rather forget.'

'What can I get you? First one is on the house.'

'Just a lime and soda, thanks. I've got a few questions for you and then a couple of enquiries elsewhere before I head home.'

Hopper raised his eyebrows but didn't ask.

He put the drink on the bar in front of her and Mia took a sip, letting her head fall backwards and taking the pressure off her neck. 'Beautiful, thanks, Hopper.'

'What questions have you got?'

'Nothing too hard,' she said. 'You got anyone booked in for the funerals yet?'

Hopper nodded. 'Yeah, two couples. I could've taken more, but the rooms aren't ready. Still renovating the other three. Well, not renovating yet. The council are taking their sweet time approving the plans for the renos. No one wants to share bathrooms anymore, the way these buildings were first designed back in the early 1900s, so I'm getting en-suites put in.' He wiped at the bar. 'Bloody council,' he muttered.

'Do you have any details on the couples?' Mia leaned forward and caught his eye, trying to let him know that this was important. Yes, he was supposed to never give out information on his customers, but . . .

'Maybe. The log is near the phone. Can you watch the bar while I shoot off to the loo?'

Without waiting for an answer, he lifted the counter and let himself out from behind the bar, disappearing into a corridor at the back of the pub.

Mia waited for a moment, then headed towards the logbook. She glanced at the old fella nursing a beer in the corner of the bar. He was someone she didn't know, but she had noticed a caravan parked on the side street as she'd entered.

Running her finger down the entries, she didn't see Charlie's name or any that raised her attention. Still, she wrote down the names in case they were useful information for later.

Hopper returned just as Mia sat at the bar and picked up her drink.

'Any good?' he asked.

'Who knows?' She slipped a photo out of her pocket. 'It's an old one, but have you seen anyone resembling this bloke?'

Hopper glanced at it then shook his head. 'Not in here.'

'Okay, thanks, Hopper. You're a legend.'

'Aren't all pub owners?'

CHAPTER 20

The caravan park in Barker had five cabins, fifteen caravan sites and no lawn.

To Mia, it seemed like a terrible place to stay. Without character and too many people in close quarters. Still, there were gum trees shading the caravan sites and everything was clean and tidy.

The reception area was empty, so she rang the bell.

While she waited Mia texted Nicole, asking if she could come out tomorrow and see her. The long, uncomfortable drive ahead didn't excite her, but she'd done it for Hallie and now she would do it for Nicole. Plus, on the way back, she could call in and see Maggie.

Kim had sent her a text yesterday, saying she'd seen Maggie in town two days ago and she thought she could be staying with family, but Mia hadn't heard anything more.

'Hello there, sorry to keep you . . . Oh, Mia! It's you. Hi.' Kate Jamison had thrown the door open and tumbled through at a jog. She put her hand to her chest, trying to catch her breath. 'Sorry, I was in the bathroom block, cleaning. Never-ending job, unfortunately. How are you? My god, what tragedies we've had over the last week.'

Mia waited until the avalanche of words had stopped. 'Hi, Kate. Yep, all pretty awful. Have you got time for a chat?'

Kate's welcoming look fell away, replaced with determination. 'Of course. Can I help you with something?'

'I'm not sure.' Mia saw a movement out of the window and looked out to see Tom walking across from one unit to another. He knocked on the door and Mick opened it, his mobile phone to his ear. Waving Tom inside, they both disappeared.

Kate followed her eyes.

'Such nice blokes,' she said. 'That Tom, he's a bit of a dish, actually. So different to the blokes around here. He held the door open for me yesterday! Pity he's got a wife.' Kate gave a wink.

'That's scandalous, Kate,' Mia said, trying not to laugh. 'What's the other one like?'

'Oh, now I think he's single because I haven't seen or heard him talking to anyone that sounds like a partner. Those walls of the cabins, gosh, they're a bit thin. If you're walking past at the wrong time, you never know what you might hear.'

Wiggling her eyebrows, Mia shook her head with a pained look on her face. 'God, what an awful thought.' Then she leaned forward. 'But have you heard lots of juicy things?'

'Well, it would be completely inappropriate to pass any of that on to you, Mia.' This time Kate had a virtuous look on her face. Then she broke out into laughter and leaned forward. 'Geez, last year I heard a couple planning their getaway without paying. They were talking about leaving at three in the morning, so I set my alarm and got up. Met them at the gate.'

'That was handy. What did they do?'

'Grudgingly paid the money they owed, and then said they were going back to bed. If they had to pay, they might as well stay until check-out time.'

'Bloody hell!'

'Oh, I get all sorts in here.'

'I can only imagine.'

'Is that what you're here to ask me about? All sorts?' Kate grinned, and her brown, wavy hair bounced up and down in time with her movements.

'Sounds like I'm here to talk to you about licorice!'

Kate burst out laughing and Mia could see why she made such a good caravan park owner. Tough, but personable, with a great sense of humour.

'But, yes, I do have some questions,' Mia continued. She drew out Charlie's photo from her pocket. 'Has anyone resembling this man rented a cabin or site from you?'

Taking the photo, Kate studied it carefully, before giving it back. 'Nope, never seen him before. I've got a fairly good memory for faces. Names not so much.'

'Right. And have you got many bookings for the funerals?'

'Oh my lordy, we are chock-a-block full. Not that I'd want two young men to die every week, but having a full caravan park is my dream. It's always busy, and there's cleaning to do and complaints to deal with, but I love being flat strap and that's what I'll be a day or so beforehand and a day or so afterwards.'

'Have you got anyone booked by the name of Charlie Dynner?'

'Hmm, doesn't ring a bell.' Kate walked behind the desk and wiggled the mouse. The light from the screen reflected in Kate's glasses as she clicked through to the reservations. 'Nope, not that I can see here. Nothing even close to that name.'

'Okay, well, if someone books in who resembles the man in this photo, can you please give us a call?'

'Sure can. Is there a reason you want to talk to him?'

'There is, but not one I can discuss.'

Kate nodded. 'No trouble.'

'Everything else going okay here?' Mia asked.

'Yep, all tickety-boo. I had to chase some of the schoolkids off last week. They were up-ending the bins before rubbish day. But they won't be doing that again.'

'Gave them a scare?'

'More than that, I called their parents. That fixed 'em!'

Mia laughed. 'The long arm of the law.'

'Little buggers swore they weren't. But I saw them walking past and then when I came back there was rubbish on the ground. I dunno why kids reckon they can get away with being a menace and lying. I guess we all had a bit of that in us when we were kids—you know, testing the rules and boundaries—but that was just messy to clean up.'

'Which kids?'

'Paul Little and Graham James. Even after their parents made 'em come back and clean everything up . . . they still swore they didn't do it. I tell you, their parents will have to keep an eye on those kids.'

Mia had fished out her notebook and was now writing in it. 'I'll keep an eye on them, too,' she said, snapping it shut.

'Oh, and while I think about it, I reckon Lainey Jackson's dog is coming in here at night. The security lights have been going on at the back of the campers' kitchen about three in the morning for the last two weeks, and one night when I got up to investigate, the bloody dog was there wagging its tail at me. There's another pain in the bum!'

'Not sure that dogs are our jurisdiction, Kate,' Mia said. 'But if it keeps happening let us know and we might be able to have a word.' Something stirred in her memory. 'Actually, while I think about it, there have been reports of someone living rough near the cemetery, but when we've checked, there's been no one around. Perhaps keep that in mind, if the lights keep going on.'

'Has there?' Kate pursed her lips as she thought. 'Well, I haven't seen anyone. And the cemetery is a long way from here.'

Mia made for the door and looked out of the window in time to see Kaylah with her toiletry bag and towel thrown over her shoulder. Stepping carefully around the larger rocks, she looked uncomfortable as she brushed flies from her face.

'Doesn't the campers' kitchen get locked up at a certain time of the night?'

Kate nodded. 'Yeah, that's why it was weird the security lights were on and why I got up to check. Ha, you should have seen me sneaking across with a cricket bat in my hand. I was ready to give someone a whack, and there's this bloody gold lab with its tongue hanging out, grinning at me.' She laughed, then cocked her head to the side. 'Reckon I could have made my TV debut on *Funniest Home Videos* with the look on my face.'

Mia crinkled her forehead, not understanding.

'Oh yeah, you're too much of a baby to remember that TV show. Forget it.'

It was Mia's turn to laugh just as her phone beeped a text message. 'No worries, Kate, I'll catch you later. Thanks for answering my questions.' She waved goodbye and let herself out, pulling the phone from her pocket as she went.

Nicole: *Hi Mia, we are in Barker shopping. We can answer your questions now if you are available?*

Mia started to tap out *yes*, then stopped, remembering Dave's words of caution.

Taking a couple of deep breaths, Mia let her head fall backwards and she looked at the deep blue sky, ignoring the flies that were clustering around her face. It didn't take long out here to stop taking any notice of the little black bastards, except to tell them to fuck off. The most Australian sentence in the history of the country. Because what fly ever fucked off when it was told?

How to answer?

'Hello, Mia. Nice day for it.'

Mia saw Tom standing near his cabin, hand raised in greeting.

'Hi, Tom. How are you feeling today?' She walked towards him as he opened the door and then leaned against the frame.

'Numb, I think is the only word for it. It's too hard to comprehend we've lost them both.' His eyes were still as red as they'd been the day they'd been sitting around the kitchen table at Hallie's place.

'Yes, it's very shocking. How's Mick?'

'He's the same. We just can't believe what's happened. I mean, these two men—'

Mia could hear his throat close over and the words stick in Tom's throat, and her heart ached. If only she could change this. Reaching out, she put a hand on his arm and squeezed. What else was there to do?

Tom turned away and cleared his throat. Fishing out a hankie and blowing his nose, he harrumphed again, then turned back. 'Sorry,' he said.

'Nothing to be sorry for,' she said.

'Anyhow'—Tom seemed to gather himself—'that's life. We'll miss them.'

'Tom, if you don't mind, I remember you mentioned that Charlie had been in contact. Do you know if he's going to come to the funeral?'

'We haven't heard anything from him again. I'd doubt it, though. I'm sure he understands that he's not welcome in our group or around our wives.' A deep frown crossed his face. 'He's very untrustworthy.'

'What can you tell me about him since he's been out of gaol?'

'Absolutely nothing. I have no knowledge of where he is or what he's been doing.'

There was a thought scratching at the back of Mia's mind, but she couldn't tease it out before Mick waved at her as he descended down the cabin stairs.

'Mia, hi. Have you got any news?' Mick took the space between them in ten large steps and stood next to Tom, watching her expectantly.

He hadn't shaved and Mia guessed it took a rare day when he wasn't in public life for that to happen.

'No, I was just asking Tom what he could tell me about Charlie. Do you have any information that could be helpful?'

'As in . . .?' Mick said.

'I was asking Tom if he knew what Charlie had been doing since gaol?'

'Ah. No. Look, Charlie hasn't been a part of our life since that terrible night.'

'Yeah, you've all said that. But now he's appeared out of nowhere.' Mia looked at them both and the itch she'd been feeling before became a full-blown thought. 'How did he know how to get in contact with you? How did he get your phone numbers?'

Tom and Mick looked at each other as if it was the first time they'd even thought about it.

'I have no idea,' Mick said, raising his hands.

'God, I hadn't even considered that,' Tom added, looking around in case someone was going to jump him.

'Are either of your phone numbers public?'

'Not my mobile,' Mick answered. 'My office's numbers are, but this one'—he held his phone in the air and waggled it—'nobody has this one unless I give it to them. I'd have all sorts of crazies ringing me otherwise.'

Mia thought hard and then stared at each man. 'How did Charlie first get in contact?'

'He rang me,' Tom answered. 'Well, I think I was his initial port of call.' He turned to Mick. 'You hadn't heard from him before I let you know?'

Shaking his head, Mick answered, 'First I knew about it was when you sent me a message.'

'Did you speak to him, Tom?'

'No, it was just a VM.' He searched his pockets for his phone and then drew it out, opening the app. 'I think I kept the message.' Tom scrolled until he found what he was looking for and tapped the icon. A tinny voice sounded through the speaker.

'*Tom? The message sounds like you, even though it doesn't say your name. Anyhow, Tom, it's Charlie. I've heard about Alex.*' A rushing noise in the background sounded like cars to Mia. '*I want to come to the funeral.*

Actually, I need to come. I need to see you all. Could you ring me back?' He recited a number and then the phone went dead.

'Play it again, please,' Mia said, getting out her notebook.

This time she wrote the number down.

'Did you call him?' she asked.

'Not on your life,' Tom answered with a curious look. 'We've told you why.'

'Had to ask, Tom. It's all part of our investigations.'

'Investigations?' Mick asked slowly. 'What are you investigating?'

Mia put her notebook back into her pocket and gave a rueful smile. 'Investigation is probably too strong a word. Information gathering. Trying to see the big picture.' Her phone beeped again, saving her from an awkward situation and she took her phone out, looking at the screen. 'Oh, sorry, got to answer this.' She paused before she lifted the phone to her ear. 'Look, guys, this is really important. Dave and I would like to speak to Charlie. 'If he gets in contact, you need to let us know. All right?'

CHAPTER 21

'Thanks for seeing me, Nicole. How are you and Rod?'

'We're fine. Thanks for asking.'

Nicole sat straight in the chair Mia had pulled out for her and reached towards the cup of tea Joan had brought into the room moments before.

'Such a tough time for you all,' Mia said. She cursed herself for saying the obvious and looked down at her notebook she had in her hand. 'Dave and I were talking yesterday and we realised we didn't really know Alex from your point of view. He's important to us and we want to get this right.'

Nicole took a sip of tea, Mia noticing her hands were shaking very slightly. When she put the cup back down, her smile was forced.

'He was his own person,' she said. 'Wayward and head-strong, but kind and considerate at the same time. A bit of a contradiction in terms, but that was Alex.'

'Alex was your second son?'

'Yes.' Nicole now folded her hands in her lap. A glance down then she found Mia's eyes again.

'You have another son who isn't living on Tirranah?'

'Sam.'

Mia was impressed with how Nicole was able to school her features to calm and serene, even when there was the smallest of tics giving away how uncomfortable she was. It was her throat that gave her away. The slim, long throat, tanned red from the vicious sun, showed a racing pulse.

'Did he decide he didn't want to be at home on Tirranah?'

'Yes. He married a girl that really didn't fit in with our way of life.'

Mia paused and thought how to phrase the next question. Dave would be proud, if only he could see her careful consideration.

'She didn't like the bush?'

'Oh, she liked the station well enough, although she never lived out there,' Nicole said. 'But she didn't really fit in with our family values. It's interesting when your children choose a partner.' Nicole was warming to her subject now. Relaxing minutely. 'More often than not, it's someone whom you wouldn't have chosen for them and, as parents, we always think we know best. I guess, over time, we'll see whether Sam has made the right decision. I suspect not.'

'Hallie mentioned something about a financial agreement when we spoke with her last. Is that part of your family values?'

'Absolutely. Those women who have no idea of the sweat and hard work that's gone into getting the family business up and running and successful have absolutely no right to any part of the land or proceeds if they only marry a son. They must earn their right to their place in the business.' Nicole gave a humourless smile. 'I can see I've shocked you. That is life out here. It's not only women who are asked to sign these agreements. If we had a daughter at home working on the station, the same would apply to her husband-to-be.

'I must tell you, Mia, I myself had to sign that agreement and I did it willingly, as Hallie did, because I loved Rod.'

'Would you have let a daughter come home and work there?' Mia was genuinely interested. The way the conversation was going, it seemed that only sons were welcome home.

'I had a daughter,' Nicole said suddenly. 'She was the first-born and I had such high hopes that Rod would want her to come home after boarding school and work. Instead he was devastated to have a girl born first. All he'd ever wanted was a son.'

'Oh, Nicole.' Mia's brain exploded with the many different thoughts and feeling running through her. 'What happened?'

'Well, Kirsty died from SIDS when she was eight months old. She was a wonderful sleeper, so different from what I'd been told to expect by all the nurses and people I knew who had already had babies. Rod's mother was a great one for giving wisdom. Not always where it was wanted.' That wan smile again.

Mia leaned forward, her pen in her hand, twisting it around as Nicole spoke.

'One night, I put her down and she went off to sleep as she always had, easily. I hadn't been well, mastitis, so I took myself off to bed with cabbage leaves, Panadol and lots of water. When I woke up the next day, I wasn't surprised that Kirsty hadn't woken during the night for a feed, but even so, I couldn't shake the feeling there was something wrong.' Nicole pressed her lips together before speaking again. 'By the time I found her, she was cold and there was nothing to be done.'

'I'm very sorry, Nicole,' Mia said softly.

'Well, again, that is life. There are lots of mothers who go through losing children.' Her matter-of-factness didn't seem to match the look on her face. There were confusing emotions crossing her whole body. But again, the control and poise she held were strong.

'I'm so sorry,' Mia repeated.

'Kirsty is buried in the family plot on Tirranah, but neither of the boys know about her. We didn't put a named headstone on her grave, only a small cross. Rod and I decided that was our secret. I didn't need my grief to be passed on to our other children.'

'Your grief?'

'I've learned, over time, that a mother's grief is different to that of a father. Because it's our job to nurture our children. Men tend to get so busy providing and focusing on their work that grief is pushed away out of sight.'

'I'm sure Rod was as devastated as you were.'

'Hmm,' Nicole said, 'if that was the case, he's hidden it well.'

There was a long silence while Nicole took another sip of her tea and licked her lips.

Mia processed her words. 'Back to Hallie and Alex,' she finally said, 'and the agreement.'

'Of course. Sorry, I've got off track. I'll continue to explain our thinking, shall I?'

'I'd appreciate it.'

'Well, this is something the Donaldsons have done for the last two generations. There was nothing untoward in it, only that if Hallie had no reason to live here anymore, she'd need to vacate the house as soon as was possible. Unfortunately, that's what has happened.

'And financially, she doesn't have any call on us to support her. I mean'—Nicole gave a small laugh—'why would she? Hallie has done nothing to improve or help on the station since she arrived. If anything, we've been supporting her, allowing her to live out here for free, even if she is married . . . um, was married to Alex.'

'Did you know that Alex had approached a lawyer to look at your agreement?'

'We did.'

'Did that upset you?'

'Not upset. We weren't adverse to Alex having his own opinions—it's good he was an independent thinker—however, we, Rod in particular, were disappointed he may have thought we didn't have his and our best interests at heart.'

Mia fiddled with a pen, flicking it from top to tip and over again as she thought about what Nicole was saying. 'What about Hallie's best interests? And Ruby's? As your granddaughter, will she be welcome at your place?'

There was a pause, only the humming of the landline and a dog barking in the distance to break the silence.

'You know what, Mia?' Nicole sounded resigned. 'I'd like to think so. Because in time, if she'd stayed on the station with Alex and Hallie, and with us as guides, she'd know this land as well as Alex does. However, I know Rod was not of the same opinion. Some city folk never come to understand the bush.'

'But you're not willing to let either of them stay and try?' Mia asked.

'That part isn't my decision. Perhaps you forget, I'm not a Donaldson by birth.'

~

It was midnight when Mia woke and jumped out of bed. A thought had been chasing her all evening and she hadn't been able to put her finger on what it was. Between Hopper and the local caravan park, there hadn't been a record of Charlie staying in town, yet Mia couldn't shake the feeling that he needed to be found. As she'd said to Hallie, '*No one likes a rapist in their town.*'

She got dressed and pulled on her boots then walked to the police station, enjoying the cool air. The whole town was getting sick of the heat of summer and was counting the days until autumn. At this time of the day the median-strip sprinklers were on, keeping it green and attractive, and the streetlights were dim, the insects clustered around them.

Quiet. The whole town was quiet.

As she walked, she replayed her conversation with Nicole. The last thing she'd said was that Rod had promised his father he would always protect the station the same way his dad had. By asking Hallie to sign that agreement, he was doing what he'd promised.

'*Rod never breaks a promise, Mia. No matter what.*'

Letting herself into the station, she disarmed the alarm and went straight to her desk to turn on the computer. Did she need to investigate Rod and Nicole further? Yes. There were questions she felt she couldn't ask Nicole yesterday after her revelation of losing a daughter. That poor woman had lost three children, one of them estranged, and yet she was still standing with a 'that's life' attitude. Mia was in awe of her strength, but uneasy about many threads that were beginning to make themselves clear.

Maybe there were more pressing things at hand.

Mia needed info on Charlie. He'd done five years in gaol and disappeared after his release. She hadn't been able to find anything on the man. Neither Tom nor Mick could shed any light on his whereabouts but now Mia had a phone number she could try to track. If he'd worked since his release, Mia hadn't found any official records. There was the option that he'd always been paid in cash or kind and also that he was thieving to keep his head above water.

'There has to be something here,' she muttered to herself. 'There has to be.'

What are you looking for?

'I don't know. Information on Charlie to keep the town safe? Information on what caused these two accidents?'

Mia completed the paperwork to track the phone number, sent it off to the telecommunications carrier and sat back. She was confused by Nicole and Rod's attitude towards their family, and Charlie . . . Because she couldn't find him to talk to, Charlie felt mysterious and sinister.

Nicole's comments yesterday had been disturbing, too—perhaps that was only because Mia didn't understand the 'eldest son' tradition. She had come to realise, as in any industry steeped in tradition, that word, *tradition*, encompassed fear of change and misunderstanding.

For Rod and Nicole, fear a son wouldn't be there to take over the family business. There was no chance a woman could do it as well as a man, and what happened if that man and woman divorced, and she tried to take their long fought for and successful business?

You don't know what they're capable of sounded alarming to Mia; yet, was that fear on Alex's behalf because he was of a different generation than his parents and didn't understand their beliefs?

Abandoned by his friends, Charlie had been left without support at the darkest time of his life.

Charlie, Nicole and Rod. Were there two accidents? Was there something darker at play here?

How could two men, seemingly not connected other than through friendship, be linked?

She scribbled some notes: *More information on two accidents ... Both were caused by a fall. Alex fell and a ute fell on Danny. Similarities and yet so different.*

Picking up the folder that held all the photos from Alex's death, she flicked through, running a careful eye over each of them.

The windmill, nine metres high. Dave had measured it. A long way to fall.

Trough and tank, footprints, birds. So many birds coming into the water.

No note, loving family. Good friends.

This man was a typical 'good bloke'. She could imagine what everyone at the funeral was going to say.

'*Such a shame. He was such a good bloke.*'

'*We'll miss him. Alex was a hard worker.*'

'*How devastating for his family. I've known him since he was a child and he was such a lovely man.*'

Running her fingers through her unbrushed hair, she sighed. 'What am I missing?'

Turning on the coffee machine, Mia popped a pod into the cavity and stood there waiting for the water to heat up. It didn't take long for the pump to kick in and run the black liquid into a cup. She added milk and took the drink back to her desk.

Her phone beeped and she frowned. Who was texting her after midnight?

Hamish: *You at the station? It's late.*

You going to work? she replied. *It's late.*

He sent back two laughing emojis. Then asked, *Coffee machine on? I'm on my way home.*

Yes.

Moments later she was letting him in the door and handing him a steaming mug. The last week had taken its toll on Hamish, Mia could see. Being a redhead, his skin was always pale, but the freckles stood out more than normal and his eyes were tired and bloodshot.

'Here's to it,' she said, raising her own mug.

'Best of health,' he answered, taking a sip. 'God, that's good. What a shift. Whoever said country nursing was easy should have been in my hospital tonight.'

'What happened?'

'We took old Mrs Ganter into care last weekend to give her carer and family some respite. She's a feisty one. Took a bit to convince her it was bedtime. Insistent on making dinner for the whole of the hospital. You know what she said?'

'What?'

'"How can you expect these men to shear sheep if you don't feed them properly? No wonder they're all still asleep. Haven't got enough fuel in their system. Now, show me where the kitchen is and I'll feed them up and get them going."'

Mia's first instinct was to giggle, then sadness hit her in the chest. Dementia was the cruellest of diseases. She knew from firsthand experience.

'Anyhow, why are you here? Strange hours for you to be keeping in a quiet country town.'

'As if there is such a thing.' Mia grimaced. 'I don't know, Hamish, there's something about these two deaths I can't shake and yet I have no idea what it is. You got any thoughts?'

'Other than totally tragic? No. What are you thinking?'

Mia looked around as if making sure there was no one listening. Silly, considering the time of day. 'To be honest, I don't think they were accidental.'

Hamish took another sip of his coffee. 'Murder?'

Feeling uncomfortable, Mia shifted in her seat. 'I don't know that I want to go as far as that,' she said.

'Well,' Hamish said, 'what else is there? They've each been signed off as an accidental death—from there, it's suicide, manslaughter, murder. Have I missed anything?'

'Not when you put it like that,' Mia said, pushing the photos towards him. 'Plus the platform on the windmill that Alex allegedly fell from was rotten so . . .'

'Why do you think he fell from there? Maybe his grip slipped when he was climbing. You know that when the pathologist was working out injuries versus height of fall, there wouldn't be much difference between being on the platform and the top rung of the ladder. One step.'

'True. However, the platform was broken from where he put his foot.' She paused. 'Why was Danny under the vehicle? I mean, he's a station kid. He's grown up around machinery; changing a tyre would be second nature to him. There wouldn't be any reason for him to climb underneath when the vehicle was balancing on a jack. Surely we all know how dangerous that is.'

'Mmm, but don't forget familiarity breeds contempt.'

Mia looked over at him. 'You think he just got complacent?'

'I am nothing but your devil's advocate.'

'Excellent because all you've been is argumentative.'

Hamish put his coffee down and picked up the file. He carefully looked at each photo. 'Has Alex's clothing gone back to the family?' he asked.

'Not yet.'

He tapped on a photo and she leaned forward. 'You've matched these boot prints to the soles of his boots? I mean, if you're thinking murder, you have to put someone else at the scene, don't you? There's nothing else to indicate there was anyone there, unless these prints don't match his, from what you're telling me.'

Mia stilled as her mind ticked over. She knew it had been on the list of things do to, but didn't remember doing so. She yanked the folder towards her and flicked through the pages until she came to the other prints she'd photographed the next time they'd gone out there. Dave had mentioned they were probably from Alex taking a leak. Now, when she checked the tread, these prints looked different.

'Hey, look at this,' she said. 'This print has no damage to the sole and yet this one looks like there's a chunk taken out from the middle. They're different footprints!'

'Hold on, hold on,' Hamish said to her. 'What about Alex's father or Danny? They were both there that night. Could be theirs.'

Mia deflated. 'Yeah, they could be. We still need to rule them out. But what if they're not?'

'Then you've got trouble,' Hamish said.

CHAPTER 22

Mia was still at the office desk when Dave came in the next morning, except she was slumped back in her chair, mouth open and sound asleep.

Dave looked at her, remembering how he used to be that enthusiastic about going to work, solving cases and investigations. That felt like a long time ago.

His mate, Detective Bob Holden, had talked about this feeling as he'd become sick. Everything hit too hard and heavy and he felt like he'd been dragging around a ball and chain of responsibility. That was after he'd accepted his cancer diagnosis and handed over the reins of the Stock Squad to Dave. Then, and only then, had he decided he wanted to concentrate on nothing but doing what he could to get well.

At the time, Dave couldn't ever imagine feeling how Bob did, but now he understood.

He pushed the button of the coffee machine, noting its warmth, and made Mia a cup.

Gently, he put it in front of her and touched her shoulder. 'Hey, sleepyhead,' he said.

Mia's eyes flickered open and she sat straight up. 'Shit!'

'What?'

'I didn't mean to fall asleep.' She blinked and took in her surrounds. 'Thanks,' she said, taking a sip of the coffee. Mia pushed the photos towards Dave then started talking excitedly. 'You'll never guess what I've worked out. Well, Hamish was here, too, but look . . .'

Not having slept much during the night, Dave had to get Mia to run through her findings twice before he could have a well-formed thought. His constable was up-ending everything they knew about the investigation of Alex's death so far—and on the day of the funeral.

'Mia, firstly, I want you to know that I am in no way disregarding what you're telling me, okay? However, the land out there stays the same for months and months. Sometimes there's little wind to cover tracks like these and unless an animal walks over them, or there's rain . . . these prints could have been there for ages!'

'But we have to check it out, don't we?'

'Of course, but please, don't get your hopes up, okay?' Dave had to admit Mia had done her job well. There was a list of differences in the soles and a printout of each brand of boot that they could match.

'What about the funeral?'

'What about it?'

'Do we need to ask them to stop it? Just until we've done this.'

Dave took a deep breath in through his nose and another sip of coffee. 'No, I don't think so. The injuries aren't going to change from the autopsy, and the pathologist didn't find anything that indicated murder. If that's what it is, then we have to prove that without an autopsy.'

'We don't want to get into a situation where we have to exhume the body,' Mia ventured. 'Wouldn't it be better to hold off for a day or two until we know for sure? Just in case. Maybe they might need to go back and look at the findings again.'

Dave was silent. 'Fuck,' he said after a moment's contemplation. 'Fuck.'

Mia was squirming in her seat, but also looking like she wanted to punch the air with excitement. She'd found something Dave thought was worthy of pursuing!

'Pass me that report,' Dave said and took his glasses out of his pocket.

For the next half an hour, he read quietly, making notes, while Mia googled Alex's blood brothers.

Dave took his pen and added to his notes, when she gave him a rundown. Mia had done a thorough job, he had to admit. She found each man's social-media profiles, relieved they were public. Unsurprisingly, Charlie's was inactive, while Danny hadn't posted much, but Maggie had tagged him in many photos, which showed up on his timeline. Happy photos: Maggie on the back of Danny's motorbike, in the sheep yards. Maggie behind the wheel of her new car.

Tom's LinkedIn feed told Dave that he was an investment banker with a large global company, which had its head office in Singapore. Exactly what he'd told them.

Mick? Well, he had been the easiest to find. As a politician, his name and face were all over the news. He had a soft spot for car accident victims and mental health, all backed up by the portfolio he held . . . Health.

Today the health minister has announced another five million dollars to expand research into mental health in rural areas, one article announced.

The minister is blinded by his country upbringing, another shouted. *He should be holding the same type of enquiries into the city hospitals.*

Alex had been quiet on social media, too, but Hallie had tagged him in photos. Although, two weeks ago, he had changed his profile picture, showing Alex standing next to Hallie, his arm around her, while she held Ruby on her hip. They were all smiling, looking like the perfect happy family.

'I've got a comment,' Dave said as he looked up from his work. 'One thing I know about these cameras is they start recording when there is movement, but only if it's within three metres of the sensor. If someone else was at the windmill, we might not be lucky enough to catch them on camera, and if they were too far away, then they won't have triggered the camera to start recording. Still, it would certainly be worth looking at it. And perhaps other bores that might be nearby or on the same track in case a ute drove there and parked a distance off.'

'I'll see if I can get the footage. Also, here, I've pulled Kirsty Donaldson's file as well. I told you about her, remember?'

Looking at Mia over his glasses, he raised his eyebrows. 'I remember.'

'I know, it's just another gut feeling and I've had too many for them all to be true, but in my defence, I'm new at this.'

Rolling his hands in a way to get her to keep talking, Dave waited.

'I thought her file was worth looking at because of Nicole's comments about Rod being upset that a daughter was born first and he didn't seem to grieve that much.'

'Jesus, Mia, not everyone gets around without feelings here. Rod is not some sadistic bastard.'

She pursed her lips. 'There isn't a file. Her name is not recorded in this database. There is a birth certificate and nothing else.'

'That's not possible,' Dave said. 'If there was an unexplained death like SIDS, there has to be an autopsy.'

'Well, maybe, but that's not what's happened.'

'How the hell?' He read quickly, seeing that Mia was right. His gut was beginning to churn. 'I don't know how that could have happened.'

'Do you want me to get Rod in for a chat?'

Taking his glasses off, Dave rubbed his eyes. 'Geez, Mia, you've really opened a can of worms here. There are too many coincidences to ignore the situation, but I'm not sure which thread to follow first. A conversation with Rod is necessary, but so is talking to Hallie and Maggie and the blokes again. Danny's and Alex's mates might know if something was amiss or if they were involved in some type of dodgy business dealings.

'Is there any chance Nicole was staying in town last night? You did catch up with her quite late in the day.'

'Funnily enough, yes. Rod was meeting her in Barker last night. They were meeting with the funeral director over in Port Augusta this morning. Something about checking finer details.'

'A viewing by the sounds of that. Get them on the phone. Hopefully they haven't left town yet.'

~

Mia glanced at her watch and then picked up the phone. 'Rod, hi. Sorry to call so early. This is Constable Mia Worth from the Barker Police Station.' She listened for a moment then said, 'I'm well, thanks. Look, have you and Nicole left to go to Port Augusta yet? . . . No? Great. Could I ask you to come in to answer a few questions for us?'

Dave was scribbling on a piece of paper and shoved it over to her. *Go to them.*

'Actually, it might be a whole lot easier if I come to you,' Mia amended. She glanced at her watch. 'Yes, if everything goes well, you should be able to make your appointment there. Okay, where are you staying?' Another silence then

Mia nodded. 'See you soon.' She put down her phone and looked at Dave. 'They own a house on Fifth Street.'

'Let's go,' he said, tucking Kirsty's birth certificate into his briefcase and his notebook into his top pocket.

~

Nicole opened the door and held it wide open to let them in.

'Good morning,' she said. 'Rod's in the kitchen. Can I get you a cup of something?'

'I'm fine, thanks,' Dave said.

'No, thanks,' Mia said with a smile.

Rod was on his feet by the time they arrived at the kitchen, his hand outstretched. 'Morning, nice to see you are all on the job early, Dave. How are you?'

'Mia and I are both well, thanks, Rod. Sorry to have to have a chat under these circumstances. Need to clear up a couple of things from Nicole speaking with Mia yesterday.'

'Of course, of course, anything you need to know.'

Rod was behaving exactly as he had when Mia had first met him: never looking at her, always speaking straight to Dave. She wasn't going to let this go on.

'Rod, good morning,' she said, pulling out a chair and sitting down. Mia waited until the rest of them had sat, then took out her notebook. Looking up, Rod was scowling. Mia smiled. 'Nicole told me yesterday you had a daughter who died from SIDS.'

'Yes.'

'To do my due diligence, I thought it was important that I read the file of Kirsty's death. Yet I couldn't find a file within the police database. Can you tell me why you took her straight to the funeral director instead of calling an ambulance?'

'The child was clearly dead. Nothing an ambulance could do.' Rod shrugged. 'Better to take her straight to the person who could help her the most.'

'Right, but didn't you think that the police might need to be involved because she died unexpectedly?'

Rod shifted in his chair and leaned forward. 'Look, what I know is our daughter died in her sleep. In the animal world, there are unexplained deaths of lambs and calves. This is nature taking out the weakest ones. Unfortunately, there must have been something wrong with Kirsty and the outcome was awful. But as to thinking the police might need to be involved? Ha!' Rod gave a confused laugh. 'No. Not at all. She died. What more was there to know?'

'To find out why?'

'Would that bring her back, Constable?'

Mia looked down at the blank page she had opened her notebook to. Clearly the answer was no, but protocols didn't change what had happened. Rules were there for a reason.

'Rod,' Dave said, leaning forward now, 'this is pretty tricky, because from what I can guess, the funeral director would have told you that going to the police was non-negotiable. I hope that I won't have to pull your financial records from that long ago and find there's been some type of pay-off.'

Rod stood quickly, his chair falling loudly to the floor behind him, and he glanced towards the door. 'I resent your insinuation.'

Dave crossed his arms and looked silently at the man, while Mia cheered inwardly. She wanted to laugh and fling her head back with joy, despite the seriousness of it all. Finally, someone could take this prick down a peg or two.

'Please sit down, Mr Donaldson,' Mia said.

Reluctantly Rod sat back down, and Nicole came over to stand behind him. She put her hand on his shoulder, squeezing gently.

'How did you feel when you found out your first-born was a girl?' Mia asked.

'Oh, I don't know. At the time, I guess I was devastated.' Rod threw his hands up in an I-don't-know gesture. 'The first-born child had been a son for generations, and I just assumed that's what we'd have. There's a difference between being upset that we hadn't a son, to being upset that we had a daughter.'

Mia blinked. 'You'll have to explain that.'

'Yes, I wanted a son, but I never didn't want a daughter. I know a lot of the blokes now say, "I just want the baby to be healthy," and that's exactly what we wanted. But back then, it was also important to have a son to carry on the family name, business, all that sort of thing.

'But it didn't take too long to fall in love with that little girl.' Rod swallowed, his tone had become soft and laced with longing.

'But there was a time you didn't want her?'

'No, that is fundamentally untrue. I always wanted her. However, if she was the second child that would have been better.'

'Did you give the funeral director money to bury your daughter without going through the correct protocols?' Mia asked.

Rod's hand snaked up and found Nicole's. 'Look, it was an awful time. Our daughter had died, and we didn't know what was right and wrong. The chap from the funeral home, I can't even remember his name, Doug, I think, said we couldn't just turn up with a body,' Rod said. 'We had to take her to the hospital.' He looked at Mia and then over at Dave. 'I couldn't understand why. Our little girl was dead. We needed to bury her. Quickly, before it got too hot. I've seen what happens to animal bodies when they're left out in the sun. I couldn't have that happen to my beautiful little girl.

'I begged him just to take her and do everything that needed to be done. We would wait for the coffin and bury her ourselves when we got home. He said he needed five thousand dollars in cash and I said no worries.'

CHAPTER 23

'Are you happy to wipe Nicole and Rod off your list of suspects?' Dave asked as they got in the car and headed back to the station.

'He seemed genuine,' Mia answered.

'I'm not so sure,' Dave said.

'What? How come?' Her head snapped around to look at Dave.

Flicking on the blinker, Dave pursed his lips. 'Come on, Mia. You're the one who's been questioning everything about these cases since the accidents happened. Are you telling me you're just going to let this slide, because Rod said yes he bribed someone? That's the oldest trick in the book! Admit to the least criminal thing you've done and gloss over the bigger crimes.'

'He was genuine,' Mia said again. 'What did I miss?'

'The smooth delivery. The way he nodded *yes*, when the word *no* came out of his mouth when I asked if he hadn't wanted Kirsty. More often than not, actions speak louder than words. If you watch people and they're lying, there's always a tell.' Dave brought the car to a stop next to the kerb in front of the police station. 'I reckon he's a slimy little fucker who might just be exactly what Alex said he was: *You don't know what lengths they'll go to*, or whatever his words were.'

Unable to take in what Dave was saying Mia turned towards him in her seat. 'Just tell me again.'

Patiently now, Dave went back through the interview. 'And when I asked if there was a time when he hadn't wanted her. Rod said that was fundamentally untrue, but as he was saying it, he nodded *yes*.' Dave paused. 'Have you heard of Joe Navarro? He's a body-language specialist who worked for the FBI. I read an article he wrote on body language recently, where he specifically talks about the person of interest talking genuinely, as you've just said, but his feet are pointing outwards because he wants to leave. Rod also continually rolled from one butt cheek to the other—another sign he was uncomfortable.'

'Oh.' Mia was stunned she'd missed so much.

Dave ran his hand over his cheek. 'I'm not sure what I think Rod has done . . .' Dave held up his hand in caution. 'If he suffocated his daughter, and pushed his son off a windmill, then he's a serial killer and I'm damn sure he's not that. Perhaps he's not guilty of anything except covering up the fact that Nicole took the baby into bed with her and she accidently rolled over and smothered her.'

Mia snorted. 'Nicole is not the sort of woman who would take a baby into her bed. She'd probably stand over the cradle and shake her finger at the baby, telling them to go back to sleep.'

'But you understand what I'm saying here, Mia? I don't believe Rod and Nicole had anything to do with Alex's death. The scene—' he broke off, frustrated. 'The scene doesn't lie, Mia. As police officers we have to prove *beyond reasonable doubt*. There is no way we can do that with the scene at the windmill, or where Danny was killed. We physically can't.'

'But there's got to be something we've missed! You can't still believe all this is random?'

'You're right, I don't, but at the same time, we haven't got enough to prove anything!' Dave held his hands palm up. 'I'm sorry, but those are the facts of the matter.'

Mia dropped her head. 'Fuck.'

'I know. That's the difficult thing about policing. What we think we can see so clearly will be laughed out of court by a judge without strong evidence. And that's where we can't rush. We have to get this right because a defence lawyer will go to town on the prosecution if we stuff up in any way.'

Mia's phone chirped with an email and she reached into her pocket to pull it out while saying to Dave, 'Where to from here? What else can we do?'

'We need to have a chat to Tom and Mick, and see what we can find out about Charlie.'

Looking at her phone now, Mia held it up. 'The phone number Charlie rang from was a public phone in Adelaide.'

'Well, he's in the state. Wouldn't be a stretch to think he would get up here somehow. Ah, look over there.' Dave nodded towards the footpath where Tom was walking along holding takeaway coffee cups.

'Wonder how their businesses are keeping going while they're away,' Dave mused. 'And Mick, being the Minister for Health. I would imagine the call on his time, while he's not there, would be huge.'

'Mick was on the phone a lot when I was at the park yesterday,' Mia said. 'Since Covid, we've all learned to work from home, haven't we? Maybe now is the right time for a chat.' Mia opened the door and, with Dave following behind, she walked across the road. 'Tom, hi,' she called out as she waved. 'How are things?'

'Good morning. What a nice day,' Tom answered, waiting for them both to catch up. 'How are you both?'

'Going to be warm again,' Dave said. 'Needing a pick-me-up?'

'Got to say I'm surprised there's decent coffee in a town like this. I was a bit worried Kaylah and I might be back to instant International Roast.'

'The couple at the cafe have got Barker powered on decent caffeine, that's for sure,' Dave said. 'How's the business coping without you?'

Tom gave a half grin before he took a sip of coffee. 'No trouble. As an investment banker, I keep strange hours and can work from anywhere. As long as I have a decent internet connection, my computer and phone, everything still goes on as normal.'

'What does Kaylah do?' Mia asked.

'She's in between jobs at present. I met her when I was on a flight from Singapore to New York. Back then, Kaylah was a flight attendant, so her job makes it difficult to be married and live together. There're a few other options, but nothing that's really taken her fancy yet.'

'Yoo hoo, Mia. Hello, Mia!' A shaky voice from across the road called out and, without turning around, Mia knew it was Mrs Granger who walked the streets every morning looking for an unsuspecting soul to have a conversation with.

They needed to get Tom into the police station before Mrs Granger started talking to them all.

'Hey, Tom, I wondered if we could ask you a couple of questions? Could you come over to the station? I know this is short notice,' Mia said, ignoring the calls from across the road.

Tom looked surprised. 'Sure, now?'

'That would be ideal.' She didn't wait for him to say yes, before Mia headed towards the police station, not turning in Mrs Granger's direction.

'Better get a move on before we get accosted in the street,' Dave said with a small laugh.

By the time Dave had shepherded Tom back to the station, Mia had the door to the interview room open.

'Just in here, thanks, Tom. I'll be right back.'

Following her back to their offices, Dave whispered urgently.

'What are you going to ask him about? Charlie?'

'Yes, but I'm going back further. I want to know about the night Charlie raped that woman.'

Dave gaped at her. 'Mia, you can't go at this like a bull at a gate. I've explained this to you over and over again. Gently always gets the best results. What are you thinking?'

'I'll be gentle, I promise. I'm following a hunch. You've always told me to trust my gut. I don't usually get feelings, but this time I have.'

'You've got a bad case of Bali Belly from what I can see. You had a feeling about Rod and Nicole, too.'

'And you said I was right in some way, didn't you?'

'Jesus!' Dave swore under his breath. 'Mia, I hope you know what you're doing, these are powerful men you're dealing with here. One wrong step and they'll go to the media and your career will be over. 'Gently does it, okay? No accusations.'

Mia knew he was feeling edgy. 'Can you trust me?'

Dave dropped his head. Of all the questions to ask. He wanted to for sure, but Mia's track record wasn't the best. She was always rushing off half-cocked or reacting to something someone had said. This request needed a solid weighing up as it could affect their reputation as police. The way they were regarded in Barker. Not to mention the possible fallout from the families.

'Let's talk to Tom and see what comes of that,' Dave conceded. 'I have to tell you, this isn't sitting well with me.'

Mia got up. 'Thank you,' she said quietly.

CHAPTER 24

'What else do you think I can help you with?' Tom asked. 'All I know is that it's beyond belief we could lose two friends so close together and in such tragic accidents.'

'Actually, I'm going to go back a little further here, Tom, if you can bear with me. Like I said to Nicole and Rod previously, we want to do the best by both Alex and Danny, and getting as much information as possible will help that.'

'Sure, I'll do anything you need.'

'Do you know if Alex and Danny were in any type of business arrangement together?'

'Ah, um, no I don't. That's out of the blue!' He smiled and took another sip of his coffee. 'I hadn't heard they were cooking up any schemes, so I'd say not. In the business I'm in, sometimes Alex would send a message and ask for a bit of advice, but I hadn't heard anything about them going into a venture together.' Then he gave a shout of laughter. 'Neither of them had any spare time. They were chained to both their family stations. It was always a bit hard for them to take a break, so to have headspace to start up a new enterprise? I'd be very suspect that was the case.'

'Right.' Mia made a note. 'Can you tell me about the night that Charlie was charged with rape?' she asked.

'What the hell?' Tom gaped at her, but Mia was getting used to that reaction. 'That was years ago.'

'I know.' Mia didn't say anything more, just waited.

'It was 2017,' Dave said. He was sitting in a chair that was against the wall, his leg jiggling up and down, letting Mia take the lead.

'Geez.' Tom ran his fingers through his hair and raised his eyebrows, clearly trying to gather his thoughts. 'Guess my memories might be a bit sketchy. Not something any of us ever wanted to dwell on.'

'We understand.'

'There was a party at the college. We'd all had a bit to drink as usual. I'd been trying to get the attention of another girl there but wasn't having a lot of luck. You know how it is.' He looked at Dave rather than Mia.

She kept her face impassive. Already she could feel the uncurling of anger inside.

'Um, anyway, it wasn't really until the next morning I knew something was up. I'd heard the girl had run in front of a car, but by the time that happened I think I'd passed out, so I don't remember anything about that part of the night.'

'Who put the party on?' Mia asked.

Tom shrugged. 'No one, really. It was just a normal party like we always had at the college. Lots of booze and bad behaviour.'

'Bad behaviour?'

'Okay, not a great choice of words. We used to get pissed, and sometimes when that happened, things would get out of control.'

'Like Charlie raping someone?'

Dave stopped jiggling and opened his mouth for damage control, but Tom got in first.

'No, not like that. Sometimes we dressed up, ah, inappropriately. You know, pretended we were females or our Indigenous cousins. That sort of thing. Politically incorrect, of course, but we were kids. Sometimes we bought cheap cars and had races, wrote them off. All sorts of things.'

'And who came?'

'Anyone, really. We could invite whom we wanted and sometimes, well . . . See, there was a pub next door to the college and sometimes towards the end of the night the people there would come over.'

'Did you know the girl Charlie raped?'

'Not really. I'd seen her around. I think she'd had her eye on Mick, because I'd seen them dancing together earlier in the night.' He looked sheepish now. 'Back when I could still remember.'

'Do you have any idea how much alcohol you consumed that night?'

'Wouldn't have a clue. Lots.' Tom looked down at the table. 'Look, I'm not proud of the way we behaved back then, but we were young blokes, you know. We were all blowing off steam, sowing our wild oats, whatever you want to call it. We weren't doing anything that other young fellas weren't doing.'

'Did you do any drugs?'

'Of course.' Defiant now, Tom brought his head up and looked Dave then Mia in the eye.

'What types?'

'Anything we could get our hands on. Weed, speed. Opioids, if we could. They were a bit harder to get.'

'Would your drug use be a reason you can't remember much about the night?'

'I'm sure it is. Along with the booze. I'm not hiding the fact that we did that sort of thing. Back then. Not now.'

'When did you last have any contact with Charlie?'

'Now that I can tell you exactly. He was charged with rape the day after the party, which was on the eighteenth of August 2017. That poor woman died the next day—nineteenth of August. That was the last time.'

'Why? Didn't you want to support your mate?'

Tom looked appalled. 'Would you? His actions ended up killing someone. We didn't want any part of that. No, he was on his own.'

Mia watched Tom carefully. He pulled away, leaning his back against the chair.

'Tom, was that the first time Charlie had done something like this?'

The silence was deafening.

'Tom? Were there other women who Charlie raped?'

'Look, there was always talk,' Tom said, finally, 'that he slipped them drugs and then slept with them.'

'While they were passed out?' Dave asked.

'Apparently. But there were never any other charges brought against him. No other women came forward when the media got hold of the story, so I don't think that gossip was correct. From what I've seen over the years, when someone is charged with this type of offence, other women come out of the woodwork pretty quickly. There was no one who did that with Charlie.'

Mia started to form a question, but then stopped and glanced over at Dave. Could she ask it? Would Dave approve? Didn't matter, she decided. 'Did you all have a go at slipping girls drugs and then "sleeping" with them?'

'Like Charlie did?' Tom's voice was steel. 'Are you accusing me of something, constable? Should I engage a lawyer?'

Dave stood and shifted his chair to the table, which told Mia she was on shaky ground.

'Not at all, just seems to me that if one mate was doing something like that, he'd be encouraging the rest of you to have a go, as well. Or at least be talking about it. But, hey, I'm not a bloke, so I might have that wrong.'

'Well, no.' Tom's face had flamed red. 'I've found it relatively easy to get women into my bed without having to drug them.'

'What about the rest of your group?'

'I think,' Tom said carefully, 'you'd need to ask them.'

'Don't worry, we will,' Mia said. 'Now, I'd like to circle back to when you last had anything to do with Charlie. You said it was 2017. You haven't heard from him since Alex and Danny died?'

'Sorry, that's incorrect. Charlie did get in contact with me,' said Tom. 'We talked about this the other day when you were at the caravan park.'

'I'm clarifying the information.'

'You weren't happy with the contact?' asked Dave.

Tom linked his fingers together and glanced from Mia to Dave and back again. He seemed to want to speak to Dave, but understood Mia was leading the charge.

'Not really. Even less that he wants to come to the funerals. It's been too long and none of us have any interest in catching up with him. We've all got our own lives and he has his.'

'Do you know if he is in town and still plans to go?'

'I have no idea.'

'Shame,' Mia said. 'As a police officer, I have a problem with a rapist being in my town. I'd like to have a chat with him before the funerals. You sure you don't know where he is?'

'Sorry, I can't help you.'

Mia looked for more questions, but came up short, so she turned to Dave. 'Do you have anything else, Detective?'

Dave seemed indecisive, but then he leaned forward and looked Tom in the eye. 'Tom, if I pulled the police report on that night and checked the rape report, am I only going to find one lot of DNA?'

~

'Geez, where the hell did that come from?' Mia asked as they stood on the street watching Tom walk back to the caravan park.

'It wouldn't be the first time a gang of blokes has drugged a woman and taken turns.'

'God, I feel sick.' Mia put her hand to her forehead and wiped sweat away. The sun had risen with fire and continued to create a furnace. In a couple of days' time, both funerals were going to be held on the stations, out in the open. What a terrible heat to have for the ceremonies. She hoped there were fans and lots of cold water. Or even a cool change. Maybe Hamish should head out there, too, in case anyone experienced heat stroke.

'Pull that file and see what forensics said. They should have taken a rape kit. Come on, we've got work to do.' Dave strode back into the station and picked up the phone. 'Mick, yeah, Detective Dave Burrows. Mate, could you come into the station, please?'

Pause.

'Yes, that would be ideal.' He put the phone down. 'He's coming now.'

'Tom would have rung him straightaway.'

'Of course he would have. They've had time to get their stories straight, so you make sure you've got enough information that puts them there at the time of the rape.' He shook his head. 'But, Mia, I'm not sure how you plan on linking Alex's and Danny's deaths back to this incident in 2017. You're right, though. I think there's more to this than meets the eye.'

'I don't know either,' Mia said honestly. 'I only know that those boot prints don't match, so perhaps someone else was there when Alex died.' She turned to Dave. 'If Alex was up the windmill, how could someone have made him fall?'

Dave stared at her. 'The footage from the computers, did you ever ask Hallie to send it through?'

'Shit, I got busy and forgot to check that. I don't think so.'

'Okay, ring Hallie and ask her if she can email the files from the bore that day. Let's go through frame by frame and see what we can find.'

Mia had picked up the phone before Dave had finished talking. 'Do you want me to tell Hallie?'

'Yeah, I'll ring Maggie and see if there were any business interests between the two.'

Mia keyed in the numbers. 'Hallie? It's Mia Worth,' she said as Hallie answered her mobile.

'Hi, how are you?' Her voice sounded strained and far away.

'Fine, thanks. How about you and Ruby?' Mia made her tone kind.

'Packing. That's all. Actually I was going to ring you. I've got something I want to bring in to you.'

Mia took a breath, not really hearing what Hallie had said to her. Her mind was too busy still rehearsing the questions she needed to ask. 'Hallie, there's been some information come to light that we need to clear up before the funeral. I really need you to send me the camera footage from Red Dirt Bore on the day that Alex died. Have you sent that through yet?'

'Bugger, sorry, I forgot to do that. My mind isn't working that well.'

'No trouble at all. And another question. Were Danny and Alex involved in any business dealings together? As partners?'

'Not a chance. Rod wouldn't have approved of that.' There was a long pause, then Hallie said, 'So I found something I think you should look at.'

'Sure, what's that?'

'This morning I was taking everything out of the bedside drawers, on Alex's side. His wedding ring was kept in a box there, and I couldn't find it, so I decided to pack everything up and look at the same time.'

'Okay.' Mia stuck her finger in her ear, blocking out Dave's conversation with Maggie.

'It's a phone I've never seen before. It's flat and I'm now charging it. I don't want to see what's on there; I'll just give it to you and you can do whatever you have to do.'

'You haven't tried to turn on the phone since you've had it on charge?'

There was silence. 'No, Mia. I can't. I thought Alex and I didn't have any secrets, but this phone . . . well, I certainly didn't know about it.'

'How do you know there's anything bad on it?' Mia asked. 'Perhaps it's an old one of his?'

'You might be right but I don't think so. I've got a feeling . . . Anyhow, I'm not risking it. If you want to have a look, that's fine, if you don't, that's okay, too. I did think you'd want to know.'

'We absolutely want to see the phone,' Mia said. 'I'm just trying to work out how I can get it. When's your mail run?'

'That's already gone for this week.'

'Did you find Alex's wedding ring?' Mia was stalling for time.

'Yeah, I did, thankfully. Hadn't looked properly in my haste, it was tucked in between some folded old jocks. Think he was hiding it, actually.' There was a slight amount of humour in her voice.

Dave had hung up by now and Mia asked Hallie to wait, while she spoke to him.

'What did you find?' he asked.

'She's found a phone that she doesn't recognise. How are we going to pick it up?'

Dave ran his fingers through his hair. 'Shit, we haven't got time to get out there.' He drummed his fingers on the table. 'Hamish might have to help out. He's been trained enough to go out there and pick it up. And Alex's normal phone—we need that as well. Ask if Hallie would be happy for us to have a look at their computer and, if she is, Hamish can bring them all in. But make sure that footage gets to us, like, yesterday.'

Mia put the phone back to her mouth. 'Hallie, if we send Hamish out to pick it up would you be able to meet him on the road somewhere?'

'Yep, I can do that.'

'Would you feel comfortable handing over Alex's normal phone and computer as well?'

'I'll package all of that up, plus the clippings he'd kept about Charlie. I don't know if they'll be useful, but there's something about the way he held on to what happened to Charlie that makes me wonder, you know?'

Mia stopped clicking the pen she was holding and thought carefully before she answered. 'What's on there that's concerning you?'

There was a silence and, in the background, Mia heard pinging of WhatsApp messages.

'Ha.' Hallie's tone was dry. 'I'm sending you some screenshots. The boys have obviously not thought that anyone is reading Alex's messages.'

'From Tom and Mick?' Mia motioned for Dave to come back over and put the phone on open speaker. 'Hallie, Dave Burrows is in the room and I've put you on open speaker.'

'Hi, Hallie,' Dave said, sitting at the desk and leaning towards the phone.

'Hello.'

'Now, what were you saying about the messages?'

'Yeah, between Tom and Mick. They're talking about Charlie. Umm, starts off with Tom.

'Tom: *Cops calling. Asking about Charlie.*

'Then Mick: *So what? There's nothing to tell them? I've been asked to go in and speak to them, too.*

'Tom: *Isn't there?*

'I don't know if Maggie is getting the same messages as I am, but I would assume so. I was going to ring her and talk to her about them, but now I've told you.'

'No, she wouldn't be,' Mia said. 'Even if Danny was still in the group chat, his phone was smashed when the ute fell onto him. He had it in his shirt pocket. It's been sent to forensics but they've got a backlog and I don't expect to get any information from that for a couple of weeks.'

'Is there anything else, Hallie?' Dave asked. 'They're not still talking?'

'No, nothing. I'll screenshot the conversation for you.'

'Great, thanks,' Mia said. 'I'll pass your number onto Hamish and he'll ring you to organise a place and time to meet. And make sure you send me that footage. Hopefully, I'll have something for you by the end of today.'

'You know what, if you come up with a reason as to why Alex died, I won't mind one bit.'

That gave Mia pause and Dave sat up straight. 'Do you have reason to think it was something more than an accident?'

'I always have,' Hallie said simply. 'I know my husband. He wouldn't have contemplated suicide, and he was too careful to have an accident like that.'

Mia deflated. Everyone thought they couldn't make a mistake, until they did.

'That's a fairly serious thing to say, Hallie,' Dave interjected. 'Why haven't you said anything before now?'

'I don't know. Probably because I was too out of it to think clearly. The shock, you know?'

'Was there any other reason?'

Mia knew he wanted to ask if she'd been scared or worried, but they had been trained never to put words or ideas into people's minds when they were questioning them.

'Not really. But I know Charlie haunted him. He used to have dreams—Alex did—nightmares. He would talk in his sleep, muttering something about Charlie.'

'Did you ever ask him what that meant?' Mia asked.

'No!' Hallie sounded shocked. 'No, I've told you, he never spoke to me about Charlie, but whatever happened that night, it really did bother him. I only found out about the rape when I read the newspaper articles.' She paused and Mia could hear her talking to Ruby. 'I won't be long, Ruby-rubes. Here, have a biscuit.'

Mia grinned, knowing that Ruby would be eating some of the hedgehog slice or a biscuit they had made together a few days ago.

Finally, Hallie spoke back into the phone. 'Sorry. And the other thing is that Alex wasn't one to have any type of keepsakes. The fact that he has those newspaper articles is unusual. There's a reason he's kept them, I'm just not sure what it is.'

Mia made a couple of notes and was about to ask another question when Hallie started to speak again.

'One thing that I always remember was something Nicole said. We've always had a pretty tumultuous relationship as you know, but one day, I heard her say to Rod she was glad I'd come along to bring Alex out of his funk. She said he hadn't been the same since Charlie had been given a gaol sentence.'

CHAPTER 25

Joan put her head around the door. 'There's someone here to see you,' she said.

'Mick Fowllis?'

'That's him.'

'Can you take him to the interview room, please, Joan? I think we'll let him stew for a while. Offer him a coffee, though. Only so he doesn't think we're barbarians out here.'

Joan grinned and left.

Mia opened the video of Red Dirt Bore and watched as a galah leaned down into the camera and pecked at the glass. 'Look at this idiot,' she said, a smile in her voice.

Dave laughed then became serious. 'Is there a date and time stamp on there?' he asked. 'How do we know it's from the day?'

Mia pointed with her pen to the left-hand corner. 'Here.'

'Good.' The galah having triggered the motion sensor, together they watched and saw Alex's ute pull up close to the trough. He got out, trough broom in hand, and undid the bung. While the water was emptying out, he went to the camera, put his face close up and waved into it. There was no sound, but Mia made out the words, '*Hello, Ruby!*'

'He must've known they'd be watching from the house,' said Dave. 'Great babysitter.'

Mia didn't answer. She hadn't taken her eyes from the screen, waiting, watching, hoping she was right. If she was, there would be someone else in this picture.

'I wonder if anyone else knew they had cameras on the trough and windmill,' she said.

'Easy to see,' Dave answered. 'I clocked the cameras attached to the tree branch when I was there.'

'But you knew what you were looking for.'

'True,' Dave said. 'But if someone wanted to hurt Alex, they would have done a sweep of the place—if they were organised. What we have to remember about these cameras is even though the recording starts when there is movement, it's only able to sense that a few metres from the camera, so again, unless something is close by, it won't set the recording in motion. Although it keeps recording for ten minutes or so after the movement ceases.'

Alex left the camera and went back to the trough. They watched him scrub the sides, getting rid of any algae and dirt, while the birds bathed in the puddles on the ground.

With the bung back in, fresh, clean water flowed through the float, then Alex disappeared from view. The camera kept recording as the birds were moving about, flapping their wings and arguing with each other.

Next time Alex was on the screen, they saw him swing his foot up to the first rung of the ladder of the windmill, some twenty metres away, then the next. He leaned down and waved back at the camera.

After five more rungs, he was out of view.

'What's that hanging down from the windmill, can you see?' Dave leaned in closer to the screen. 'Looks like a rope dangling there. Swaying in the wind, doesn't it?'

'Would that be a safety harness of sorts?' Mia asked.

'Hmm, maybe. I don't remember seeing it when we picked him up, though. Is it in any of the photos?'

Mia paused the video and opened the file, quickly checking through the photos. 'Not that I can see.'

'Make a note of it,' Dave instructed. 'Hit play, can you?'

Doing as she was asked, Mia drew in a breath, not sure if she wanted to see him fall and hit the ground.

Minutes went by, then more minutes and more. The birds continued to preen themselves, but they were Alex's only companions.

Mia blinked and as she did, Dave let out a soft groan. 'Shit.'

Alex's feet were on the screen.

Mia hit rewind and then the slow-motion button.

Together they watched Alex's final moments, cringing as he hit the ground and his feet twitched and then were still.

No words passed between Mia and Dave as they continued to watch for another five minutes. Ten.

Nobody else entered the frame, and then the video stopped recording.

~

'Thanks for coming in, Mick,' Dave said as he put his cup of coffee on the table. 'Can I get you anything?'

'No, thank you. I'd like to get this over and done with if you don't mind. I've got an online meeting that can't be delayed. Then Tom and I were thinking about driving out to see Maggie. We've only seen her once since Danny had the accident.' He looked annoyed and put out, but not stressed. 'It's a long drive out there.'

'We'll make this as quick as we can,' Dave told him as Mia came into the room and shut the door. 'But I'm sure you want the right outcome for Alex and Danny, as we do.' Mia made herself comfortable, sitting against the wall, notebook in hand.

'What? The right outcome?' Mick looked stunned. 'What does that mean?'

'There're some inconsistencies we need to clear up. That's why we've called you in.'

Mick frowned and crossed his legs, then rested his elbows on his knees. 'I think you'd better explain yourself, Detective,' he said.

'Of course.' Dave inclined his head. 'We're going to ask some questions about Charlie Dynner, and the night he was accused of rape and, subsequently, manslaughter.'

Mick scoffed. 'Not only accused. He was found guilty and went to gaol for both crimes. If you think you're going to undo those charges, it's a bit late.'

'Well, let's have a chat about it anyhow. Can you remember much about that night?'

'Of course I'll humour you, Detective, but I hope you make yourself clear very soon.' He took a breath and wiggled in the hard, plastic seat, trying to find some kind of comfort.

'It was August 2017. We were all pretty young and loved a drink, so I was fairly pissed, if that's what you want to know. But as for remembering in detail, not really. Not the first part anyhow. I remember the ruckus when he came back into the boarding house. I'd been asleep—not alone—in my room, so I have a witness, in case you need to know that. God knows where she is these days, though. Anyway, I heard screaming. I guess I'd started to sober up by then. I put my head out the door and saw Charlie yelling for us to help. That there had been a woman hit by a car. I didn't know anything about the rape until later, when the police came and arrested him.

'I'm a bit foggy, but I think it happened at the back of the pub, not inside. There was a lot of bush there—the college made the decision to clear it after this happened, just to open up the area and so there was nowhere for anyone to hide. That would make sense, because she was hit on the road that ran along the back of the college.'

'Had you taken any drugs?'

'Can't remember, but I would assume so. Drugs were available at most of those parties.'

'I see, and what can you remember about that night and Charlie?'

'Charlie was Charlie. He was the same as the rest of us—pissed—and trying to get a woman into his bed. That's what we all did back then. There's nothing illegal about that.'

'True,' Dave agreed. 'But as you saw with Charlie, rape was and still is. Have you heard from Charlie lately?'

'Yes, I had a message from him—on social media—asking about the funeral. Not a peep since.'

'This is on top of the contact he had with Tom?'

'Yes.'

'Is he here in Barker at the moment?'

'Not a clue. Do you know? I'd like it if he was. A chat wouldn't go astray. At least we'd be able to put to bed whatever you've got happening in your overactive imagination.'

Dave ignored the jab and continued with his questions.

'Mick, if we asked you for a DNA sample, would you be happy to give one?'

'Of course! I don't know what you think I have to hide, but there's nothing in my background you'd be interested in. As an MP, I had to make sure I kept my nose very clean.'

'Fantastic. Mia, would you like to do the honours?' Dave indicated for her to pass over a form for Mick to sign, stating he was voluntarily giving a DNA sample.

Mick signed it with a flourish then opened his mouth. Mia swabbed the inside of his cheek and sealed the test tube.

'Thanks. Now, Tom indicated there had been rumours about Charlie drugging women and then raping them. Had you heard those?'

'Of course.' Mick shrugged. 'But that's all they were—rumours. I think a lot of the boys were jealous he could pull better than they could. Charlie was never without a girl on the weekends. Never the same one, mind you. We called him the Stallion because he was a stud. Bedding whomever he liked, whenever he liked.'

Dave couldn't see Mia's face, but he was sure she'd be as revolted as he was, yet he knew this world well. Dave had been to ag college and knew how stupid crazy the fellas used to get. This statement also didn't match what Tom had told them. 'If he was able to get any woman he liked, why would he have raped someone? And why would there be rumours about this being a common occurrence?'

Mick shrugged. 'Maybe he wanted to try something new and it went wrong. I don't know. I wasn't there. The only person who can answer that question is Charlie himself.'

'Do you think Charlie would have a grudge against any of you, ah, blood brothers?'

Mick burst out laughing. 'Now, why would he have had that? He was the one who fucked up, not us. We chose not to support him, because who wants to have a rapist as a friend?'

'I understand but until the court found him guilty, I would have thought the boys' code was to stand by your mate. You guys dumped him the minute he was taken into custody.'

'That's true,' Mick conceded. 'I guess that could've been my fault. See, I always wanted to go into agri politics and even though we were young and stupid back then, I knew this wouldn't sit well if a journo ever wanted to look up my past, so I distanced myself pretty much as soon as I heard what had happened. It was me who suggested to the others they do the same. That was their decision, not mine. And look, since time has gone on, I've never once regretted my judgement call on that. I've had a meteoric rise to where I am today and some of that has to do with "people you know", which I know would shock any outsider looking in on politics.' He gave a self-depreciating smile. 'The other part is via sheer hard work and timing. The party was down on decent politicians as I joined, and I saw an opportunity. Having come up through the ranks and gone from agri to federal politics, I'm glad I made that decision regarding Charlie. To have a close friend going through the court system as he did would have caused me no end of career grief. Didn't matter how much I liked the guy. He stuffed up, and I wasn't going to let that stain my future.'

'You're pretty successful as a politician, I understand?' Dave said.

Mick grinned. 'My dad was a pollie, too. It always helps to have a mentor in this business. He taught me how to deal with people, to listen. I make a difference to people's lives and that is why I do what I do.'

'And all the while Charlie has been languishing in gaol. I wonder if he watched you on the nightly news and got angry.'

'What?' The word came out as a half laugh, half snort. 'Charlie wouldn't be angry with me,' he said. 'Or any of us. We had a pact, right from the start when we all met each other. We gave each other the freedom to do what we liked and not to judge.'

'Yet you have judged. You didn't want Charlie's conviction to'—Dave checked his notes—'stain you.'

'Completely different.' Mick flicked the words away with a wave of his hand. 'Self-preservation.' He stood. 'You know, I'm not really sure what you're insinuating here, but if it's that Charlie is pissed off with me or any of us because we've made successes of ourselves and he made bad choices, and now he's come to pass on his wrath to all of us for abandoning him, why am I still here and it's Alex and Danny who are dead? If I was Hallie and Maggie, I'd be furious with your incompetence and allegations.'

'Have you thought Charlie might be here for all of you?' Dave asked. 'Are you watching your back?'

'Oh, don't worry, Detective, I've had enough experience to know when to watch my back and I'm watching it right now.' His eyes narrowed as he stared angrily at Dave and Mia. 'But not from Charlie—from you bastards. Have you finished with me?'

~

'If he was worried about us finding his DNA anywhere, he wouldn't have let us take it so easily,' Mia said as she packaged the test tube and addressed it to the forensic lab in Adelaide.

'Not necessarily. He didn't really have a choice, so he just went with it. In fact, I'm half waiting for there to be an injunction sent in to stop us from sending the swab in for testing.'

'Mick'd have a lawyer somewhere on the payroll, wouldn't he?'

'Without a doubt. If he didn't, the party would. Mick might have been thinking he was going to throw us off the scent by being agreeable.'

'Mmm.' Mia wasn't sure. 'I don't think he's that stupid.'

'Tell me what you thought about his interview.' Dave leaned back in his chair and waited.

'He's arrogant and thinks he's untouchable,' Mia said straightaway.

'But so is Tom.'

'Not in the same way. I feel like Mick thinks he's living in a bubble or that he's covered in grease and everything is going to slide off him. Which is a typical politician.'

Dave steepled his fingers and put them to his mouth. 'I don't know. He's certainly arrogant.'

'What's his crime?'

'Actually,' Dave said and gave a laugh, 'I don't think he's done anything that a good pollie wouldn't. He's distanced himself from the problem and built firewalls for protection. He started that pretty early on in life by the sounds of things.'

'Exactly.'

'Has that file you requested come through from forensics yet?'

'Yeah, about half an hour ago. The interesting thing is that the woman didn't have any semen anywhere in or on her. They could establish she'd had sex—consensual or not, it's hard to tell because even though there was bruising, that could also be consistent with drunken, rough sex she was compliant with.'

'So he wore a condom?'

'Yep.'

'What about under her fingernails? Anywhere else?'

'Well, this is where it gets interesting.' Mia traced the words on the computer screen. 'The skin scrapings they got from under her fingernails don't match Charlie's DNA.'

Dave looked up. 'Sorry?'

'They don't match Charlie's.'

'So why was he convicted?'

'Because everyone saw him with her. The witness accounts say that he was half dragging, half carrying her across the dance floor. They disappeared outside and later, much later, she was running onto the road half-naked.'

'That is all circumstantial!'

'Not really, she was seen with him.'

'He could have been trying to help her! Did anyone see him chasing her onto the road?'

Mia referred back to the computer. 'Doesn't look like it.'

Dave scratched at his face, frustrated, then turned back to the image of Alex lying on the ground and hit play again. Silently he watched the bird, the trough cleaning, Alex climbing up the windmill. He made the images move in slow motion as it got closer to the time Alex fell.

'I wish I could work out what that rope was doing there,' Dave said. 'Some type of crude safety harness makes sense, but why wasn't it there when we arrived at the scene?'

'Could have Rod or Dan taken it down?'

'Of course, but why would they?'

'What it detached and just slid to the ground.'

'We would have found it.'

'I'll text Rod,' Mia said, getting out her phone.

Dave grunted, transfixed on the screen. Nothing new, except the rope. The video images were useless to them. He rewound the file to the previous recording, which was three hours earlier, the recording kicking in as the friendly galah appeared for its continual assault on the shiny thing in its backyard that it couldn't chew to pieces.

'Got to give that galah five stars for perseverance,' Mia said. 'Play it again. We've missed something. I'm sure we have.'

Again, they came up with nothing.

'What about after the fall. Is there any footage afterwards?' Dave asked.

'Nope. And there's nothing on any other camera recordings.'

'This is where we are getting into trouble, Mia,' Dave said, as he rubbed his hand across his eyes. 'There is nothing to prove that this was anything but an accident. We've been back over the photos and videos of Danny's incident. It's the same. Totally clean.

'With the information we have, there is no way to prove our theory "beyond reasonable doubt".'

'Shit!' Mia flopped back in her chair, frustrated, as her phone began to vibrate on the desk. 'Ah, Rod has texted to say there was always a rope attached to each windmill platform. Supposedly a safety mechanism.'

'That didn't work for them, then. Coffee?' Dave stood.

'Please.' Her phone buzzed again. 'This is Hallie calling. What are we going to tell her? Should I answer it?' she asked.

'Absolutely,' he said. 'Just tell her there aren't any updates but we're working as fast as we can.'

'Hi, Hallie,' she said.

'Hello, Mia. Um, sorry to bother you.'

'That's okay, although I don't have any answers for you yet.'

'I'm not calling about that. Maggie is with me, and we've been talking about the messages that have been coming through on the group chat. We're meeting Hamish in about an hour, but we thought . . .' Her voice trailed off. 'We wanted to talk to you.'

Mia put the phone on the desk, hit the open speaker icon and leaned over it, listening hard. Dave stopped in the doorway and turned back to listen.

'Okay, is there something we need to know?'

'Well, it's really small but maybe.' There was indecisiveness in her voice. 'Hang on.' There was a scuffling and then the tinny sound of the open speaker.

'Hi, Mia. This is Maggie. We're both here now.'

'Maggie, hi.' She stopped short of asking her how she was.

'This is going to sound strange, but I think Dan might have been going to meet someone after we left here the day he was'—she cleared her throat—'um, killed.'

Mia caught Dave straightening up and moving towards the phone as she spoke.

'Do you? How come?'

'Well, he said something like he'd only be gone an hour or so, just enough time to have a beer with someone. I didn't think anything of it because, well, Mick and Tom are around. Yet they were with us. I've only just realised. I don't think there would have been anyone else he was catching up with. His other mates from around here would come to our house, but sometimes he's been known to meet people on the side of the road for a beer.'

'Maggie, it's Dave here. Is there anywhere on that road Danny would have gone, just to sit by himself and chill? Have a beer on his own? A lookout or special place on the station?'

'Yeah, there is, but he wouldn't go there by himself. He'd have to be meeting someone, Dave. Dan wasn't a big drinker, hasn't been ever since I met him. And I'm sure he mentioned when he left Hallie's that day, he was meeting someone. I've forgotten so much, though, I can't be sure.'

'Alex is the same,' Hallie chimed in. 'He always said he drank enough in college to last him a lifetime. They both drank, but I don't think I've ever seen either of them drunk.'

'Who do you think he could've met, Maggie?'

'I don't know. But Dan's phone was smashed, right? That's what you told me?'

'We did,' Dave confirmed.

'I'm about to head home. Dan had an Apple phone and we've got an Apple computer. I'm wondering if his text and WhatsApp messages might have synced to the computer. We had that set up.'

CHAPTER 26

'Get an arrest warrant issued for Charlie,' Dave told Mia as he stood quickly and gathered his keys. 'This is sounding more and more like a vendetta, but we need more evidence. I'll go and refuel the car and meet you back here so we can get out to Maggie's.'

'Should we bring in Tom and Mick? Ask them if they knew who Danny might've been meeting?'

Dave paused then shook his head. 'No, let's get a few more facts here.'

'Don't you think they're in danger if it is revenge on Charlie's behalf?'

Dave banged the desk. 'You're right. Pick 'em up and we'll keep them here until we can get a bead on Charlie.' He turned. 'Joan, can you do the paperwork for an arrest warrant for Charles Dynner? All the information is on Mia's desk. We need it as quick as you can. Also, pull the phone records of every one of those blokes—texts, phone numbers, WhatsApps. Anything you can get your hands on. Can we get social-media messages as well? Tell forensics to put a rush on Danny's phone. We haven't got two weeks to wait. Hopefully, we'll see Hamish on the road and get Alex's other phone from him.'

'You'll need a warrant issued from a judge for the extra guys' stuff,' Joan said. 'I'll put the information together.'

'What else, *how* else would they have communicated?'

'Well, maybe they've all got second phones, if Alex had one,' Mia said.

'Yeah, see what other phones can be tracked to all five of the blood brothers. Joan, you right with that? Maybe if you can think of something else, whack it on there.'

'Of course.' Joan was in the office before Mia had stood.

'We're going to bring Tom and Mick in. Can you keep an eye on them?'

'I won't be able to stop them from leaving.' Joan looked nervous.

'I'll make sure they don't go anywhere,' Dave promised.

Mia was in the car and at the caravan park before Dave had pulled the troopy out onto the street.

She rapped on the first unit she came to, with no answer. In the second one she found Tom.

'Tom, we really need you to come into the station. We think you might be in danger. Do you know where Mick is?'

'I'm right here,' a voice behind her answered. 'What's all this?'

Mia turned and saw Mick coming from the shower, his hair wet and a towel thrown over his shoulder.

Dave pulled up in the troopy.

Mia started again. 'We think both of you could be in danger. Maggie has just rung to tell us she thinks Danny was going to meet someone, possibly Charlie. We'd like to bring you into the station until this is cleared up. Kaylah, too. Where is she?'

'Here.' Kaylah stood in the doorway of their cabin looking frightened. 'What's going on?'

Tom put his arm around her shoulders. 'It's okay, babe,' he said, giving her a squeeze.

'Our precautions could be entirely unnecessary, but we'd rather be safe than sorry. Just in case Charlie is unravelling,' Mia continued.

Mick looked troubled and agreed quickly. 'We'd rather we were safe than sorry, too. Neither of us has a death wish, do we, Tom?'

'Absolutely not. Do you think Charlie is here? I don't understand why he might want to hurt us, though.' He looked around the caravan park as if he thought Charlie might appear at any moment.

What Mia knew was that, if they were on the right track and Charlie was close by, he wouldn't be allowing himself to be seen.

'We're not certain,' Dave said. 'But let's play it safe. If you could come with us, we'll make sure you're protected. We're pretty keen to talk to Charlie and we've issued a warrant for his arrest. Tom, we also need a sample of your DNA. Don't worry, it's just procedure in this type of investigation. Mick has already supplied us with his.'

'Let me get my computer,' Mick said.

'I'll get my things, too,' Tom said. 'And, yes, no trouble about the DNA swab.'

Moments later both men were back, casting wary glances around.

'Good to go?' Dave nodded towards the troopy. 'Hop in. Joan will look after you at the station. Please understand you are not to leave under any circumstance.'

'But we're not arrested?' Tom asked.

'No, we're keeping you safe.'

'Revenge killings,' Mick said. 'That's what they think is going on here, old boy. Revenge killings.'

~

'Call Hamish and find out where he is,' Dave told Mia as he slid behind the steering wheel. 'Let him know we're on our way out of town and he needs to stop when he sees us, to give us the phone.'

Mia dialled his number.

'I'm nearly at the town boundary,' Hamish answered.

'Pull over, we're on our way out.' She lowered the phone and told Dave to watch for Hamish. 'What did Hallie have to say?'

'Not much. She, Ruby and Maggie were going back to Maggie's place to meet you guys, by the sounds of it.' The tension in his tone told Mia he wanted to ask what was going on.

'We need you to be on call, Hamish,' she told him. 'We're beginning to think this Charles Dynner might be looking at revenge killings, which would include Mick and Tom. We've got them at the police station.'

'Clever,' Hamish said.

'What?'

'Well, think about it. Kill one bloke and the rest come running to the same location because there's going to be a funeral. Then start picking them off one by one.'

'Can you tell me why you decided to become a nurse rather than a detective? Oh, there you are.' Mia put down the phone as Dave pulled off to the side of the road.

Hamish got out of his ute, holding a plastic bag in his hand. 'Here you go,' he said, leaning in the window. 'One phone. One computer. This,' he held up a single phone in a bag, 'is what Hallie called you about. She's going to give you Alex's phone when you see her shortly. Maggie said something about comparing messages on her computer.'

'Cheers, Hamish.' Dave handed it to Mia, who immediately pressed the on button through the plastic.

'Dead,' she said, turning it over to look at the charging port. 'Have you got one of these?' she asked Hamish.

'Not in the car.'

'Come on,' Dave said hurriedly. 'I want to get out to see Maggie and Hallie. We can charge it when we get back to the station. Have you got the paperwork there, Hamish? You did get Hallie to sign, didn't you?'

'Sure did. You've taught me well, Dave.' He passed the page over and Mia scanned it, checking the signatures were in the correct place, before placing it in a folder.

'Thanks,' she said.

'Yeah, good job, Hamish. Thanks for that. You heading to the station?'

'If that's where you'd like me to go. I'm here to serve.' Hamish flashed a grin, but it was tinged with concern.

'That's where I'd like you for the moment,' Dave said. He put the vehicle in gear. 'See you a bit later.'

Hamish stepped back and nodded.

~

'Look here, I don't know whose this phone number is,' Maggie said, pointing at her computer screen, 'but whoever it is says, "*Meet you at Heyquar Knob*". That's a lookout about another eight kilometres from where you found Dan. He must have been going there to meet whomever he was seeing.'

'Have you tried to call the number?' Mia asked.

'No.' Maggie tried to smile but failed. 'To be honest, I don't want to know whose it is.'

Dave frowned. 'Was everything all right between you and Danny?' he asked.

'We were solid as far as I know,' Maggie told him. 'But there's so much going on now, I don't know what to think.'

Mia jotted down the number and went out to the troopy to make a call to Joan, who would put that detail on the paperwork for the judge.

'Hallie, I don't suppose you've found anything else of interest in Alex's phone? Was he going to meet someone when he went to Red Dirt Bore?' Dave asked. 'We have one phone, but we haven't gone through them yet.'

'Here, I've brought Alex's phone for you to look at.' She handed it over. 'Alex never said anything to me about meeting anyone, but'—Hallie looked over at Maggie—'Danny turned up when Alex was supposed to be back. He said that Alex had asked to catch up with him. I always took that as one of their normal catch-ups, but maybe there was something more to it. Alex wanted to meet with Danny, when he, ah, died and Danny was going to see someone else, when he died. Does that mean it's the same as what Danny was going to do?' She shrugged. 'I'm not sure, but—'

Maggie gasped. 'That's right. Dan told me that Alex called him on the day he passed away and said he wanted to see him. He mentioned that Alex sounded upset on the phone, so he went right across.'

Mia came back in and stood next to Dave.

'Danny didn't do anything to hurt Alex,' Hallie said.

Maggie glared at her friend. 'Well, of course he didn't.'

'Ladies,' Dave said, holding up his hand, 'this is highly emotional. Can we take a breath and hold on a moment.'

'Sorry,' Hallie said to Maggie. 'I wasn't meaning anything by that.'

Maggie reached over and grabbed her hand. 'I know.'

To bring everyone back on track, Mia said, 'Danny was on his way to meet Alex when Alex died. Danny was on his way to meet'—she floundered for a word—'Person X when he was killed. It sounds like Charlie—if it is Charlie—is luring them to remote locations to kill them? Possibly. Which would put Tom and Mick in danger as we have already suspected.'

'Are we in danger?' Hallie asked in a small voice.

'No, I don't think so,' Dave replied. 'This is about the men. Something in their past.'

'But we've been reading the messages.'

'I believe it's Tom and Mick who need to be kept safe. They're the ones who have a history with Charlie.'

Maggie's shoulders sagged in relief. 'I thought that, but at the same time, I was still frightened.'

'We're going to have to get the STAR team up here.' Dave spoke in a low voice to Mia. 'Start knocking on doors, issue a media release looking for Charlie.' He straightened and looked at the women. 'In the meantime, you ladies are coming to town with us. I'm going to ring Rod and Nicole to come into town as well. No one is staying out here by themselves.'

CHAPTER 27

'We think it's Charlie hunting previous members of his friendship group,' Dave told his boss, Steve, on the phone. 'Revenge killings, although reprisal isn't sitting well with me. I can't work out why. What is he trying to retaliate for, unless it's that he's gone to gaol and they abandoned him?'

'Possible, I guess. Who knows what goes on in a twisted mind? What other info do you have?'

'Very limited. We've got a few WhatsApp messages, and Mia is charging up a second phone that Hallie has found. There's sure to be more on that. We're short of people on the ground here, Steve. We need to be door-knocking and seeing if there're any reports, but at the moment, I need Mia in the office going through these phones. You're going to have to send more people than you have already. As you know, there're thousands of hectares of nothingness here and we're going to need help. Without any sightings of this bloke, well, he's a ghost.'

'But you're keeping everyone safe?'

'They're in the footy club rooms. The five connies you've already sent up from Adelaide are on the grounds and they're under strict instructions to call me if anything looks suspicious.'

'I'll see who else I've got spare, but I've asked for the STAR team to be deployed ASAP. I suspect you'll be hearing choppers very soon. Are they right to land on the oval?'

'Yep. No trouble.'

'Dave?' Mia was standing in front of him, a phone in her hand. Her face was pale as she held it out.

'I'll have to call you back, sir,' he said and dropped his phone. 'What's on there?'

Mia passed it over. 'Read the text messages. I'll be back in a sec.' She slipped out of the room, while Dave focused on the screen.

Alex: *Charlie, this is Alex Donaldson. I got your number from the employment agency you're using to look for a job.*

Alex: *Mate, I've got a massive apology to make to you.*

Charlie: *Yes, you do.*

Alex: *Can we meet somewhere?*

He continued to scroll on, reading, but looked up as the door into the station creaked. Dave's mouth dropped open. 'Can I help you?' he asked, standing up.

'I'm Charlie,' the man said. 'I hear you're looking for me.'

'I am. How did you know?'

'Been listening to the ABC news on the wireless.' His eyes shifted from one side of the office to the other. Stubble covered his chin and he was very thin. 'Heard my name. Mate, I've done enough time in the clink to know I don't want to go back, so here I am. What do you want me for?'

'Come around here, if you like?' Dave said quietly. 'Can I get you a cup of coffee?'

'That'd be grand.' His English accent was very faint, but it was still there. Dave hadn't known he was from the UK.

'Mia,' he called. 'Mia?'

'Here,' she answered and came into the front room. 'Fuck!' The word seemed to slip out.

'This is Charlie.'

'I know.' Mia was staring.

'He heard on the news we were looking for him.' Dave was speaking quietly, as if he was worried that Charlie was going to bolt. The man was certainly looking agitated and fearful.

'Coffee?' Mia asked brightly.

'That'd be grand,' Charlie repeated.

'Come this way.' Dave opened the door and ushered him towards the back of the station. 'What about something to eat?'

'I haven't eaten in two days.'

'Well, we'll get you a sandwich.' He texted Kim, asking for something good and hearty, and put his phone away. 'Do you know why we're looking for you?' he asked as Mia put a strong coffee in front of Charlie.

Charlie ignored the question and lifted the cup to his mouth. Dave had to look away as he saw his shaking hands. This man had his spirit broken, and Dave was furious for him, after what he had just read on the text messages.

They waited and finally, after five sips straight after one another, Charlie put the cup down. 'No,' he said. 'I came for Alex's funeral, but I don't know why you're looking for me.'

'Charlie,' Dave said softly, 'do you know that Danny has passed away as well?'

The man stared at him. 'Sorry?' he asked, swiping at the hot tears. 'Danny's dead? I hadn't heard that.'

'Yeah, there was an accident—'

'It wasn't an accident,' Charlie cried. 'It couldn't have been.'

'Why would you say that?' Dave felt the thrill of the chase run through him. The reminder he needed as to why he was a police officer.

'Because Alex's death wasn't an accident. I was there when it happened. Hiding. We'd organised to catch up. I wanted to talk to him. We'd already been communicating via text message.' He fumbled in his pocket and brought out his phone, waving it at them. Then he swiped at the screen. 'See here, I'd asked him for a job, then hitched a lift out in the hope that I could talk to him. We'd been organising to catch up, but initially without anyone knowing. There was unfinished business we needed to talk about before anything else.'

'What unfinished business?' Mia asked.

Charlie looked at them steadily, then shrugged. 'Don't reckon it matters now, if Alex and Danny are both gone.' He slumped at the table, looking down. 'They were good mates to me, until they were turned against me.'

Dave and Mia looked at each other above Charlie's head, and then Mia picked up his cup and went to refill it.

'I reckon it would be a really good thing for you to tell Mia and me what's happened in your life, Charlie. We can help you.'

'Bit late for help now,' he said. 'Could have done with that back in 2017.'

Deciding to start with the easy parts, Dave asked, 'What did you do when you first got out of gaol? That was a couple of years ago?'

'Yeah. Bummed around for a bit, tried to get work. Pretty hard to do that when you've got a record like mine. No one wants you near a woman, which is understandable. Except I didn't rape anyone.'

The smell of hot coffee reached them as Mia came into the room. She put the cup down on the table and pulled out a chair. On her knee, she rested her notebook and waited for Dave to start talking again.

'Pretty tough not to be able to get work,' Dave said.

'Yeah, it is, but I'm patient, you know. You have to be when you're in gaol for something you didn't do.'

'If you didn't commit rape, then who did?' Dave asked.

Charlie shook his head. 'I don't want to go into it. Like I said, if Alex and Danny are dead, it doesn't matter. You haven't told me why you want to see me.'

Drumming his fingers on the table, Dave thought about the text messages, then got up and left the room. Moments later he was back.

'Charlie, I'm going to read some texts to you and I'd like you to tell me if they're true or not. Okay?'

Shrugging, Charlie picked up the mug. 'Thanks.'

'Right, here we go. "*I've got a massive apology to make to you.*" Text answer: "*Yes, you do.*"'

Charlie's head came up and looked at the phone in Dave's hand. Slowly he put his cup down and picked up his own phone.

'"*Can we meet somewhere?*"' Dave read.

Flicking open the messaging app, Charlie answered: '"*Yeah, I'll come to you. Send me a pin drop to your closest watering point.*"

'"*There's been a pin drop sent.*"' He turned the phone around so Mia could see it.

'Then the message says,' Dave continued, '"*I know it wasn't you who raped that woman.*"'

Charlie's face became red and his eyes bright as he read. '"*How do you know?*"'

There was a silence and Charlie's face came up to look at the police officers as Dave started to speak.

'"*Because I was there.*"'

'Did you get to talk to Alex?' Dave asked, putting the phone down.

'No,' he said quietly. 'No, we didn't get the opportunity to speak.'

The door banged and Kim came in holding a dish of roast lamb. Dave could tell by the smell. He waved her in and thanked her, giving Charlie the plate.

'Eat,' he said to him. 'We'll talk when you're finished.'

He and Mia walked out, leaving Charlie to his meal.

'We've got who we want over there in the footy club rooms,' Dave said. 'Get two of the connies to bring Tom and Mick over here. Put one in each cell and call off the STAR squad.' He turned to Kim. 'You need to go home and stay there,' he said. 'Lock the door and ring as many people as you can. Tell them to stay inside with their doors locked. I'm not anticipating any trouble, but if Tom and Mick realise we're coming, we might have a fight on our hands.'

Kim's eyes widened but she didn't say a word, just left to do as she was asked.

'They're not armed,' Mia said.

'We didn't check,' Dave replied. 'So, we can't be sure.'

Mia nodded and headed out of the station.

'Thanks for the feed,' Charlie called.

Dave put his head around the corner. 'Good bit of grub?' he asked.

'Tops,' Charlie answered, his mouth full.

Dave came back into the room and sat there, waiting for Mia to return. She needed to be in this because it was her tenacity that had got them to this point. A man would have got away with two murders, manslaughter and rape if it hadn't been for her.

He was incredibly annoyed with himself. How had he missed the signs? Was he so tired of policing that he hadn't wanted to dig that bit further as he would have twenty years ago?

Moments later, Mia appeared, and he heard the commotion of Tom and Mick being dragged to the cells, protesting.

'Take your hands off me.' That one sounded like Mick.

'I'm calling my lawyers.' Tom, for sure.

Dave indicated for Mia to sit down then turned to Charlie, who was wiping his plate clean with the bread Kim had put on the side.

'Do you know how Alex found you?' Dave asked.

'Not really and I don't care. I'd seen the family was looking for a farmhand and I was going to apply, but he got in contact with me first. Told me about the job when we were talking on text.

'Still, he said I needed to apply properly because the applications were going to his mum and dad,' he said. 'I'd gone to the library to apply—they've got internet in there, see? And while I was there I had a read of a few copies of the *Stock Journal*. Just so happened that Alex was in the social pages with his wife, so I read a bit about them.'

'So you had texts but you didn't get to speak to him?'

Charlie shook his head. 'No, he died before I could, and then I hightailed it away from the bore. Didn't want anyone to know I was around. I was scared.'

'Why were you scared?'

Charlie stared Dave straight in the eye. 'I'd just watched Alex die. That was enough to frighten me. But also, I've spent too much time on the inside to want to be near anything bad ever again. For all I knew, I could get framed for Alex's death and I certainly had nothing to do with it.'

'Fair call,' Dave said and paused before asking, 'Charlie, who was at the windmill other than Alex?'

Charlie looked at Dave. 'Tom. He pulled the rope and made the platform Alex was standing on fall.'

CHAPTER 28

'I don't know what you're talking about,' Tom said as he sat down at the table in the interview room. 'I'm glad you've found Charlie, but what he's telling you is a heap of crap.'

Dave pulled out a chair and sat down, too. Mia settled next to him.

'We were as surprised as you are, Tom. But you understand, we have to go through the protocols. Charlie has voluntarily come forward and then made a fairly serious accusation, so bear with us while we clear you.'

Tom relaxed into the chair and held up his hands in a *go figure*–type gesture. 'What do you want to ask me? Let's get this over and done with as quickly as we can. Poor Hallie and Maggie need to bury their husbands. This is very unfair on them.'

'Sure.' Dave leaned forward and put his elbows on the table to look straight at Tom. 'Where were you the night that Charlie was accused of rape?'

'We were all at the party. You know that.'

'Okay, where were you at the time that Charlie was accused of rape?'

Tom laughed. 'I don't know how you expect me to know the answer to that after so many years.'

'Have a go.'

'Probably either passed out in my room or busy, if you understand my meaning.'

'And when did you first hear that Charlie had been charged?'

'First thing the next morning. It was all over the college and the police had been there asking questions, looking for people who might have seen the accident, but as for an exact time . . .' He spread his hands out again. 'I don't know.'

'What was your relationship with Charlie like?'

'We were great mates. He was a typical Pom, always had something to say about something, but he was good value.'

'Why did you move to Singapore?' Mia asked.

His eyes slid to Mia and then to Dave. 'Because that's where my job took me.'

'Would I be right in saying you know a woman called Leah Tack?'

Tom frowned. 'No,' he said slowly. 'That name doesn't mean anything to me.'

Dave looked surprised. 'Are you sure?'

'Of course I am!' Tom was huffing, annoyed now. 'That's not a name I recognise.'

'Interesting. Because when I rang my counterparts in Singapore, I found there's an outstanding warrant for your arrest, which is dated two days after you left Singapore for Australia. Ms Tack has made an allegation against you for rape. Now from those dates, I can establish you arrived in Adelaide a week before Alex's death. Would that be right?'

'Not sure of the dates, but I remember thinking it was fortuitous that I was here when it happened.'

Mia wrote the dates in her notebook and resisted the urge to smile.

'Yet you told Mick that you were flying in as soon as you could get a flight,' Dave said.

'Mick didn't need to know I was here. I had business meetings.' He fixed Dave with a glare. 'And I do not know a Leah Tack.'

'Why did you need to kill Alex?'

'What? I didn't do anything of the sort. If you're going to ask questions about ridiculous stuff, how about you put them in some sort of order I can follow?' He crossed his arms and glared at them.

'Here's my theory,' Dave said. 'And I'm going to admit, some of this is guesswork, because Alex isn't here to verify anything. Somehow Alex knew it was you who raped that young woman.'

'That's preposterous.'

'Then Alex approached you about coming clean and you decided you needed to get rid of him so he couldn't tell anyone. I believe, after speaking to the police in Singapore, that you are a serial rapist. Your MO is to drug, rape and leave. You use a condom, so there isn't semen to connect you, yet you're sloppy enough not to realise that everything you touch leaves traces of contact. You've been lucky so far that there's been nothing to connect you to your victims.'

'Then why am I here?' Tom snarled.

'Because there's one thing you don't know. Underneath the fingernails of that young woman was some skin. It was found during the autopsy, yet we couldn't match it to Charlie and, back then, the police didn't DNA test the whole of the agricultural college.' Dave gave a stern smile. 'You were lucky, because if they had, the match would have been to you.'

'Load of rubbish.'

'You willingly gave Mia a sample of your DNA. Now again you seem to have Lady Luck smiling on you because I haven't received the results of that test yet, *but*'—Dave checked back to his notes—'Singapore have your DNA on file and that has been matched to the 2017 rape. I wouldn't have to be a detective to realise who was the offender here.'

He pushed a piece of paper over towards Tom. 'You're cooked, mate. You'll stand trial here, do your time and then you'll be tried in Singapore. I hear their gaols are pretty unfriendly.'

Mia leaned forward now. 'Why did you kill Danny? That's the bit I don't understand.'

Tom weighed up his options and seemed to sag. 'I thought Alex had told him all of this,' he finally said. 'When I saw Danny underneath the ute, I just acted. I had arrived as he was wiggling underneath and I pushed the ute and it fell onto him.' Tom looked down at his hands, then up at the two police officers. 'I was scared they were both going to turn on me and that would be the end.'

Dave shook his head. 'I reckon you've ended yourself, Tom.'

EPILOGUE

Two funerals and many weeks later, Hallie hugged Dave and then Mia.

'Thank you,' she said. 'Thank you for everything.'

'It was all Mia's doing,' Dave said, glowing with pride that his constable had cracked a case. 'She was the one who had the tenacity to keep going, keep digging.'

'We think you're both wonderful, don't we, Maggie?'

Maggie, her eyes wet with tears, nodded. 'At least Tom'll get his just deserts.'

'I still don't understand why he did any of this. I mean, look how pretty Kaylah is. It's not like he couldn't get a girlfriend,' Hallie said.

'Unfortunately, some men like power,' Mia told her. 'Tom is one of those.'

'Not that that is any excuse. I hate him and I always will, but maybe, in time, I might be able to have some kind of empathy towards him.'

'You're a better person than me, Hallie,' Maggie said.

Mia agreed with Maggie but she wasn't allowed to say that.

'It's nice to see that Nicole and Rod have allowed you to stay on,' Mia said to Hallie.

'I don't know how long for,' she said. 'Something has changed for Rod, too. He thinks Ruby should be able to grow up there and see if she at least likes the station. Of course, she's far too young to know now, but in time she will.'

Dave smiled, knowing the stern conversation he'd had with Rod had paid off. 'That's great to hear. Maggie, what are you going to do?' Dave asked.

'Guess I'll try to go back to life as it was before, except without Dan.' She cleared her throat, giving them a wan smile. 'I wasn't on the station a lot, was I? I guess moving to town won't be as difficult as I thought it might be while Dan was still alive.'

'I hope everything works out for you both,' Mia said. 'You can call me anytime you need.' She hugged both women again.

Hallie tooted the horn as they drove away, back towards their different homes. It was nice that the two women were such close friends. They would need each other even more when the trial for Alex's and Danny's murders came around.

Mia turned to Dave. 'Right, so you're off? Western Australia, here you come!'

In the distance she saw Kim outside their house, two suitcases on the ground.

Dave looked at his watch. 'Yep. Got five hours before we need to be at the airport and, if I know anything about my wife, it will take us all of that time to get there.' He grinned. 'I'm so proud of you, Mia. You've done a great job.'

Mia kicked the ground, hiding her flushing cheeks by lowering her head. 'Who would've thought I'd be doing this one year ago,' she said.

Dave leaned against the fence and looked out over the main street of Barker. 'I came back here ten years previously,' he said softly. 'Ten years. That time has gone so bloody fast and I never thought I'd say it, but you're just starting and I'm on the way to finishing. We're at opposite ends of our careers.' He looked at Mia. 'You've got a great future ahead of you; don't ever let anyone tell you otherwise.'

Mia frowned. 'You're not retiring, are you? There's nothing you haven't told me, is there?'

Dave smiled and shook his head. 'Just reflecting.'

'Are you excited to see Bec and Alice?'

As she spoke, a car indicated into the police station and pulled up next to them.

'To be honest, I'm as nervous as all get out. I want to see them and I'm looking forward to catching up with Mum . . . but Melinda? Too many wounds. However'—he tipped his head to the side—'that's life. I'm sure we'll cross paths. Ah, look, here's your offsider for the next few days.'

A smile spread across Dave's face as Kim walked down the street towards them. 'You know what, Mia? Whatever happens this weekend won't matter, because I've got Kim. She's my life.' Dave held Mia's eye. 'You should have a think about that. Fellas like your mate, Chris, don't come along very often.'

He turned to the young constable getting out of the car. 'G'day, Chris. Thanks for filling in for me.'

ACKNOWLEDGEMENTS

A massive thanks to everyone at Allen & Unwin—those who have left, those who are no longer with us and those who are there now. Fifteen years of fun and laughter. Of learning and teaching. Of gratitude. There is and always will be a special place in my heart for every single one of you.

Special thanks to Christa for your careful edits and patience.

To Gaby Naher from Left Bank Literary—I've always been in good hands with your care of my career. With deepest thanks.

Rochelle, Hayden and the ever-ageing Jack. With love.

DB, Anna and Nic, secret weapons! Or perhaps not so secret!

I spent a lot of time in hospitals writing this book, while my dad was very ill, and I want to acknowledge the doctors who saved him, the nurses who cared for him and the specialists who continue to work with him—thank you for the extra time. And the insight into the inner workings of a hospital. I'm sure you all will appear in a book further down the track.

To Val for the strawberry jam!

To you, the reader—I love that we have been on this journey for twenty-four books. Dave has been alongside us for most of that time. We make a good team—you, Dave and I. Thank you for continuing to love him as much as I do.

With love,

Fleur x

Shock Waves

FLEUR McDONALD

'Fleur McDonald is a master of the rural suspense novel, her characters and storyline crackle with authenticity.'
Family Circle

Detective Dave Burrows has longed for the top job in the Stock Squad but never thought he'd be acting in that role while his partner and best mate, Detective Bob Holden, is treated for melanoma.

Bob is keen to get back on the road and Dave can't wait to go bush either, expecting the trip will be much the same as usual.

But the trip doesn't play out that way.

Multiple bomb blasts in the small country town of Kallygarn send shock waves through the state of Western Australia, and Dave and Bob are once again drawn into the criminal underworld.

ISBN 978 1 76147 009 7

Voices in the Dark

FLEUR McDONALD

'A family drama at heart, the book is an authentic exploration of grief, family estrangement, and life on the land (fans of McDonald's previous novels will enjoy the return of Detective Dave Burrows).'
The AuReview.com

When Sassi Stapleton receives a middle-of-the-night phone call to tell her that her beloved grandmother is unwell, she quickly puts her job on hold, packs her ute and sets off on the long drive home, knowing her grandfather will need her.

Less than an hour away from Sassi's home town, Barker, she swerves to miss a roo and her car rolls down an embankment. By the time Sassi is found, her grandmother has already passed away.

On the other side of the world, Sassi's estranged mother, Amber, receives a similar call and shocks the whole family when she flies home from South Africa.

With everyone under the same roof, tensions escalate as Amber's secrecy and odd behaviour become unsettling. What is she really doing at home with a father she's barely spoken to since she left years ago? And will Amber and Sassi ever be able to reconnect?

ISBN 978 1 76106 648 1

Broad River Station

FLEUR McDONALD

'With a quintessentially outback South Australian setting, Aussie slang aplenty and a great mix of characters, *Broad River Station* will delight new and long-time readers of McDonald, who shows once again why she is known as the Voice of the Outback.'
Better Reading

Mia, a newly graduated constable, is assigned to the small country town of Broad River. And as certain as she is about her ability to do the job, on day one she's already in conflict with colleagues who believe that women shouldn't be coppers.

It takes the shine off coming home, where her grandmother, Clara, is in the early stages of dementia. Mia is accustomed to their conversations often not quite making sense, but when Clara gives Mia a mysterious key and hints at veiled family secrets, Mia isn't sure what she should believe.

In the midst of all this, a local child goes missing and Mia is confined to barracks. When Detective Dave Burrows realises she has skills that could be put to use, Mia's career takes a new turn, and she must decide which road to walk down.

ISBN 978 1 76147 057 8

Fiction *with* heart

Craving more heartwarming tales from the countryside? Join our online rural fiction community, **FICTION** *with* **HEART**, where you'll discover a treasure trove of similar books that will capture your imagination and warm your soul.

Visit **fictionwithheart.com.au** or scan the QR code below to access exclusive content from our authors, stay updated on upcoming events, participate in exciting competitions and much more.

See you there!